The Russian Affair

Michael Collier

This book is dedicated to my wife Linda, with endless thanks for her love, encouragement and support.

My thanks also go to Eve for her wonderful book cover design; and to Paul for all his enthusiasm and help.

Chapter 1

John Paul Matteson had arrived in Hong Kong in 1992 to work at Dentons, a long-established trading house. Matteson specialised in trade analysis and development, and after nearly three years, he was seconded to the Governors offices in Upper Albert Road, reporting to Major Andrew Trivett.

"We've been asking Dentons for copies of your reports and we're very impressed with what you've been doing," Trivett had explained. "Nobody really knows what will happen after the handover in 1997. Not just here in Hong Kong, but also the Far East in general. China will end up with one of the strongest established trading centres in Asia under their control. We want you to continue what you are doing but with full emphasis on the effects of the handover on the region, not just commercial but political as well."

After that, Trivett came and went, discussing reports and directing attention where needed. Anything seriously political or military was taken away "for other eyes". Matteson got on well with the Major, with his easy smile and that shock of sandy hair.

Matteson had returned to Hampshire every summer to spend his annual leave at home and was in his office thinking of his next trip back and maybe flying the long way round and route via California for a change, when the phone rang. It was Aunt Mary, his mother's sister from Yorkshire. She told him in a faltering voice that both his parents had been killed in a car crash. The memory of that call and the days that followed still haunts him - the numbing disbelief, the grief mixed with the frustration of the long journey home, the arrangements, the funeral. His Aunt Mary and her daughter, cousin Ruby, were a comfort and he spent some time after the funeral with them in Yorkshire. But, on the plane back, it hit him how his parents had been such a major part of his life, even with him living abroad. On the way back, he hoped life in Hong Kong would take his mind off things and was relieved when the big plane began its sway and dip through the apartment blocks of Kowloon down to Kai Tak airport.

From then on, Matteson's life in Hong Kong continued apace with a packed social life of parties, dinners at Landau's and nights out with the old Dentons crowd. But pressure was mounting as the 1997 handover got nearer, and there was an undercurrent of unease in the Colony.

It was October 1995, and the oppressive heat and humidity had started to retreat. Matteson had slipped out of the office one Thursday morning to go to Lane Crawfords department store in Central and was looking at Christmas presents to send back to Yorkshire. He turned suddenly in the aisle and collided into another shopper, sending parcels spilling onto the floor.

Before him stood a young, elegant Chinese woman in a knee length blue and red cheongsam. She was staring at him with a look of annoyance and contempt.

"I am so sorry," Matteson said, flustered and embarrassed. "I just didn't look….I….Please let me get these things for you."

She just stood, continuing to stare at him as he bent down and gathered up the parcels on the floor.

"I will of course pay for any damages," he said forlornly.

He needed a gesture of forgiveness but there was none. She walked past him and headed to the exit, and he had no choice but to follow, the parcels clutched firmly to his chest. He emerged from the subdued light and air conditioning of Lane Crawford into the heat, noise, and traffic of De Vouex Road, one of the main arteries of Hong Kong Central. Despite the "no parking" signs which he knew to his cost were rigorously enforced, she had left her silver Mercedes randomly parked outside the main entrance. She unlocked the car with a remote and waited as he placed the parcels inside. She looked at him for a moment, her eyes having changed from contempt to indifference, then got in and drove off. All Matteson could do was stare, mesmerised, after the departing Mercedes as it weaved its way through the traffic, his young face still flushed with embarrassment and his heart pounding. He walked off heading back to his office, leaving the Christmas presents for another day.

On Friday evening of the following week, Matteson walked into the foyer of the Mandarin Hotel in Central and headed to the bar. He knew some of the crowd would turn up there later, but first wanted some time on his own, not least to contemplate what will happen to him when that Hong Kong lifestyle comes to an end in a couple of years' time. As he entered the bar, he saw her, the woman from Lane Crawfords. She was sitting alone at a table at the back of the room. He tried to hide his surprise and excitement as he turned to the barman, ordered a drink and walked across to her table.

"Hello……do you remember me?" he asked hesitantly.

She looked up at him. She had her hair down, and was wearing a black cocktail dress, offset by a diamond necklace contrasting her dark liquid eyes. He thought at that moment that she was the most beautiful woman he had ever seen.

"Yes. How could I forget the man who crashed into me," she said flatly. Her English was almost perfect.

"It was really stupid of me. I'm so sorry. Was anything broken?"

"No," she replied.

Her face had softened just a little and it was enough to encourage him.

"May I buy you a drink….unless you have a friend…." He stumbled over the words. She paused before replying.

"Yes, you may."

She looked across to the barman who nodded and proceeded to mix a cocktail which he brought to the table.

She gestured to Matteson to sit down opposite her.

"What is your name?"

"John…John Matteson. I work at Dentons."

"I am Suen Ling." She sipped her drink. "You are young. How old were you when you came to Hong Kong?"

"Twenty four. I've been here for three years."

"And what will you do in 1997? Go back to your life in England?"

"I suppose so. I don't know. It depends on what happens at Dentons."

Matteson was mindful about any mention of the Governor's office where he now worked.

"Will you stay here in Hong Kong?" he asked.

"Maybe. I don't know. I know the States but I need to learn more about life in Europe. Then I will consider my options," she said. For the first time, she smiled at him.

"But now I must go."

She rose gathering her shoulder wrap.

"Thank you for the drink."

Suen Ling moved as if to leave and then paused and looked at Matteson.

"I would like to know more about living in England. And other countries in Europe. Would you like to meet again and talk?"

"Yes. Yes, certainly. I would love to."

"Here is my number. Call me."

Suen Ling had pulled out a small gold backed note pad and pen, wrote down her number, and handed the slip to Matteson. One more smile, and she turned and left, with a nod to the barman who responded with a head bow.

Matteson called for another drink and sat at the table thinking about Suen Ling and wondering how soon he could phone. Some of the crowd came in and he joined them at the bar, choosing not to mention his earlier encounter. After a few drinks, and with the noise level rising, the group set off to Kowloon and the bars of Nathan Road.

Over the next few days, Matteson tried hard to contain the undercurrent of excitement as he concentrated on his work. Although the transfer to China in 1997 was an obvious fact of life, every interested party – political, commercial, military, police – everyone down to the street vendors, were grasping at any snippet of information, any shading of colour, that might indicate what life in Hong Kong would be like under mainland rule.

Finally, on Wednesday evening, he could hold back no longer. He retreated to his bedroom in the flat in Leighton Road and dialled her number.

"Hai." The tone was hard and blunt. It was not Suen Ling.

"May I speak to Suen Ling."

"Wait." Same tone, but in English this time.

Matteson heard some talking in the background, and someone coming to the phone.

"This is Suen Ling. Who is that?"

"It's me John. In the Mandarin?"

"Ah, John. How are you?"

"Yes, I am well, thank you. I wondered whether you still wanted to meet. To talk about England and Europe?" The phone went quiet for a moment.

"Yes, I would like that. One minute............" Suen Ling left the phone for a few minutes.......... "I am free on Friday. I will take you somewhere special and we can talk."

"Er.......fine, yes. What time shall I pick you up....and where, of course?"

"I have other things to do before. It would be better to meet at the restaurant at eight. It is in Aberdeen Street. It has a Chinese name only, but it has a white serpent on the front window. I will tell them to expect you."

"OK. I'll be there."

"I must go now. I am pleased you phoned John." Suen Ling spoke with a warmth he hadn't heard before.

Chapter 2

On Friday evening, he found the usual taxi at the rank near his apartment and headed to Aberdeen Street. He had been there before but more to look at the gift shops. The taxi moved slowly in the evening traffic along Causeway Road, past the Star Ferry terminal, before cutting up into the western end of Central and stopping at the bottom of Aberdeen Street. Having paid the driver, Matteson set off up the steep incline looking for the restaurant. The road was dominated by the shops and stalls busy selling souvenirs, many of which were finely crafted and were bargains, even at the inflated tourist prices. He worked his way through the crowd of evening shoppers and was almost at the top when he saw the lit window with a very large white serpent covering most of the glass. He hesitated, realising that the customers were all Chinese and he would be the only "gwailo" there. But he went in and was immediately spotted by what he presumed to the manager.

"Suen Ling?" the man asked.

Matteson just nodded, and was taken to a small room at

the back, conscious of the sideways glances from the tables as he passed through the main restaurant. He sat down at the round table, and as his eyes grew accustomed to the subdued lighting, he saw that the walls depicted snakes in various mythological guises, and was trying to work out what they might mean when the manager came back ushering Suen Ling to the table.

She smiled at him.

"Hello John."

No evening dress, no extensive jewellery – she wore jeans, a shirt, her hair loose, with just a little make-up. She looked lighter, more youthful, and confirmed his original belief that she was thirty or less, certainly no more than five years older than himself. He smiled back with a slight shake of his head.

"What?" she said, querying the gesture.

"I'm just amazed how different you look."

"Do you approve?"

"Yes. But then you always look….well, amazing."

Suen Ling smiled at him again and turned to the manager ordering in Cantonese. The man nodded assent at everything she said and left.

"I hope you don't mind but I have ordered for us. Drunken prawns…….it is the speciality of the restaurant. I have also chosen some wine, but would you prefer a beer John?"

"No, wine is fine. Drunken prawns? Sounds interesting."

"It is. Wait and see."

At that point, the manager returned with the wine in an ice bucket, and plate of appetizers of miniature dimsum, crab claws and sliced abelone. One of the waiters brought in two small tables which were set up alongside them. Having poured the wine, both left to come back almost immediately and set up a small burner on one table with a copper dome shaped pot with a small hole in the top; and a large china bowl on the other into which they poured two bottles of Chinese "whiskey". Finally, a bag of large prawns was dropped into the bowl. The prawns started thrashing around noisily. Matteson looked on in astonishment.

"What are they doing?

Suen Ling laughed.

"Getting drunk! That is the dish – Drunken Prawns. Here have some of these," she said gesturing to the plate of dim sum and crab.

There were only chopsticks. Fortunately, he had got used to them and was able to pick up the dim sum. He avoided the abelone which he did not like and, more importantly, could never pick up with chopsticks – too slippery.

The thrashing in the bowl had slowed.

"Well, John, tell me about England. I know London – I have visited there several times – but would I be able to live in England? I don't know. What do you think?"

"Language would obviously not be a problem. Your English is excellent. But London is unique. It's an action city for which you need money. The rest of England is different. Outside the cities, it's quieter, plenty of space, and the countryside is very beautiful."

"Is that where your parents live? In the English countryside?"

"No". He paused before saying quietly, "My parents are

both dead. Killed in a car crash last year."

The smile went from her face as she reached for his hand. "Oh John, I am so sorry. I would not have asked…."

"No, it's all right. You weren't to know."

He felt the softness of her hand on his, as she looked at him differently.

The moment was lost when the waiter appeared and started to drop the "drunken" prawns one by one into the pot through the hole at the top. More thrashing but briefer. When all the prawns had been cooked this way, the pot lid was removed and the prawns taken out of the boiling water, drained and placed in a large flat bowl in the centre of the table. The waiter retreated with a nodding bow.

They both tucked into the feast of prawns, which Matteson had to admit tasted delicious. They talked amiably through the meal, with Matteson telling Suen Ling of the countries in Europe he had visited, his early years, and his work at Dentons, but with no mention of his current location and function. In turn, Suen Ling had told him of her childhood in Hangzhou in China, and that she had married young to a rich trader who died of a disease – she didn't say what – some years ago, leaving her wealthy enough to live in comfort in Hong Kong.

The meal had finished. Matteson detected that Suen Ling was winding the evening down, readying to leave. He didn't want it to end. She stood up.

"I think we have finished, John."

"Yes. Of course. I'll get the bill."

"No. There is nothing to pay. Come."

She linked her arm into his and they walked out through the restaurant, with the staff again head bowing. When they got outside, she turned him to look at the front window.

"You know what this white serpent is John?" He shook his head.

"It is Bai Suzhen. Known as Madame White Snake. In Chinese mythology, this poisonous white serpent became human and found love. But lots happened. In some stories, she was able to change when she wanted from a beautiful lover back to wicked serpent."

She turned and looked straight into his eyes.

"Can you imagine that happening, John?"

He was puzzled by the question but responded quickly. "In mythology, yes. We have similar tales in England." They turned to walk away from the restaurant.

"My car just around the corner. I can give you a lift."

"Yes, if it's not out of your way. Thanks."

"Or…… It's still early. Come back to my place and we can have another drink and talk some more. I can get a taxi to take you home later."

Matteson's heart raced.

"Yes. That would be great."

She smiled and squeezed his hand, steering him towards the waiting Mercedes. Soon they were crossing over the Peak down to the lights of Repulse Bay. Suen Ling chatted away asking him questions about his upbringing and schooling. She drove to the eastern end of the bay, now strewn with high rise, the old Repulse Bay Hotel long demolished and redeveloped. The car turned up a drive and approached double gates which opened automatically, leading into a large courtyard. When he got out he was surprised to be in front of a beautiful three storey old colonial style building, lit with subdued floodlights. She took him through the large carved front door, up a marble staircase to the first floor landing, and on through double wooden doors into the lounge which seemed to run the whole length of the building.

"Come, look at this," she said, leading him to the balcony.

The balcony also ran the length of the building but was split in the middle by an enclosed round turret with table and chairs, and windows facing towards the sea. He was looking at the lights of yachts and pleasure craft gently swaying in the water. Lamma island was lit up in the distance. There was a clear starry sky above. He turned to look at Suen Ling.

"This is……absolutely magical! What a beautiful sight."

She smiled at his delight and then lent up and kissed him softly on the lips, but pulled away before he could take it further.

"I'll get us some wine. Please….sit."

She gestured to the long sumptuous couches in the lounge. They were soon settled in, up close, sipping cold white wine.

"Do you have all of this house?" Matteson asked, looking around at the lounge.

It had a parquet floor, most of which was covered by an enormous carpet with a white serpent running its whole length. There were two more clusters of easy furniture, chandeliers, and a mixture of Chinese and classic paintings on the wall.

"Yes. The bedrooms are on the top floor, and Wei and her husband live on the ground floor. There is also the garage and storerooms there."

"Wei? Was that the lady who answered the other night?"

"Yes. She has been with me for over twelve years – since I got married. Which was very young." She laughed. It made him smile. "She can be bossy but it is only because she cares for me. Like a mother. Her husband, Liu does things around the house and also drives if I don't feel like it."

"Well, this is a wonderful home, Suen Ling. But I expect the developers would love to get their hands on it. Knock it down for a high-rise apartment block."

"I have offers constantly. But my husband bought it in the eighties, planning for us to move here later with a family. But, well fate intervened as it does. No, I will not sell it. Not ever."

Her face took on a distant look, but she was back smiling at him within a minute.

"Do you dance? Yes, I think you do. I will put on some music."

The music started, but it was not the disco sound he had expected from her, but a slow, romantic, almost wistful sound. She came to him, nestled her head into his shoulder, and they started moving together, her body pressed to his. The sensation of holding her so close, the feel of her hair on his face, and the faint scent of her perfume made him feel for a moment lightheaded. When the music stopped they stood still together, and then she looked up from his shoulder and they kissed. This time she stayed with it – a long lingering kiss. Without a word, she took his hand and led him out to the landing, up the stairs and into the bedroom. His mind fleetingly took in a fusion of colours and silks, but his whole being was lost in the moment and the longing for this woman before him. They quickly undressed and were soon lying on the silk cover of the bed.

"Slow John. Slow," she whispered, her hands easing down on his arched back and moving her body to restrict his movements. It worked to a degree, the love-making lasting longer than usual, but he realised that nothing had happened for Suen Ling. And she obviously wasn't going to fake it. However, she still snuggled up close into his chest, her fingers enticingly stroking the flat of his stomach.

"I'm sorry…I just wanted you so much," he whispered.

"You mustn't worry, John. I will teach you."

Chapter 3

They usually met two times a week, always ending at her house in Repulse Bay. Matteson would take a taxi from his flat in Kung Lee Mansions – he had started using the new guy who seemed to know the way better – and Suen Ling would order one for his return, usually before midnight. She did not want to be seen in his flat even though his flatmate Simon was on long leave through Christmas and he was on his own. And she did not want Wei, her maid, to find the "gwailo" in her bed in the morning. Not yet at least.

One night they had met early and gone straight to bed. Matteson tried hard to put her pleasure first, moving slowly and low inside her as she had taught him. She was, as always looking at his face, when he heard her make a small gasp. Her eyes began to glaze over, as she breathed more rapidly, clenching and unclenching him. Their movements together accelerated, until she reached her climax, with a loud moan, her back arched, and her fingers digging into his shoulders.

They both lay on their backs panting. She turned to him and touched his face.

"You learn well."

She laughed and leaned across to kiss him.

They showered, put on dressing gowns, and came down to the lounge where Suen Ling laid out an early supper, prepared beforehand by Wei. They took their plates of food and some wine out to the balcony turret and sat eating and talking.

"By the way," Matteson said sipping the wine, "I saw you the other night in Kowloon. You were going into the Peninsular on the arm of a rather elderly man." There was no reproach in his voice – just curiosity.

"Yes. That was a business meeting John."

"What kind of business?"

"I have lots of business interests and deal with a lot of people – men, women, old, and young. But this is my pleasure time, John, so lets not spoil it. It has been a wonderful evening so far."

"Yes. Of course. Sorry."

"Anyway, "Suen Ling rested her chin in her hand, "I saw you the other day coming out of the Governor's building. Did you get a medal?"

She laughed. Matteson tensed a little but managed to hide it.

"No. I had to deliver a trade document from Dentons. The Governor likes to be kept in the loop. But, of course, I just deal with the admin staff."

"Ah" She paused, and then continued," enough of those things. I think we should have a holiday away together, yes?"

"Yes, that would be fantastic."

With that, the conversation moved on to where and when and for how long, which they broke off only to go back to bed.

It was the second week in December when she phoned to say that her maid, Wei, and her husband were away that weekend visiting relatives in the mainland, and there would be just the two of them. Excited at the prospect of spending a whole night and day with Suen Ling, he arranged to be there Saturday early evening. He took the now regular taxi, with the large Chinese driver just nodding, knowing where this particular passenger wanted to go. When he arrived, Suen Ling took him straight up to the second floor, and out onto the bedroom balcony where she had a bottle of champagne waiting in an ice bucket.

"To celebrate our first proper night together," she said with a somewhat wistful smile.

He opened the champagne and poured two glasses. He now knew her well enough to know that she was not her usual self. Perhaps this wasn't what she really wanted?

"Are you OK? We don't have to do this if you don't want to."

"No...no John. I really want you here. I've just had a difficult day. I will snap out of it."

Then, leaning forward, she kissed him gently, and raised her glass.

"To us," she said smiling.

"Yes. To us, and our wonderful time together. And the holiday to come."

She looked at him for several moments, and then stood up.

"Excuse me. I need to make an urgent call. I won't be long."

With that, she turned away from the surprised Matteson and went out to the next bedroom. He assumed that this had something to do with her subdued mood and perhaps it was best that she sorted it now, so they could enjoy their much anticipated weekend together. He heard the muffled sound of her speaking next door, and suddenly her voice rose as she seemed to get agitated. Concerned, he went to the corridor and listened. It was not Cantonese, he knew that. He recognised the odd word of Mandarin, and she seemed to be pleading with someone. He wanted to run in and help her with whatever was causing this distress, but he heard her finish the call and rushed back to his chair on the bedroom balcony.

She came back in. She had been crying. He went to her and held her tight.

"What has happened? Why are you so unhappy?"

She looked up at him as he gently wiped away her tears.

"I am losing someone I love."

"You mean at home. In China?"

She hesitated.

"Yes, at home in China."

She clung to him for several minutes and he was happy just to hold and comfort her.

"Let us enjoy our champagne, John. Can you go down to the lounge – I left a tray of things for us. If you could bring them up," she said kissing him softly on the lips.

He came back with the tray which he set down on the

balcony table and returned to his champagne. Suen Ling had pulled her chair close to his and was holding his hand.

"You know how much you mean to me, don't you, whatever happens."

He was feeling slightly dizzy and confused by what she had said. He tried to speak, but stumbled as the dizziness grew, and the images blurred. He heard her say "I am so sorry, John. I am so sorry." There were tears on her face. Then he passed out, his head spinning off into a rollercoaster of dreams – his parents, Suen Ling, school, Trivett – in the middle of which he sensed a loud noise coming from somewhere off in the distant clouds.

He started to come to. Someone was shaking his shoulder. He wanted to slip back into the fog, but this person wouldn't let him.

"Wake up Mr Matteson. You must wake up."

He forced himself awake, opening his eyes, to see a large square, Chinese face shouting at him.

"Hurry, hurry. Mr Matteson please. You are in much trouble."

The man helped him to his feet and he started to take in his surroundings. He was still in the bedroom and had been lying across the bed. The man before him he vaguely recognised, but from where? There was another person in the room, a large Chinese man – the taxi driver!

He then looked down at a third Chinese man in a suit sprawled on the bedroom floor surrounded by blood. This last scene brought him abruptly to his senses.

"What is happening? Who is that man? And where is

Suen Ling. I must find Suen Ling!!".

"She has gone. You must move quickly out of here. The Major is waiting at your flat."

"The Major? Yes, I remember you! I have seen you with Major Trivett. Where has Suen Ling gone? I need to talk to her."

He was confused and anxious and needed answers.

"I work with Major Trivett. I am Michael Ho. And that is Newman. Stand in this sack and take all your clothes off—everything. Put on these things, and then the plastic gloves. We have to get you out of here immediately or you could be spending your time in jail," said Ho, waving away Matteson's protests.

He stepped into the large gunny sack open on the floor and did as ordered, whilst Michael Ho continued to talk.

"We know Suen Ling has not been harmed, but where she has gone to....that's impossible to say right now. The Major may have more news for you when you see him."

He handed Matteson the black trousers and shirt, and slippers.

"Get dressed. Newman will take you back to your flat. The Major is waiting. I have work to do here."

Newman led him onto the path of sheets laid around the body and out of the building. He sat in the back of the taxi as it sped through the Aberdeen tunnel to Causeway Bay. It was mid-evening, and the streets were still crowded. Newman went with him into the apartment building, and then up the lift to his flat.

Major Trivett was sitting in one of the armchairs. No

uniform, dressed casually in shirt and trousers. He got up to meet Matteson.

"There you are, John. I was getting worried." Then turning to Newman, "Everything taken care of downstairs?"

"Yes. Should I go back now?"

"In a minute, Newman. John, get those clothes and gloves off and get showered now please."

It was an order, not a request, and ten minutes later, Matteson emerged from the shower in a towelling robe. He handed the clothes to the waiting Newman, who following a nod of thanks from Trivett, left to return to Repulse Bay.

"Sit down John. You must be devastated by what's happened. But let me tell you first that no harm has come to Suen Ling. She is at this moment waiting to board the night flight to Vancouver. Where she goes from there, I don't know."

"But what happened? Who was that man on the floor? He's dead, isn't he?" Matteson was shaking his head in bewilderment at the whole sequence of events. "And how do you know......why are your men there?" Trivett handed him a glass of whiskey.

"Here. First drink this. It will make you feel better and I'll explain."

"Firstly, let me tell you about Suen Ling. She has come across our radar before...not for anything criminal but more because of who she knows. She comes from a wealthy and influential Sun family in Zhejiang Province in China, and married young – she was just fifteen I think – to an equally prominent figure in Hangzhou who just happened to be a gangster. Very powerful. Very rich. Running legitimate businesses. But, nevertheless a gangster. He died when Suen Ling was in her early twenties. He was poisoned, and some believed at that time that she did it, but it was never proven. He had put most of his property empire – and it stretched from Vancouver to Hawaii to Hong Kong and elsewhere – in his wife's name. And Suen Ling has lived an independent life of luxury ever since, mainly based in their home in Repulse Bay."

Matteson still ached inside for her, but his head was clearing with the help of the whiskey.

"So how did I fit in? And again, who was the dead man on the floor of her bedroom?"

"Well, we're within eighteen months of handover and there are a lot of people jostling for position, trying to get an edge. I think that someone saw an advantage in discrediting the Governor's office and British interests. I believe you presented them with that opportunity. They knew you worked out of the Governor's office and I think you were to be set up in a compromising position – sexual presumably – and photographed. Those photos could have been used to blackmail you, but I think they must have known that you had no access to any real secret information. It is more likely that the plan was to publish the pictures in several newspapers. The captions would highlight you as part of the Governor's staff."

"What!"

Matteson stood up aghast.

"This was all a trap. Suen Ling? No….no. She wouldn't."

"John, take it easy. She didn't go through with it. The dead man on the floor? Suen Ling shot him."

Matteson slumped back down into the chair.

"Suen Ling killed that man?"

"Yes. She cared for you John. More than perhaps you realised. In the end she couldn't go through with whatever had been planned for you."

Matteson remembered the phone call and her pleading. And the tears on her face as he passed out. Then he suddenly knew she must have put something in his champagne when he went downstairs to get the food.

"What will happen now," he asked forlornly.

"We can't do anything about the dead man. Our main concern is to get you clear of the scene. If your name is linked to this, it could still do a lot of harm. The maid is not back until late tomorrow night so Suen Ling will be well away by the time the alarm is raised. She must fend for herself. You, on the other hand, need to prepare for the police who will undoubtedly learn of your affair with Suen Ling and want to question you. You must rehearse your story that she did not want to see you tonight – to emphasise that she had made other arrangements with this man, and you went out to the Lanes for presents for family and friends for Christmas. That bag on the table has some things that we got for you. The camera at the front is broken, so there is no record of your coming in at this time to contradict your story."

"But, who was that man, Andrew? Do you know?" Matteson kept going back to the scene in the bedroom.

"No. We don't think he has anything to do with the Chinese government. They've got Hong Kong, so they don't have to get involved in such theatrics. He may be from Suen Ling's past. We will learn more as time goes on."

Matteson persisted.

"Suen Ling will be blamed. The Police will search for her and charge her with murder. They will get her back from Canada."

"I don't think the police will catch her. She will move on under a different name and disappear into the Chinese community."

Trivett stopped there, about to say that it will be the people she was working for who will hunt her down. She double crossed them and killed one of them and will probably end up paying for it with her life. But he kept it to himself.

"Now," continued Trivett, "lets run through your story. I'll be the police."

"Just one last thing" Matteson interjected, his brain getting back into gear, "your man Newman has been posing as a taxi driver for over three weeks. So, you were aware what was going on. Why didn't you tell me, Andrew? I would have stopped or been on my guard, and maybe none of this would have happened. No dead body, and Suen Ling not running for her life."

His voice had taken on an angry tone. Trivett looked at him, not used to being spoken to by his young protege in this manner.

"You're right, John. Perhaps I should have told you what was going on. But at that time, there was nothing going on except you having a relationship with a beautiful woman. Why would I stop that? It was just that we knew Suen Ling had certain connections, and since you worked out of the Governor's office, that alone made it sensitive. I thought we should just make sure no harm came to you. Newman would take you to Repulse Bay and wait close by until he saw you safely on your way back in the other taxi. Thank heavens he did just that.

He saw the man arrive, and then later saw Suen Ling leave in her Mercedes. But no you. He hadn't heard the shot but came to see if you were OK and found the scene in the bedroom. Newman contacted Michael Ho who called me. If we hadn't been watching, you would have ended up in a lot of trouble, my friend."

Matteson just nodded. He looked glum.

"What happens to me now? I presume I'll be sent back."

"Not immediately. It would look too obvious to both the Police and whoever was behind this set up. We'll wait for a few months." Trivett paused. He knew his young friend's world had just imploded. "You would have been going back anyway before the handover. I presume Dentons would have had to do a big reshuffle."

"I suppose so."

"Listen, you weren't to blame for all this. And I like the work you've been doing. I'll speak to a few people in London and see what I can line up for you. OK?"

"Yes. Thanks."

And thus, it was that Matteson left in the summer of 1996. The dead body in the Repulse Bay flat was discovered by Suen Ling's maid and the story was prominent in the South China

Morning News but only for a few days. There were more serious concerns on the minds of the expat community. Most were concentrating on any news items that would help point to the future of the colony. Others believed that the end of their way of life was fast approaching. Matteson had been interviewed only once by the Police, a Scottish Inspector Munro, who accepted his rehearsed story, perhaps too easily, but Matteson was pleased it was all over. He tried to get back into the spirit of life in Hong Kong with the younger set, but inside he still carried a sadness over Suen Ling. Despite pressing Andrew Trivett, he got no further with the explanation of who and why on that fateful night.

The long flight back London gave Matteson time for reflection, and he knew he had to sort out a future in England. Following a number of interviews, he ended up in an office in Whitehall working under Graham Stokes providing analysis and forecasts of commercial shifts and developments in the Far East. He knew that this opportunity had a lot to do with Andrew Trivett.

He had sold his parents' house – he could never live there with all those memories – and had bought a flat in a new development in Battersea. He watched the handover ceremony at the end of June 1997 on his TV, the lowering of the British flag, and Governor Patten and the Prince of Wales departing on Brittania, ending two centuries of British rule. Matteson felt very emotional, his mind swirling with the memories of his years in Hong Kong, and, in particular, his time with the beautiful Suen Ling.

But he was to meet Suen Ling one more time.

Chapter 4

An hour after dawn on a Thursday morning in April 2015, Phillipe Turan, an ex-Legionnaire marksman, was up and fully alert. He loaded his bags into the boot of his hire car and cleared everything from his rented room at the Swan Lodge in the Surrey countryside. He wiped the obvious fingerprint points, confident that, even if any investigation ever reached Swan Lodge, the room would have seen many subsequent guests with a room clean at each changeover.

Turan then drove the Ford to the public wooded area adjoining the Valley Golf course, reversing his car into the corner of the car park at an angle which obscured any clear sight of the front number plate. He loaded his jacket pockets with a compass and distance scope put on some gloves and set off carrying a fishing bag in one hand and swinging a dog's lead in the other. He went through the woods to the service track around the perimeter of the course, and pausing to ensure no one was about, he crossed to the mesh fence and pulled back the flap that he had cut the day before, putting the securing wire strand back in position. He then made his way to the hide, guided by the oak with the crooked limb, where he laid the camouflage net on the ground. Keeping the right side of the net clear, Turan fitted the silencer to the Mauser rifle which he placed in position with the skeletonised butstock on, and the front bipod folded down. He eased the weapon forward to front of the hole he had cut in bush, which was just enough to sight down the fitted telescope and train the weapon on the 4th tee. He wasn't completely comfortable but stopped moving to lie still and listen for any sound. Only when he was satisfied no-one was in the vicinity did he move again getting himself settled for the wait, fitting the magazine, and putting his pocket distance scope ready at his side. He pushed the fishing bag down to the bottom of the incline and checked his watch – it was just after seven. He had calculated that if the Russians teed off at eight, they should clear the first three holes in an hour and a half, arriving at the 4th tee at around nine thirty. He had just over two hours to wait. His longest wait had been over five hours on a twisting hillside road in Andelucia – hot, dry, and dusty, so this was no problem. His eyes and ears stayed on the alert, but his mind went to other things. He wondered how his sisters were and his two nieces whom he hadn't seen for nearly two years. When this was over, he would take a long break, get his visa, and spend some time with them in Teheran. He then started to go back over the past few days.

On the previous Sunday morning, Phillipe Turan had been sitting in his armchair in the flat above the shop in Place Clichy that he had inherited when his father died.

Turan's parents had moved to Paris from Iran in the fifties and his father had started the shop dealing in Persian antiques and rugs which he sourced through his family contacts back home. They had three children, Turan being the first, followed by two girls. They had given him a French name, Phillipe, but they always called him by his middle name, Sami. His two sisters had eventually returned to Iran and were married and settled with families. Turan had volunteered for the Legion when he was 24 years old, and despite his father's protests, spent 6 years learning how to use weapons and how to survive. Then he started working contracts He had never in all this time met the man who controlled the operation. He did, however, meet the burly Englishman Beck, who told him he had once heard the man call himself "Essex", but like Turan, Beck's instructions were always anonymous. Beck was an explosives expert and Turan was involved when gun cover was needed. He also negotiated some Semtex for Beck from a fellow ex-Legionnaire whom he knew had access to some of the Libyan stockpile. The only other member of the ring he had dealings with was the German, Stils who was involved in electronics. On most contracts, Turan worked alone.

Turan's cellphone pinged. He checked the message – an asterisk and the number four. He knew it was a communication from the man, a new job and the instructions were en route. He immediately deleted the message.

Chapter 5

On Monday morning Turan left the shop and walked along to the main Poste Restante on Boulevard Clichy to collect his mail. Mainly work related with one letter from his sister in Teheran, and a small slim cardboard package posted from London on Saturday. He returned to his apartment above the shop.

The package contained a recording of Vivaldi's Four Seasons by the Slovak Philharmonic. He put the disc in his CD player and selected track 4. The languid music of the Summer Allegro ran for about forty seconds, followed by a lengthy period of static. Then, after a faint whirring sound, the static turned into a synthesised voice.

"We have been asked to take care of a Russian, Lanskoy. The client wants it done outside the territory and not using a cheap Eastern gun. Lanskoy is in England this coming week but only for a few days. The best location is the Valley Golf course in Surrey owned by another Russian, Garnovski. The course is to be locked down on Thursday morning and Lanskoy will be playing with Garnovski and two other

Russians. A black Ford saloon will be parked in the far right corner of the car park next to the Guildford Theatre on Tuesday for one hour from one o'clock with all you need. If you are not there by two or you signal a problem, it will be removed. Use your Belgian name. It is short notice and won't be easy, but I have negotiated a fee of one million dollars. Let me know if you accept the contract".

Turan fired up a laptop and went into search first for Guildford Theatre noting the location of the car park and the nearby railway station, and then Lanskoy. The photo in the article he found showed a youngish man, dark haired and medium build. Andrei Lanskoy ran Interlansk, specialising in nickel and non-ferrous metals, and was a major player in the Russian economy. His wealth was estimated at over $10 billion, and his company employed 86,000 people. Lanskoy was 42yrs old and gained the momentum for his success in the "loans -for-shares" auctions in mid-1990s Russia. He owned properties in London, New York, and Hong Kong. Turan could find no mention of Lanskoy's political affiliation nor his relationship with President Putin.

He then searched for English golf courses in the area outside London and soon located Valley Golf Course. Valley was a private club with 216 members, located in the countryside north of Guildford, and the publicity shots showed rolling fairways with wooded areas at the back. Turan scoured the website and eventually found what he was looking for – an aerial plan of the course. He went through the plan zooming in on certain parts and began to concentrate on hole 16. The plan showed a service road running alongside the course and splitting an area of woodland. The woods outside the course appeared to be public land with paths running through. Inside the service road was around thirty metres of woodland before it opened up onto the fairway of the 16th hole. Across the fairway and on rising ground was the tee of the 4th hole. Turan nodded to himself. He had found what he was looking for.

He sat back frowning. The message said the car would have "all you need ", which must include the gun. There was no way he could have arranged a weapon or got his rifle into England at such a short notice. This would undoubtedly be a one shot kill and it would be difficult and dangerous to practice with whatever was provided. Not good, he thought. Moving on in his mind, he would need to get through the woods where other people may be out and about. The sun rose early in May, so maybe get there not long after dawn before too many walkers appeared. The 4th hole would be at the beginning of their round so if they reached the tee at around nine, he would have been in position for up to three hours. He didn't play golf himself but had seen enough to know that players paused on the tee before swinging to strike the ball. That would give him the seconds he needed to shoot. The Russians would undoubtedly have a number of bodyguards, all armed, some of whom would sweep the course ahead of the play at each hole, so concealment had to be good. Also escape had to be swift and silent, and hopefully he would get some precious time out of the initial confusion and shock of the group.

As the man said, it won't be easy. Not enough time to

prepare. But one million dollars was a lot of money. He still had misgivings about the weapon but nevertheless sent a double hash text to London indicating he accepted the contract. If, when he saw the gun they were providing, he had any doubts, he would have to opt out. There was no way Turan would end up on a suicide mission, no matter how much money was on offer.

He then printed off the plan of the golf course, but nothing else. It was too risky to be carrying a photo of Lanskoy if stopped for any reason, and there undoubtedly would be something on the target in the car. All searches were deleted, and Turan unscrewed and bagged the hard drive, ground the cd in the shredder, and started preparing for the trip to England.

In London, Derek Beck had also received his instructions. Beck was a big man in both height and weight and had started out with more humble beginnings. His skill with explosives working for a private demolition contractor had brought him to the attention of the man. He had never met him face to face although he suspected he had been watched for some time before he received the anonymous call with the offer. He had now been carrying out these contracts for over 4 years and had the funds to indulge his passion for wine and build up a respectable business as a wine broker.

His instructions were to get a black Ford saloon which had to be cleared and cleaned to look like a hire car; and make a fake hire contract in in the name of Beaume – Beck immediately knew Turan was involved. The car had to be delivered by Monday afternoon to a lock up garage on the outskirts of Sutton; then collected on Tuesday morning to be taken to the Guildford theatre car park to wait from one o'clock for one hour. If there was no show, the car had to be returned to the Sutton lock-up. Finally, Beck had to book a room for Beaume for two nights, Tuesday and Wednesday, in the closest thing to a motel that he could find near Woking. For this he would be paid two hundred thousand dollars.

The first thing Beck did was to phone the Irishman Farrell, who he had used before, to get the car and a blank hire contract, making sure that the cash he offered was more than enough to get Farrell moving that week-end. He then scoured the web for recent bankruptcies until he found a car hire firm that had gone under and would use their details to knock up a passable hire car document. He also searched the web for the accommodation but found nothing suitable. So, he abandoned his plans to spend the week-end with girlfriend, Janice, and set off on Sunday for Woking to hunt down a room. After an extensive search and a few discreet enquiries, he managed to locate the Swan Lodge a mile from the centre of Woking. It had a central hub with a run of terraced cottage type rooms either side, each with their own front door. He avoided going into reception and phoned from his car to book a room in the name of Beaume. On his way back to London, Farrell phoned to say that "the goods that he had ordered were ready for delivery". Beck diverted to Bermondsey to the motor works garage run by Farrell who opened up and let him in. He checked out the Ford which had been deep cleaned and had that familiar hire car look and smell.

The next day, Beck met Farrell outside Clapham Station collected the car and drove it to the lock-up in Sutton. He had completed the urgent part of his assignment and was able to text a double hash to the man in London.

Less than a mile to the west on the borders of Knightsbridge and South Kensington, that man had received the confirmation texts from Turan and Beck. He waited until dusk and then drove to the garage in Sutton. The garage was a single unit with an electronically operated shutter, and a side door. He had bought it using a false name, some twenty months before as a standby. He stayed only long enough to check that the car met his demands, and to deposit a large canvas fishing bag and an envelope in the boot.

Chapter 6

Turan had risen early on Tuesday morning to travel to Surrey. He had packed a carry-on with essentials and a change of clothes, including a light-weight green hunting jacket, pocket compass, and a small distance scope. He checked the money in his safe and found he had six hundred and twenty English pounds which he pocketed together with a wad of Euros. Turan accepted any currency in his shop which also gave him foreign funds for his trips out of Europe. He also took the bag containing the hard drive, locked up the apartment and shop, and walked to his garage in Dames. He drove his Peugeot to his workshop in Colombes where he dropped the hard drive into a large glass container of acid which he kept on the bench with a piece of slate as a lid. The acid was already bubbling at the edges when he left to travel north on the AI autoroute, branching off on the A2 and crossing the Belgian border just past Valenciennes . He drove on and into Mons and found a long-term car park near the station where he parked and locked his car, hiding his French ID card in a floor compartment in the boot, together with the knife that he usually kept in the glove compartment. He patted the passport in the inside pocket of his jacket to almost trigger the psychological switch to Maurice Beaume, citizen of Belgium, and strode off with his bag to the station.

He boarded the commuter train to Brussels, in time to catch the 9.56am Eurostar from Midi to London Waterloo. The journey went smoothly and he arrived at Waterloo only six minutes behind schedule. There had been a cursory check of his Belgian ID at Brussels and the French police did a tour of the train at Lille, but there was virtually no immigration at Waterloo and Turan passed quickly through into the main station hall. He boarded the first train heading south and was soon walking out of Guildford station and crossing the road towards the signed Yvonne Arnaud Theatre. He found the adjacent car park bordering the river and he made his way to the far right corner and saw the parked black saloon As he drew closer, he recognised the bulky shape sitting in the passenger seat reading a newspaper. Beck saw him coming in the mirror, put down the paper, and unlocked the doors, allowing Turan to slide into the driver's seat and deposit his bag over the back.

"Good to see you again." Beck said smiling.

"Yes, and you."

"OK. We don't want to be here too long so I'll quickly run through what I've got."

"This is a rental car and here in the glove compartment is a hire contract I've knocked up. The company has gone into liquidation but only recently, so it should be OK. I've also got you a room for tonight and tomorrow not too far from here – a place called Woking. It took some time to find the right place but this should suit. The rooms are individual units with their own front door opening onto the car park so you should be able to come and go as you please. I've asked for an end room for you. It's seventy pounds a night – have you got enough sterling?"

"Yes, plenty."

"When you've finished, you've got to drive the car to a place called Sutton where we have a lock-up garage and it will be taken care of from there. You have to leave everything in the car – except your own bag that is -and catch a train back to London and away. The station is nearby." Beck paused but no question came from Turan. "I've written down the addresses of the hotel and the garage. I've also loaded into this SatNav on the dashboard the postcodes and saved them as recent searches. So, all you have to do is this........."

Beck set about showing Turan the workings of the SatNav and how to get the recent searches. Turan knew all about SatNavs but let Beck do his thing.

"You'll see that there are other entries on the list. One is the Valley Golf Course which was put on by the boss. The other is a DIY supermarket near Guildford."

Turan had not settled enough into his English to fully understand and gave Beck a quizzical look.

"DIY. Bricolage – you might need some things and it is big enough not to be personal", Beck explained.

"I understand. What about the weapon? Where is it and what is it?" asked Turan.

"I don't know what it is, but it is in the boot in a bag. I had nothing to do with that part – he had the car overnight and added his bits. I believe there is also a large envelope for you back there."

"OK. I'd better get to this hotel and check everything out. Thank you for this."

"No problem, my friend. But oh…wait…," Beck said reaching into his pocket, "here, a prepaid mobile fresh off the line. I'll get back to London. Bonne chance, mon ami."

With that Beck handed the phone to Turan, got out of the car, and ambled off towards the main road and the station.

Turan found the hotel, the Swan Lodge, on the SatNav and set off. He drove slowly and carefully, getting used to the car and the "wrong" side of the road, and finally reached the Swan Lodge. It was as Beck described, a bit run down but with individual access rooms, like an American motel. Turan parked the car away from the main entrance and checked into Reception paying cash.

The room was small – bed, wardrobe, side table with coffee, tea, and longlife milk, TV and an old DVD player. He dumped his overnight on the bed and checked out the bathroom. It had a bath with an overhead shower and plastic shower curtain. Turan grimaced, but knew it was perfect for his need. He pressed the side panel of the bath and found it was sprung. He then went out to the car, opened the boot and brought in the long canvas fisherman's bag. He locked the door, closed the curtains, and unzipped the bag, What he saw made him smile - it was a Mauser SR 93. He had used one of these in the early days before he got the Arctic.

Few and far between. Why the boss had one he couldn't imagine but he was glad that he did.

A luggage label was attached the gun. "Zeroed in". He felt a lot easier about the assignment and began checking out the other contents of the bag– day and night scope, suppressor, a sheet of camouflage netting, and two mags of .300 WM.

There was no sign of the envelope Beck had mentioned, so he went back out and located it under the spare wheel cover. When he opened it inside the room he found a large photo of Lanskoy, and three smaller photos with names Garnovski, Orlov, and Krupin written on the back together with their age, build and height. There was also a DVD, and the same aerial plan of the Valley Golf course that he had found on the computer. A sheet of paper listed the addresses of the golf course, and the garage in Sutton, and at the bottom were the words "Tee off time booked Thursday 8.00am". Turan studied the details on the photos noting that Orlov was taller and thinner than the rest, whereas Garnovski, the host, was older, balding and quite short. Turan was concerned that Lanskoy and Krupin looked similar. He needed to know that he was shooting at the right target. He took the DVD out of the sleeve and put it into the player and, after some fumbling with the controls, managed to start the recording. It showed several different sequences of the same man – striding into an office building, sunning himself on a yacht, and walking with a crowd of colleagues. The face matched that of Lanskoy in the photo, and the limited dialogue was in Russian. The yacht photos were of no help, but the shot of Lanskoy entering the building showed a man with a purposeful walk.

This was confirmed by the sequence where Lanskoy was with the others, taking longer strides out of pace with his companions.

He had a quick look at the aerial plan and then checked his watch – just after three – and decided he would take a first look at the golf course. He wrapped the gun and shells in the camouflage net, sprung the panel off the side of the bath, and manoeuvred the bundle in between the bath cradle before putting the panel back into position, pressing a thumbnail of soap into the join. The photos were torn into shreds which put down the toilet, flushing several times. He hid the DVD inside his bag.

The SatNav guided Turan towards Valley Golf Course. He had come off the main road and was cruising slowly along the secondary road which then looped left passing the gated entrance to the golf course. Turan noted the cameras guarding the gate and also the wire mesh fencing running from the gate round the perimeter, before the road swooped back right and down away from the course. He followed the road round hugging the wooded area to his right until he found an entrance with signs indicating a picnic bench and walking trails. He parked the car and set off in the direction of the course with his pocket compass and distance scope.

He made his way through the wooded area, alert to any other walkers, but most had brought dogs and were sticking to defined paths. He eventually reached the dirt track used to service the perimeter fence but could see little of the course through the trees inside the fence. He noted a point further along the track where a bush was growing through the fence and then returned to the car and activated the SatNav for the DIY store and was guided to a retail park on the outskirts of Guildford where he bought wire cutters, and a gardener's combination tool with secateurs and knife blade. As he reached his car, he noticed a pet store on the site and came out with a long leather dog's lead.

He returned to the Swan Lodge, doing a cautionary drive past, looking for any unusual activity, and more importantly, any unusual silence. But there was none, and he found the room as he had left it. The evening was spent with a take-away he had got en route, going through the Lanskoy DVD again, and checking, cleaning, and getting the feel of the Mauser.

The next morning, Turan went back to the golf course, having given a message to Reception that he did not need his room serviced. He cut a flap in the fence by the protruding bush, climbed through, and teased out a wire strand to close the flap behind him. He walked through the wooded area of the golf course until he saw the open fairways through the trees ahead when he dropped down and crawled to the edge of the rough and peered through with the scope. It took him some time to get his bearings, but eventually he was able to confirm that he was alongside the rough area adjoining the 16th fairway with the 4th tee off to his right. He crawled up a slight incline to the edge of the fairway and could see the tee area in his scope, raised and clear of any bushes. The scope showed a distance of 170 metres. The Mauser was designed to penetrate body armour and with that velocity at such a short distance, the chance of being off target was greatly reduced. Turan shifted around on the ground, taking a shooting pose, looking for a comfortable lie where he could stay for a number of hours. When he was satisfied, he pushed the scope through the foliage until it was accurately set on the tee, and then cut a small circle with the secateurs for the rifle, and lay still, waiting. At just after eight, he heard the distant sound of golf balls being struck and, shortly afterwards, a men's foursome came trundling up to the 4th tee. He watched each man drive off clearly visible on the flat tee surface and all pausing still before starting their swing.

After they had moved off up the fairway, Turan returned to the car. There were several cars parked in the area, and he could hear dogs and people in the distance. He drove back to the Lodge and spent the rest of the day running through his plan looking for anything that he had missed, breaking off only to go out and eat.

Chapter 7

Turan was still deep in thought in the nest when he was suddenly interrupted by noises in the distance. He looked at his watch to see it was almost nine. The time had raced by! He picked up the pocket scope to check any movements. He could see through the foliage to the area in front of the 3rd green where the four men were taking their approach shots. Each man had a golf buggy nearby driven by an armed guard. No caddies. The older Garnovski and the tall Orlov were easily distinguishable. Not so the other two men at first sight. But then he saw them walking up to the green and the man in the powder blue sweater was striding purposefully ahead of the others. Turan focused the scope on his face and confirmed in his mind that the man in the powder blue sweater was the target, Lanskoy.

Then he froze! Two other men had suddenly appeared on the 4th tee – two of the armed guards, one of whom had binoculars which he used to scan the fairway ahead then sweeping down the nearside. Turan put down the scope and pulled the rifle back before the guard switched the view to the wooded area where Turan was hiding. He remained still, not breathing until the sweep had finished and the two men had retreated back to the group. He then eased back into position with the sight on the centre of the 4th tee, and slowly bolted up the round, cursing himself for not doing so earlier. The party came into view, moving in and out of sight, laughing with good hearted banter going on between them. The guards brought the buggies, parking off the tee, and took up strategic positions by the four Russians. The tall Orlov went first, and after a few practice wiggles, paused before swinging back and then down again striking the ball with roars of approval from his colleagues for what was apparently, a good drive. Turan then saw the blue sweater move forward to the front, bending down to put his tee in the ground and his ball on it. Turan moved the Mauser slightly to the left on to Lanskoy's face. He also came down a fraction. The Russian took a couple of loose swings, steadied to address the ball, looking up to the fairway ahead a couple of times. With the slight crouch into position, Lanskoys head was now plumb centre in the sight and as he paused concentrating on the ball, Turan steadied the cross hairs on the bridge of Lanskoy's nose. He applied pressure to the trigger, easing it back, and followed the shot through to target. The bullet punched into Lanskoy's skull, shattering the brain, and traveling on through, taking part of the rear of the head with it, just missing one of the guards standing at the back. Lanskoy crumpled to the ground, amid shouts and screams from the other Russians.

Turan held position ready to re-bolt if the guards came

racing to find him. But they didn't. They were professionals and their first duty was to protect the three Russians whom they hurriedly got down onto the ground, shielding them with their bodies, guns drawn. They were also not stupid – no one runs towards a sniper's rifle in the open. So Turan folded up the bipod dropping the rifle onto the netting, which he brought together gathering all the bits and pieces and started to belly crawl back down the incline using feet and elbows, and dragging the bundle with him. Still at ground level he put everything into the fishing bag and crouch walked back to the bush at the perimeter fence. Making sure there was no one about, he slipped through the gap and used a gloved thumb to press the strand over and hook behind. Not foolproof, but at least there was no obvious gaping hole to see. With the dog lead at his side, Turan walked steadily back emerging from the woods alongside his car. There were now several cars parked, but only one active with a middle-aged woman striding away with two Yorkies scampering ahead of her. With his back towards her departing into the distance, he loaded the bag and the lead onto the back seat, buckled up and drove out of the car park. Anyone who knew guns might have recognised the muffled crack of a shot, but to the dog walkers, it was just another distant noise from the golf course, and that man just another dog walker. Turan knew the way onto the A3 and that this would lead him to the London peripherique, the M25, and from there east towards Sutton. He wanted to clear the area without delay and would wait until he got close to Sutton to stop and activate the

SatNav to guide him to the address he had been given.

The guards had ushered the three Russians off the tee area to a line of trees and bushes separating the 4th and 16th fairways and providing some form of cover from the supposed line of fire. They shielded the three men from the top moving forward like a rugby pack. The three Russians were short of breath and cursing, ranting in their native language. Garnovski took charge.

"We need to go back to my house and sort things out."

"But who did this, the bastards!" shouted Krupin.

"I don't know. But we will find them, I promise you." replied an angry Garnovski. "We must get out of here – there are things to do." He turned to the guards. "Two of you get a buggy each and go back and fetch the limos."

"You mean drive across the golf course?" the guard said.

"Yes, I mean drive across the fucking golf course! Move! Now!"

Two of the men set off traveling as fast as the buggies allowed, heading back on the most direct route to the clubhouse.

"What about poor Lanskoy? What shall we do?" It was the first words Orlov had spoken and he was visibly shaken.

"We will take him with us."

"But his head is blown away."

Garnovski looked at him hard, before replying, "He is my friend! I am not leaving him there on the ground for the animals. He comes with us!"

Just then they saw the limos approaching, bouncing over the dips and mounds of the fairway.

"You two!" barked Garnovski at two more guards, "get

Andrei and put him in the boot – gently!"

The two men went to the 4th tee to collect the body, guns drawn, and scanning the wooded area for any sign of the sniper even though they knew he must be long gone by now. They stooped to pick up Lanskoy, then remembered that the rear of the skull was at the back of the tee, but shook their heads in unison, and carried the damaged corpse to one of the limos and placed it carefully in the boot.

The two cars moved off, Garnovski in the one with Lanskoy's body, and Orlov and Krupin in the other. They approached the club house and moved onto the gravel drive where a number of the staff were staring with alarm at what might have occurred and, as far as the groundsmen were concerned, aghast at the unprecedented action of driving over the course and the damage to the fairways. The club secretary came racing up to Garnovski's car, shocked at what had happened and ready to complain, owner or not. Garnovski told the driver to stop and wound down the window.

"Mr Hinks, there has been an incident and the police will undoubtedly be here very soon. You must keep the club shut and do not let anyone on to the course no matter what. NO ONE! Mr Hinks, do you hear!?"

He waited for a nod of compliance from the startled Hinks and then ordered the driver to move off. The two limousines swept out of the opened gates heading to Garnovski's mansion near Esher, its occupants silent, each with their thoughts and fears about what they had just witnessed. The cavalcade arrived at Longmoor, Garnovski's sprawling estate on the edge of the village of Oxdown. The massive spiked gates were buzzed by the driver in the first car and slowly opened, closing behind the two limousines after they had passed. The domestic staff had been alerted to the arrival and were waiting at the portico entrance for the arrival of the party. Garnovski quickly led Orlov and Krupin into the Regency drawing room, poured himself a large whisky, and gestured to the other two to help themselves from the extensive drinks cabinet. He dismissed the hovering butler and shut the door, leaving the three men alone in the room.

"What are we going to do?" Krupin said gulping on his drink.

"Firstly", replied Garnovski, "I have to phone Moscow."

"And what if Moscow is behind it?" Orlov said quietly. He had declined the offer of a drink and was sitting at the table, hands clasped under his chin.

Garnovski was quick to break the silence that ensued.

"I don't see how. Or why. They have a hundred ways in which they can silence someone. It's not their style to use guns in Western countries. And besides, look at Khodorkovsky. No weapons there, but he will soon no longer be a threat. No, I'm OK about phoning Moscow.

Anyway, what else can we do."

It was a statement, not a question.

"And the police? What about the police?" Krupin asked.

"We leave them until I have spoken to Moscow. I will phone now, and you can hear what is said."

Garnovski walked across the room and picked up the

phone, dialed the number, and switched the phone to speaker. The other two watched intently now both standing nearby.

"Da?"

All three recognised the deep throaty voice on the other end.

"This is Garnovski. May I talk?"

"Of course, Stepan. It is good to hear from you."

"I am here with Orlov and Krupin at my house in England."

"I know. And Lanskoy too, I believe." The tone was unhurried and amiable. Krupin and Orlov looked at each other but said nothing.

"It is Andrei that I need to talk about. He was killed this morning.......murdered by a gunman on the golf course."

All three heard the intake of breath at the other end.

"Who did this?"

The voice had lost its warmth, the tone now hard and demanding.

"We don't know. We have brought his body here and are deciding what to do. The police need to be told at some time."

"Yes, Stepan, you must follow the procedure."

The three men heard a long sigh of despair before the voice continued.

"I will speak to the President. He, like I, will be shocked and distressed at this news. All three of you need to return here as soon as you are able. I am sorry Stepan. I know Andrei was like a son to you."

The phone went dead. All three men were silent for a moment.

"OK," said Garnovski to the other two, "I need to contact the Police."

"What about our business meetings. Shall we abandon those now?" It was Orlov who spoke.

"No, I don't think so. We need to continue setting up the trust. We should announce an opening date for the first hospital and I would like us to name it after our dear friend, Andrei Lanskoy."

Both men nodded in agreement.

"And the other business?" Krupin asked.

"We cannot go ahead now." said Garnovski. "I know you wanted to see about getting someone of our choice in power in 2008, but what with this trial of Khodorkovsky", He paused before continuing…"and now poor Lanskoy dead. We have to be careful."

"I agree," said Orlov. "It is too dangerous at the moment."

"Yes. You are right." Krupin put down his glass. "But we do not give up. We come back to it, if and when the time is right."

"So, we are all in agreement. Now I must phone the Police. The sooner their business is done, the sooner we can all get out of here."

With that, Garnovski went to the phone and dialed 999.

"Yes. I would like to report a murder at the Valley Golf Course."

***

Turan had turned off the M25 at the intersection signposted for Sutton and drove along the A217 until he found a place to pull in at the side. He fixed the SatNav on the dash and activated the stored postcode for the garage. Whilst he was waiting for the Sat Nav to start, Turan sent a text on the mobile given to him by Beck. It was a double hash.

He was guided into Sutton, with several turns until he came to the run of garage units which seemed to be at the back of some light industrial units. He drove up to the end garage, pressed the fob on the key ring, and eased the Ford inside, closing the roller after him. Turan wasted no time. He put everything in the boot – the bag, fishing jacket, documents – everything, except his jacket and carry-on. He turned to the side door and saw a note with a drawing of the immediate streets and the route marked to the railway station. There was also a single ticket from Sutton to London.

Less than twenty five minutes later, Turan was on the train to Waterloo, arriving well in time to catch the 1227 Eurostar to Brussels. Once again, there were hardly any formalities at Waterloo and he left England without any delay arriving at Midi late afternoon, and then on to Mons where he said goodbye to Maurice Beaume forever. All documents would be destroyed when he got to Paris. Turan needed to lie low and had no intention of undertaking any more contracts for some time.

On the drive back from Mons, his thoughts turned to Simin. It had been nearly three months since she last visited, and he missed her. She had first come to the shop a year ago with her companion, both dressed in fashionable trouser suits with headscarves, and speaking faltering French. She was about the same age as him, in her early forties with wide eyes and a gentle smile. The two women were visiting Paris with their families and were looking for any small Persian artifacts to take back. The conversation was cordial but formal and they left after twenty minutes having bought nothing. He was surprised and delighted when she returned alone one month later. He offered to speak Farsi but she wished to improve her scant French, and so they conversed hesitantly, often breaking the linguistic deadlock with Farsi and sometimes even English. He learned her name was Simin.

She stayed longer with each visit, wanting to talk and learn of life in Europe, and France in particular. Whilst the meetings were always warm, Turan knew they would never progress beyond tea together in the shop which he closed whenever she came. And it was enough for him. She usually bought some small item -a stone seal or plaque- before she left.

She was hesitant at the last goodbye and as she left, she said softly, "We will meet again in the garden."

He wondered sadly if it had been her way of telling him that she could not visit him anymore.

When Turan got back to his shop in Clichy, he was still pumped up by the whole venture, and he needed a release. So, he phoned to make sure Sophie was available, and then showered and changed, and walked down to the house just past the Moulin.

Chapter 8

John Matteson was in his office in Whitehall late Friday reading the news on the marriage of Prince Charles and Camilla Parker-Bowles. Matteson headed up the Economics Intelligence Unit, which comprised himself, an assistant, Frew Douglas, and "half" a secretary.

He had been pressing Graham Stokes for more staff, and with it, full use of the secretary, Lindsay. The usual excuses of budget and costs had been thrown at him, but at long last, it was agreed that he could start looking for someone. Matteson put down the paper and began thinking what to do over the week-end. It should be something to look forward to, but since he had split up with his last girlfriend, Ruth, there was not a lot happening in his life.

Most of his friends were partnered. He could visit his Aunt Mary in Yorkshire – she was getting quite elderly and he ought to see her soon. He was weighing up his options, as limited as they were, when the phone rang. It was Stokes, sounding unusually agitated.

"Matteson, I need you over here urgently. And bring

your man, Douglas, with all the info he has on those Russians."

"Yes, Sir, what……" Matteson tailed off as he realised Stokes had put down the phone. He knew something serious was up and found Douglas in his office.

"Frew, we're needed. It sounds as if war has broken out. Bring everything you've got on the four Russians".

Douglas nodded, sensing this was not a time for questions. He was a tall Scot, a linguist who specialised in Europe and the countries in the old Soviet Union. He gathered up his laptop and two files, and the two men walked quickly down the road to Stokes' building. Their passes got them into the lobby where Andrew Trivett was waiting - tailored suit on a stocky frame, but without his usual amiable smile.

"Good, you're here. Let's go."

Trivett waited until they were riding up in the lift. It was slow, but it gave time for him to explain.

"One of the Russians has been murdered on the golf course. It looks like a professional hit. An assassination."

"My God!" said Matteson. "Which one is it?"

"Lanskoy. We're here. I'll check you through."

They emerged onto the fifth floor. Douglas had said nothing, just taking in the shocking news. The two men were signed in through another manned barrier check and followed Trivett along the corridor past busy partitioned offices until they reached a large ornate wooden door.

"Come in", barked the unmistakable voice of Graham Stokes in response to their knock. They entered a large impressive room, richly carpeted and decorated. The interior of the building had been redesigned to accommodate as many functional offices as possible, but not Stokes' office which retained its original features. Stokes looked up and nodded at them to sit in the chairs in front of his desk.

"Andrew has told you the news, I presume. All hell has broken loose. The Home Secretary wants answers, and so do I. The Police are already on the case and no doubt Special Branch will be involved. The official line will be outrage that this….this assassination because that's what it was….has taken place on British soil. And of course, full sympathy with this man's family. But that is their job, the Police. My job is to get to the bottom of who ordered this hit and why. I have convened a meeting for this evening with all services involved. But I need you to tell myself and Andrew everything you know about this group."

"Well," Matteson started, "we know they have been meeting over the last nine months. Because of their importance in the Russian economy, Frew has been monitoring their activities and has background files on each of the men. So, Frew, can you take over now."

Frew Douglas started to relate the movements of the Russians. He didn't need to refer to his laptop or the files which he had placed on the floor.

"Yes. There are four of them. Garnovski, Krupin, Orlov, and Lanskoy. They all control major industries – metal, coal, chemicals – and are immensely wealthy. They have met three times over the last nine months – once at Orlov's place in Spain, the second time on Krupin's boat in Monaco, and again this morning at Garnovski's golf course. They have appeared to avoid each other in previous times, so why the sudden cosiness."

"What about the dead man, Lanskoy. Tell us about him," said Trivett.

"He runs…or ran…I should say, Interlansk. A large company dealing in metals, and an important one too. Lanskoy is of course very wealthy, somewhere around ten billion dollars, and is a favourite of the Kremlin. I know there are rumblings in Moscow about the power of the oligarchs, but I see no reason for a hit on Lanskoy. They have, after all, effectively dealt with Mikhail Khodorkovsky of Yukos without resorting to violence."

Graham Stokes thought for a moment.

"Could Lanskoy have run foul of the Russian mafia? They've murdered industrialists before."

Matteson stepped in.

"No. I don't think so. Not even the mafia would risk the wrath of the Kremlin by taking out one of their favoured sons. And also, why here? They could have just shot him down in Russia somewhere or hired a Chechen gun. It wouldn't make sense to go through such an elaborate plot here in England. It would be too risky."

"Good point. But if it wasn't Moscow and it wasn't the Russian gangsters, then who did kill Lanskoy? I need to find out. Right, Matteson I want you and Douglas to go through everything you've got and work out every possible outcome of this murder. I want to know who will benefit and who will lose financially. And of course, highlight anything more sinister that you may come across. I want you to get your report to Andrew by first thing Monday morning. Clear?"

"Yes Sir, we will start right away," replied Matteson, rising with Douglas to leave. Stokes nodded his thanks, as Trivett rose also to show them out.

"I'll walk you through the top checkpoint. I'll be back in a moment, Sir."

The three men left the room and walked back along the corridor.

"You both did well," smiled Trivett. "I was impressed." He saw them signed out of the fifth floor.

"I'll leave you both here – I've got a long night ahead. Remember that report. Monday please."

Matteson watched him as he turned back along the corridor, and then entered the lift with Douglas down to the ground floor and through the front checkpoint. They exited the main entrance and walked back along Whitehall to their own building to work on their reports.

***

Garnovski sat slumped in an armchair in the lounge of his Surrey mansion. The day had been spent with the Police, both uniformed and plain clothes, going over the evidence and taking statements from himself, Orlov and Krupin. The other two Russians had left for London, having agreed to stay available if needed, and Lanskoy's body had been removed to the mortuary. The investigation and forensic teams were returning the next day, and Garnovski had decided to remain in Surrey until their initial enquiries had finished. He had updated Moscow and it was accepted that none of the trio would be back in Russia for at least a week. He had also cancelled his appointments for the next few days, too pre-occupied with the events of the last twelve hours to even think of business.

Chapter 9

Ed Barrow stood looking out through the large sliding doors onto the scene of a placid Lake Geneva. He was at peace and content. He had come a long way since those early days in the hills of Tennessee, a crack shot hunting in the backwoods, who had risen through the ranks of the US Army as a marksman and had gone on to make his living with a sniper's rifle. Using the money he made, he was able to set up a protection and security firm in Europe with Mel Carter, an old friend from California. They built the firm up into a successful business, eventually selling the company after twelve years, and both retired wealthy men. He had met Veronique, who was much younger than him and they had married and set up home in Veronique's native Switzerland. Now in his mid fifties, slightly portly, with close cropped hair, he gazed out at his wife, elegant and stylish even when tending their garden that backed down to the lake's edge, and he knew he was indeed a lucky man.

His land line rang, and he turned away from the scene and picked up the phone from the hall table.

"Yes?"

"Edward, it is you yes?"

Barrow had no difficulty identifying the deep, gruff voice of the Russian.

"This is a surprise. It must be over ten years."

Barrow had lived in Europe long enough to mask his Tennessee drawl but still had a slight warming American tone.

"Yes, a voice from the past, eh."

"Indeed." Barrow was cautious. "As I said, this is a surprise. I won't ask how you got my number. But I will ask how you are – well, I hope – and more importantly, the reason for the call."

"I would not have troubled you if it was not important to me. I know you are married and settled in Switzerland and I am pleased for you. But I need your help."

"How? I'm not in that business any more, as well you know."

"It is not a contract, Edward. A friend of both mine and the President, Andrei Lanskoy, was shot and killed in England this morning. It was a professional job and I need to find out who did it. So, I need your help."

Barrow knew the caller of old and knew how he could play games. But there was, he felt, a real sadness in the Russian's voice.

"I am really sorry. I did meet Lanskoy once and he seemed a genuine guy. But as I said, I am retired and I don't move in those circles anymore."

"I know. But you know how these people work – you

were one of them. I just want you to look at the situation maybe ask around. Even if I get to know which country this shooter came from, it would help."

Barrow pondered the request for a few minutes. The Russian remained silent. Finally, Barrow answered.

"I will look into it. But, if there is any hint of danger coming to my doorstep, to my wife and my home, I will shut it all down."

"Thank you. I understand. I will leave it to you. You can get the details from the English press. Please phone me as soon as you have some news. You know where I am. And Edward, whatever you find – everything or nothing at all - I will be grateful that you helped."

The line went dead. Barrow replaced the receiver and went back to the lounge to look again at his wife in the garden. Anyone else and the answer would have been an emphatic "No".

But the General had intervened once behind the scenes in Georgia to save his life. Nevertheless, Barrow was determined that he would not cross any line that would bring any threat near his beloved Veronique. He needed to get to England and check out the scene but that would have to wait until Monday. He had already planned his weekend with his wife – sailing on Saturday and a social dinner in town. In the meantime, he would get as much as he could from the internet.

***

On Friday evening, Beck collected the car from the garage in Sutton, making sure that everything connected to Turan's trip was inside the boot, including the gun. He drove to the outskirts of Bermondsey and parked a hundred metres from The Tops car crushing plant. Fallon arrived twenty minutes later and took over the Ford. The two men didn't speak, just nodded at each other. Fallon removed both the front and rear number plates which he threw onto the back seat, and then drove the car the short distance into the breakers yard. Beck did not want to be seen by anyone in the yard but walked close enough to the gates to look in where the large crusher stood ready. He saw the grappler lift the Ford into the gaping mouth and watched as the car was slowly crushed, rocking and screeching, until all that remained was the block of metal which was lifted out and dumped unceremoniously onto a pile of scrap.

A large sum of cash was handed to the owner for this "no questions asked" deal, and Fallon left the plant to return to his own car joined by Beck. The two men drove back into London where Beck was dropped off again at Clapham to make his way to his flat on the South Bank. He used his mobile to text a double hash to the London number.

The man in Kensington was relieved that the final part of the operation was over His client was now aware that Lanskoy had been successfully eliminated, and the three million dollars should shortly be transferred into his Swiss numbered account. He would arrange payment to Turan and Beck, but first sent a text – a capital X -to the two men, and also to Stils. This was his instruction to lock down all operations in Europe, a procedure he had adopted after completion of any difficult contract. There would be no further contact until he was satisfied things had quietened down. That could be anything up to six months. On receipt of the text, all three men destroyed their pay as you go cellphones.

***

Matteson and Douglas worked through the weekend to complete their report which was on Andrew Trivett's desk early Monday morning. The report stated that there was no real gain for anyone from Lanskoy's death. Moscow would not allow any of the other oligarchs to take over Lanskoy's business as it would make them too powerful. At the same time, the State could not be seen to be engineering nationalisation of a major industry, especially using assassination as the means. Lanskoy's family would naturally inherit his estate, but it was obviously inconceivable that they were involved in his murder. The two men had concluded that there was no obvious financial gain for anyone in particular; and the likely outcome was that the State would monitor the running of the business until an "approved" candidate from within Interlansk takes over control.

Chapter 10

Barrow was working on Monday morning at his home in Geneva, gathering all the information he could on the killing from the various news items on the internet. He then researched the history of the four Russians, in particular Lanskoy, and also downloaded the layout of Valley golf course. On Tuesday morning, he kissed Veronique goodbye saying that he would be back in a couple of days from this unexpected business meeting in England. Although she understood perfectly, he hated leaving her and hung on to the farewell embrace for as long as he could.

The hire company courtesy car was waiting for him at Heathrow, and he was soon driving down the A3 to his hotel in Guildford. After check-in, he went off immediately to look at the Valley golf course.

He followed the road round the course and swept down the bend leading to the parking area of the adjoining woods. He left the car and walked through the woods towards the Valley course, until he reached the service road, and saw in the distance the distinctive Police tape across an area of the perimeter fence. He worked his way through the woods until he reached the point opposite the taped off area. The opening in the fence was now clearly visible. Barrow took out his plan of the course and checked the aerial photo and was able to identify the point of entry and the probable route to the hide. There was no one around and Barrow stayed hidden on the fringe of the service road, pondering the probable actions of the gunman, before he left and made his way back to the car. He drove to the hotel and went up to his room.

His problem was that it had been some time since he was in the game and the players that he had known were like him, well past it – or dead. He could make a few phone calls but doubted that it would elicit anything useful. Plus, he would prefer to let sleeping dogs lie. You never know what an awakening could lead to. No, there was nothing more he could do here. He phoned home.

"Veronique, it's me Edward."

"Edward......I didn't think you were phoning until this evening."

"I know my love, but the meeting has been cancelled so I'm getting the first flight back. I should be there later today."

"That's wonderful. I will go and get something special for dinner. Oh Edward, I thought you would be away tomorrow, so I have asked my mother to come for the day. Is that all right?"

"Of course. I have some work to do in my office, but I shall be free for most of the day. It will be nice to have your mother over. I'll see you later. Bye darling."

"Bye Edward. I love you."

Barrow put the phone down, smiling at his wife's obvious delight that he was on his way home. He checked out and drove back to Heathrow where he returned the hire car, before catching the afternoon flight back to Geneva.

The next day, after he had finished coffee with Veronique and her mother, he retreated to his office, leaving the two women to enjoy the early summer day in the garden. He telephoned the Moscow number, waiting until the re-routing was finished, and then heard the gruff voice answer.

"Da?"

"It's Edward."

"Ah Edward, I did not expect to hear from you so quickly. Do you have anything?"

"I've been to the site and looked around. My best guess at this stage is ex-military, brought in from outside England, probably the EU, and with help from inside England."

"Interesting. Can you tell me what makes you think that?"

"Yes, sure. Britain is small place with the security service and Police almost always on a constant alert for one thing or another. You wouldn't give this to someone living in England, and I doubt whether any resident professional – if there are still any left in the UK – would accept the contract. No, it makes a lot more sense to go outside England. In which case, who can travel in and out of the UK without immigration checks - European Union nationals. I don't think it was one of your lot – that would have been too obvious."

"I agree," the Russian growled. "I would certainly have learned of something like this or got a whisper at least. But nothing at this end."

"And someone had to provide a car and then make it disappear. There has apparently been no trace, but that is based on newspaper reports only. And the same people would have come up with the gun, one that they knew suited the shooter. So, all our man had to do was to travel from an EU country into England, almost definitely by train – less stringent checks than planes – pick up the car and the gun, do the job, leave the load to others to get rid of, and jump on his train back to whichever EU country he came from."

"Yes Edward. Yes, I see that. Very good."

"Look, this is not one hundred percent certain. I mean, someone from America or anywhere could have easily got a false EU passport, but that would mean additional travel in and out of Europe that could be avoided. So, this is my best guess with the information we have at the moment. I just hope it helps."

"More than you realise, my friend."

The old Russian paused, before resuming.

"Edward, I have work to do. Thank you for this. Would you please continue to look for any other information that will help. If we can speak in, say two weeks time, I would be grateful."

"Yes, certainly. I'll contact you in two weeks."

"Good."

The line went dead. Barrow leaned back, pleased that he had helped the old man, but at a loss to think what else he could do. Anyway, that could all wait for now. He got up and went out into the spring sunshine to join his wife and her mother.

***

General Leonid Shepilev sat back in his chair, thinking. He had spent his life on the front line defending the State and the President. He should be retired now, with his suburban flat and country dacha, but they said they needed his experience and his still active brain to protect the President's office. In the three years in this job, he had foiled a number of conspiracies with the help of his network of informants, and people who owed him favours, built up over many decades.

The General knew that 2005 should have been a good year for the President. He was in his second term and the economy was growing thanks mainly to rising oil prices. The President had taken various measures to restore stability to Russian society and to reinforce his position.

The upcoming Khodorkovsky trial should put a stop to the political meddling of the oligarchs. But Ukraine's "Orange Revolution" last December, and the street protests about changes in welfare benefits, had unnerved the Kremlin, and the emphasis now was to maintain the President's approval rating and ensure a smooth transfer of power to a nominated successor after the end of his second and last term in 2007.

The General coughed, patting his chest with his hand. He had given up cigarettes six years earlier, but it had been hard. He had smoked since he was a boy, and at times, a cigarette had been his only companion. Even the cardboard Belomorkanals that roasted his throat had been a welcome friend in the bitter cold mornings out on manoeuvres. But no more. Now his only vice, if you could call it that, was coffee, endless cups of coffee.

Right now, his mind was on this shooting in England which puzzled him. The killing of Lanskoy was bad enough in its own right, but he knew there was something more behind it. Something lurking in the shadows. At the least, he had to be ready for it, but the best solution would be to expose and crush it altogether. He had people, including Barrow, dredging the bottom layer to identify the man who pulled the trigger. He needed to work on the top layer, find the person behind the conspiracy who ordered the assassination, and the reason why.

The information from Barrow confirmed his original conclusion that the person he was looking for was not someone whose mind remained behind the old iron curtain, but someone whose thought process could easily slide to the West, who was comfortable with Europe both mentally and probably physically. The other three in England with Lanskoy would obviously fit that description, but were they too obvious? And would they risk their own lives being in touching distance to Lanskoy when the bullet was fired. Garnovski sounded truly distressed and angry at the loss of someone he was close to. But he would give that order if he had too, I'm sure, thought the old General, leaning back in his chair. Maybe his anger was feigned; or possibly real because the shooting took place dangerously close to him and on his own golf course.

He looked at his watch. He still had forty minutes before his meeting with the President. He took a sheet of paper and started writing, looking up from time to time and the big clock on the far wall. When he had finished and was satisfied with what he had written, he pressed the buzzer on his desk. His aide, FS Major Ivan Guragin, came in and stood formally in front of the desk.

"Take this list. I want you to find out all of the names of the support group for each of these eleven individuals. In particular, their fixers. In fact, underline that name in each group so I can see it immediately. Go, and I want this done quickly."

"Yes, Sir. Immediately."

The aide turned and left. Three of the names on the list were Garnovski, Orlov, and Krupin.

Chapter 11

A week after the incident, Matteson received an internal memo for his eyes only outlining the results of the investigations so far. The bulk of the report related to Police enquiries, and despite being for him only, he called Frew into his office to run through the findings.

"I can't give you the report Frew, but basically, nobody has uncovered anything positive. The Police have located the sniper's nest, and it looks like the man parked up in an adjoining wood and cut a hole in the boundary fence. The only thing is two sightings of a dark car, possibly a Ford, in the area at the time. One was in the car park of the woods opposite the golf course. A woman was walking her dog on that Friday morning around the time of the shooting and says that she saw a man getting into a car in the corner of car park. She thinks it was a Ford but she could not be absolutely certain of the make and as far as she was concerned, it was just another early morning dog walker. The other sighting was more definite as to the make – definitely a Ford and dark colour. It was seen in the corner of the car park next to the

Yvonne Arnaud theatre in Guildford about lunchtime a couple of days before the shooting. The witness was a guy eating his lunch in his car. He noticed it because a big man sat there for some time reading a paper, and was then joined by a smaller man, and after about ten minutes talking, the big man left and walked out of the car park and the other man drove off in the car. He thought it was odd, but really none of his business, until the Police advertised for any information about any suspicious sightings of a dark car, possibly a Ford in the area around the time of the murder. But that's it. There's been no subsequent sighting of the car or the men. What? Why are you frowning?"

Frew Douglas was searching his memory, and his face suddenly lit up.

"Yes, JP. I've got it. Do you remember that incident at the Titanium plant in South Africa? Early last year?"

"Yes. I think so. Some sort of explosion. But what's that got to do with this, Frew?"

"Well, I got friendly with a Police Inspector down there – we talked rugby together – and I remember him mentioning that the explosion was thought suspicious and two men were seen sitting in a car off the main road on the evening of the explosion and near to where the body of a worker was found shot dead. The two men were described as one large and bulky and the other smaller and slight. Coincidence? What do you think?"

"Yes probably, Frew. But I don't remember reading this in your report."

"No, I know JP. Our brief was to report to Defence on

the effect of the shortage of titanium following the explosion. Shrinking supply and rising market price, and how best to source the raw material to keep defence projects going. The Ministry would not want the report cluttered with Police suspicions."

"No, that's true. Are you still in touch with this Inspector?"

"Yeah, sort of. Christmas cards and things. Well maybe more. He's planning a visit to England with his family and I think we might meet up some time.

"Give him a call. Find out if anything else cropped up about these two men. I won't raise it elsewhere at the moment. I think you were absolutely right not to mention it in the report to Defence, Frew, but you know what it's like upstairs when they're under pressure – they'll criticise anything. Let's wait and see what you come back with first. As you say, it may just be one of those co-incidences and totally unrelated."

But unrelated it was not.

***

It was early evening on a warm Spring day in 2004, in South Africa. The evening shift had just started at the massive titanium plant near Durban. Two men were working at the smelter on the No 2 electric arc furnace where the titanium slag reaches 1700 degrees centigrade before being tapped off. Suddenly there was a small explosion and a section of the furnace wall bulged and then erupted. The liquid metal hit both workers and they died instantly. The slag gushed from the furnace smoking and hissing as it snaked its way across the floor spreading widely as it went, engulfing everything in its path. The sensors picked up the breakout at the same time as the supervisor saw it from the overhead gantry. The klaxon blasted furiously and the whole evening shift stopped and listened with a mixture of fear and apprehension. By the time the emergency crew reached the area, the two workers were partially immersed, and the river of molten metal had spread into the cable trays causing an immediate shortage. The plant in the area stuttered to a halt and the emergency lighting kicked in.

Kanele had just finished the afternoon shift and now stood off the approach road, hidden from view, looking back through the dusk at the factory site in the distance. He heard the klaxon alarm and smiled to himself. Now his family would never worry about money again. They had promised him more than he could earn in ten years working the slag. All he had to do was smuggle in the small package and leave it in the dark spot by the furnace wall just before he left. He turned away from the plant and headed up the road to where they would be waiting.

Turan and Beck were in the car, lights off, down a sidetrack off the approach road. They had been in South Africa for three days on alias passports, outwardly visiting vineyards on a business trip, mixed with some sightseeing. They had made plans earlier to meet a local fixer who had told them about Kanele and his sometime involvement in petty crime. Part threat but mostly money had persuaded the worker to co-operate. They too heard the explosion at which point Turan got out of the front passenger seat and into the back behind Beck.

Kanele turned into the sidetrack and saw the dark outline of the car ahead. As he drew alongside, the back widow wound down and he was still half smiling when he saw the flash and felt the sudden pain in his chest and fell. Turan got out of the car and fired three more shots at the groaning figure, with one aimed at the head. The body went still. Beck got out the front and the two men dragged the dead worker off the road and into the undergrowth, got back into the car, and drove off. Further along the approach road leading away from the plant, the car slowed and Turan hurled the gun into the undergrowth. The Z88 handgun and the explosive used at the plant had been sold to them by the same gangster who recruited Kanele, and who now lay shot dead in his Durban apartment. Turan peeled off the latex gloves and put them in a carrier bag to be thrown out along the main highway. They then drove to the airport where they left the hire car in the rental car park and the keys in the drop box. The two men were just in time for the evening flight to Johannesburg where they would catch the night flight back to Amsterdam. Before boarding, Beck sent a text to London. There was no message, just a double hash.

The man receiving the message smiled to himself. This was a good line of work, sabotage to influence share prices. It was a contract that paid a good fee, with a bonus promised by the client when the market price reacted favourably. He would check the movement of the price of titanium and make sure he received that bonus.

Chapter 12

Two weeks had passed, and it was now late May. The Police in England were dealing with the death of Lanskoy as a murder enquiry, and all efforts were directed to finding the person who killed him. Other interested parties in London were more concerned with who was behind the assassination and why.

Matteson had to prepare a report on future trade relations with Spain in the light of the continuing Gibraltar problem, and although not strictly necessary, he arranged a trip to Madrid to discuss matters with the Embassy staff, pleased to get away from the pressure of London. He had to point out to Andrew Trivett that this was his proper job and what he gets paid for, and that he would be back in a few days. Matteson had arrived the day before and spent most of that day and the next with the Embassy staff with an early evening flight booked back to London. He was in his hotel room packing to leave when the phone rang.

"Mr Matteson?"

"Yes. Who's that?"

"It's Clark from the Embassy, Sir. We've just heard that Air Traffic control has gone on strike unannounced as always, so unfortunately you won't be flying to London tonight, or possibly not even tomorrow."

"Oh, no!" Matteson slumped.

" … but, " continued Clark, "I've managed to get you on the overnight train to Paris and you can get back to London from there tomorrow. But you have to get a move on, Sir. The train leaves in forty minutes."

"Thank you so much, Mr Clark. You are a life saver."

"I've arranged for the ticket to be delivered to reception for when you check out and booked your taxi with the hotel. I couldn't get you a single berth so you'll be sharing with one other."

"That's fine. And thank you again…I really appreciate it."

"That's OK Sir. Have a good trip."

Matteson was now in a rush to catch the train and carried his bag down himself to reception, where he collected his ticket and checked out. The concierge had been alerted by reception to have a taxi ready outside, and he was soon on his way to Chamartin station.

After what seemed like an interminable taxi ride through Madrid's early evening traffic, Matteson made it to Chamartin with just fifteen minutes to spare before departure. The departure hall was busy with weekend travelers and Matteson noticed the queues at the ticket centre and silently muttered another thanks to Clark. He made his way to the platform where the overnight Paris train, the Francisco de Goya, was waiting. Clark had managed to get him in Gran Clase and he was duly shown to his compartment in the sleeping car by the attendant. After the formalities of passport and breakfast vouchers, he booked dinner with attendant for the 8pm sitting.

His travelling companion for the journey was already in the compartment.

Peter Veldt, who, like Matteson, was supposed to have flown home but was now training it to Paris and then on to Amsterdam. Veldt had eaten a long Madrid lunch and declined Matteson's invitation to join him for dinner but agreed to an early drink in the bar. The two men made their way to the bar as the train started its journey out of Madrid heading north through the hills. Veldt was friendly enough and it turned out that he owned a restaurant in the centre of Amsterdam.

"Were you in Madrid checking out the food, Peter?" asked Matteson, putting his glass down on the bar.

"No, not for any business. I was there for a pistol competition."

"Really!"

Matteson was surprised, not associating this slight, unassuming man with guns.

"Yes," continued Veldt, "my father taught me when shooting did not carry the stigma that it now has. I belong to a club in Amsterdam. To me it is a sport and I just want to hit the target and win the game."

"And did you win, Peter …… in Madrid, I mean."

"On no! Too good for me, but it was an honour to be invited. It was nice to visit Madrid, but I shall be pleased to get home to my wife," he said smiling. "And you my friend, what about you?"

"No, I have no involvement with shooting" replied Matteson.

"No, not shooting. I mean do you have a wife to get back to?"

Matteson laughed at his misunderstanding.

"No, Peter. No wife. Not yet anyway."

The conversation continued amiably with Matteson giving a limited explanation of his work and visit to Madrid. Just before eight, he left Veldt at the bar and went on into the to the dining car. To the south west, the last of the sun was giving a red hue to the Sierra de Gredos. The diner was elegant and relaxing, filled mainly with tourists, the Spanish preferring to stick to the later sitting. He was shown to a side table for two but with only one place laid, and settled in thankful to have room to stretch his legs.

"Excuse me, may I sit here?"

Matteson looked up from the menu to see the smiling face of a young, attractive woman.

"Well, may I?" she said, questioning with a tilt of her head.

"Oh, forgive me. Please do." replied Matteson, pulling his legs back and climbing to his feet. "I don't know why it's been laid just for one."

"Perhaps you're a VIP," she said smiling.

"Far from it. My name's …John."

"And I'm Lillian."

She had settled in the seat opposite and he had a moment

to take in the short brown hair, brown eyes, and the strong face of a young woman he guessed to be in her late twenties dressed in a loose top and jeans. He manoeuvred to give her more room and their legs touched as they fumbled for position.

"Excuse me," he said, "I'll get them to lay a place for you. I've looked at the menu so it's all yours."

Having given their orders to the waiter, they settled back into the rhythm of the train with Lillian chatting away.

"I'm travelling with my best friend Jaz....Jasmine, but she's not feeling too good. She's lying down. We've been to Barcelona which was fabulous - I want to go back one day but stay a lot longer - and then we came on to Madrid. We're now on our way to Paris where we were going to stop for a few days, but if Jaz is no better by the morning, then I'll have to take her straight back home to London."

"What has she got, some food bug?" Matteson asked sympathetically.

"No, the food's been fine - she's got a really bad chest and is a bit fluey."

"Has she seen a doctor?"

"No," smiled Lillian, "we're both doctors! We work together in London. No, it only came on badly today. If she gets a lot worse, I'll get her to a medic in Paris, but I know Jaz - she'll just want to get home." Lillian paused. "But enough of that - what about you, John? What do you do?"

"I work in Whitehall....a sort of liaison for trade. Boring really, but I do get to travel occasionally."

"Was it work that brought you to Spain?"

"Yes, something in Madrid. I was supposed to be on a plane back, but air traffic control decided otherwise."

"And where do you live in London?"

"In Battersea. I've got a small flat there. And you?"

"I'm north of the river, in Islington. Jaz and I share. But you're not originally from London are you?"

"How do you figure that out?"

"Oh, it's just the way you say some words."

"Oh, I see. But yes, I was born in Yorkshire. My family originate from a small place called Nethertong. It's near Huddersfield, where we ended up moving to and where I went to school."

"And do your parents still live there?"

Matteson hesitated before answering.

"No, both of my parents are dead. They were killed in a car crash ten years ago."

Lillian put her glass down.

"John, I am so sorry. Really I………"

"No, it's OK. You weren't to know obviously."

The waiter arrived with their food and Lillian took the opportunity to change the conversation, not wanting to cause any more discomfort to the handsome man she had just met.

"Jaz and I needed this break. It's been very hectic at work. We're both junior doctors and it's been non-stop for us. If we hadn't got away, I think we both would have collapsed with exhaustion."

"Which hospital do you work at?"

"Barts. St Bartholomews. We more or less went through

the whole five years together, and we were both pleased to end up at Barts. Though I don't know how long Jaz will stay – she's going steady now and there could be wedding bells soon."

"Are you not with someone?" he said as nonchalantly as he could, hoping she would say no.

"Was. But it didn't work out. This fish is really good."

"Yes, it is, isn't it."

End of conversation. Not going there any further, Matteson thought. She didn't even want to ask me if I had someone.

Matteson's evening with Lillian ended all too soon. She had lingered over the dessert and a second glass of Rioja, but then readied to leave.

"I'm sorry, John, but I have to get back to Jaz," she said, slightly forlornly. And then touching his hand, "It's been a wonderful evening. Thank you so much."

Matteson was taken aback at the apparent sudden end to their evening together, and although Lillian paused as she rose, all he could say was, "No, thank you, I enjoyed it too."

And with a smile, she turned and left.

He slumped back into his chair, bewildered that she had gone so abruptly, and annoyed with himself for letting her go like that. He poured out the last of the wine and sat thinking about her and knowing he needed to see her again. She would be tending her sick friend now, so it would have to wait until morning. Matteson sensed the waiters were preparing the vacated tables for the late sitting, so he downed his wine and went back to the bar. It was quite full, with the waiting diners, mainly Spanish, having a predinner drink; and some English and German travelers whom he partly recognised from the first sitting. He found space at the end of the bar and sipped a brandy, pressing himself into the corner, steadying against the gentle rocking of the train. The surrounding chatter faded into the background as his thoughts meandered across the girl he had just met, work, Hong Kong, and his parents whom he still missed. He deliberately broke away from his thoughts, finished his drink, and headed to the sleeper compartment.

The beds had been made ready by the attendant, and Veldt was already asleep, turned away from the light and gently snoring. Matteson quietly changed and got into his bed, intending to shower in the morning. He turned out the light and lay there, thinking of how to see Lillian in the morning before the train dispersed. The rhythm of the track coupled with the wine and brandy began to slow his thoughts, and it wasn't long after before he was fast asleep.

When he awoke, the curtains were partly drawn and daylight was streaming into the compartment. Veldt's bed with empty, loosely made up with his case on top. Matteson grabbed his watch. Nearly eight! Oh no. He looked out the window - he didn't know where they were. It was still countryside, possibly the Loire area he thought, and a beautiful spring morning. He was annoyed that he had slept so long and hastily shaved and showered and dressed. He then worked his way along the train to the bar. He was greeted by the smell of strong coffee and a mixture of travellers, seated and standing, but no sign of Lillian. He went quickly to the restaurant car where a more sedate breakfast scene prevailed, but still no sign of her. He did however see Peter Veldt and went to join him at the table.

"John….," said Veldt, looking up from his plate, "good to see you. I hope I didn't wake you - you were fast asleep."

"No, Peter, I didn't hear a thing."

Matteson ordered coffee from the waiter.

"You're not eating. Everything is really good. You have no problem, I hope," Veldt said showing a gesture of rubbing his stomach.

"No, I'm fine, Peter. The food was excellent last night. Do you know what time we arrive in Paris?"

"Yes, about nine."

"Ah, I've still got some time. I'm sorry, Peter, I have to leave you. I need to pack and be ready to get off as soon we get to Paris."

"Of course. Please don't let me hold you up. But, before you go". …Veldt reached into his inside pocket… "here is my card, John. If ever you are in Amsterdam, please call me. It would be good to meet up again. I've put my private number there, so you can get straight through if the restaurant is busy."

"Yes. Thank you. And the same if you come to London, Peter. I don't have a card on me but if you have a spare one, I'll write my number on the back."

Matteson left the Dutchman to continue his breakfast and returned to the sleeping carriage. He packed, checking that his work papers were still secure in the portmanteau pouch, and then made his way along the swaying train to the front. The scenery had changed in the time since he awoke, and there were now clear urban signs and the beginning of the suburbs outside Paris. The train eventually slowed winding its way through Paris and finally coming to a halt in Gare d'Austerlitz. Matteson left the train as soon as the doors allowed and went to stand alongside the platform exit, looking down the line of the train for any glimpse of Lillian. Eventually he saw her pushing one bag, whilst carrying another, and walking closely alongside a fair haired woman buttoned up and looking decidedly rhumey. She caught sight of him approaching and touched her friend's arm to stop.

"Hello," she said smiling broadly. "I didn't think I'd see you again. This is my friend Jaz."

"Hello," he directed to Jaz, and then turning back to Lillian, "I wanted to make sure you were both all right. Are you still heading straight back to London?"

Lillian gestured sympathetically towards Jaz who gave a wan smile behind her coat top.

"Yes, we need to get back. We've managed to switch our Eurostar tickets and we're just off to get a taxi to Gare du Nord. What about you?"

"I've got to fly – my car's parked at Heathrow. But let me help you with your luggage."

Matteson took the heaviest of the bags from Lillian and they walked through to the taxi rank where the queue was moving quite swiftly. The conversation was mainly niceties with Jaz staying silent apart from the odd snuffle. When they were near the front of the queue, he finally asked her.

"I'd like to see you again….in London, I mean. That is

if you are free at any time."

She looked at his face for what seemed ages to him before slowly smiling and saying, "I would like that, John. Can you call me if I give you my number?.......but I must warn you, I do work all sorts of odd hours."

The next taxi would be theirs. He hastily pulled out his mobile and tapped in the number she gave him. Smiles and even a hug. Then they were in the taxi and gone. Matteson spent most of the week-end thinking about the woman who had just come into his life. He hadn't had a serious girlfriend for some time, and he was both curious and excited about where this was relationship would go.

Chapter 13

Matteson was back in his office early Monday morning, catching up on an accumulated "in- tray", mostly on the computer when his assistant, Frew Douglas, knocked on the door and came in.

"Morning, JP, how was Madrid?" asked Frew, peering over the top of his specs.

"It was fine, Frew. Much the same as the last time – a lot of posturing but I doubt whether there will any dramatic impact on our trading relationship. What about you? Anything happen whilst I was away?"

"Nothing further on the Russian business. I doubt whether there's anything more we can do to help. It's really a matter for the Police and whoever else is involved. Has there been anything from Andrew Trivett?"

"Not that I can see, but I still have a few memos to run through. OK, I'll get on. Thanks Frew."

Matteson was starting back on his computer when Frew Douglas stopped at the door and wheeled round back into the room.

"I've forgotten to mention my last conversation with the South African Police Inspector. We had a long chat on Friday. He did remember the two men – the big one and the smaller one - and said that enquiries at the time showed two men fitting that description were Dutch wine brokers touring the vineyards on business. They had left for Amsterdam by the time the Police checked up on them, but they seemed to know their wines and were supposedly reputable businessmen. The sighting must have been purely co-incidental."

"Yes, I agree, Frew. I think we'll just leave this for the moment. But good work. And a useful contact for the future."

Douglas smiled and left his boss to get back to work. Matteson broke off just after noon, searched his mobile for Lillian's number and pressed dial. It rang six times and switched to answer phone. He recognised her voice immediately.

"Hi, this is Doctor Lillian Culver, I'm busy at the moment, but please leave a message and I'll get back to you."

Matteson hesitated through the answer phone invite until it was too late. He stared at the wall, thought, shrugged, and dialed again. This time he was straight in with the message.

"Hi Lillian. This is John....we met on the Madrid train. I was just wondering if you got back OK. I'll try and catch you later. Bye."

After the call, Matteson sat remembering the dinner on the Francisco de Goya and wondering if anything would develop with Lillian or was it just ships that passed in the night. She would probably immerse herself back into her world and make no contact. He came out of his thoughts and went back to his workload, accepting the offer from his secretary, Lindsay, to bring a sandwich in for him. She also reminded him that he needed to approve the short list of candidates for the second assistant so interviews could be arranged. He switched to that task immediately, knowing how long it had taken him to get Stokes to underwrite the cost and did not want any delay in getting someone installed to help in the overworked section. In the end, he short listed two names as definite. One was Russ Sterne, in his fifties, fluent in Arabic and immersed in Arab affairs, having lived and worked in Saudi, and travelled extensively throughout the Middle East, and also Pakistan. The other was a young woman Rebecca Howard who was already working in the Foreign Office. She was a business graduate, fluent in Spanish and Portuguese, and just what he needed to cover the markets in South America. He added a couple of reserves in case neither of these two wanted or suited the part, then took the list down to Lindsay to agree the interview day and start making the appointments.

Matteson broke off work part way through the afternoon and decided to try Lillian again. This time she answered straight away.

"Hello, Dr Culver.".

"Hi, Lillian. This is John. Did you get my message?"

"Oh, hello John". Her tone softened. "I'm sorry, we've been really busy. Rushed off our feet. This is the first real break I've had. I was going to call you."

"That's OK. I understand. Can you talk now?"

"Yes, sure. I would love to meet but this is a busy time and my shifts are all over the place."

OK. Shall I call you next week?", Matteson said with a hint of disappointment in his voice.

"No….wait. Let me look. I'm free Thursday evening but not until gone seven. We could meet then."

"That would be great. You live in Islington, if I remember. I can pick you up."

"Do you mind if we meet at a restaurant in Islington. It will be a lot simpler. There's an Italian in Upper Street called the Bella Luna. We go there a lot and it's great. Can I meet you there at say, eight?"

"Yes, sure."

"Hang on John……….."

Matteson heard voices in the background, and Lillian saying, "OK I'll be there right away".

"John, I'm afraid I have to go. Another emergency. But I'll see you on Thursday. I'm looking forward to it. I've got to rush. Bye."

The phone went dead. He had wanted to talk more, but he was happy, and returned a little more enthusiastically to the Chinese infiltration of our markets abroad.

***

General Shepilev sat hunched over his desk going over the sheets of paper that his aide had brought him. They contained the names he had requested, each with a photograph and personal details. He looked at the underlined names first – the fixers for each of the main suspects, grunting from time to time and muttering to himself. Nothing unexpected, so the old man started looking at the long trail of other individuals associated with each man. He stopped part way through to rest his eyes and called for some more coffee. His habit was to sit back, sip his drink, and think of something totally removed from the task in hand. This time it was his granddaughter, Natalia. He smiled, then sighed, and went back to the list with a slightly clearer mind. He was getting near the end when he stopped at a man called Neylev. He peered closer, and then got out his big magnifying glass and put it over the photo.

"I know you," he muttered. But from where. The General stood up and started pacing up and down his office, casting his mind back, searching for a name. It was hard. The old brain was slipping, he knew that. But as often happens, it suddenly shone through the fog.

"Zorich!" he said out loud. "Grigor Zorich."

"Ivan!" he yelled for his aide who came in immediately.

"Yes, General?"

"Get me everything you have on this man Neylev, and also a man called Grigor Zorich. He's not on the list but he's somewhere in our records. He will be the same age as this man, Neylev. This takes priority, understood?"

"Yes, Sir, completely. I will have everyone working on it immediately."

The aide left, and the General stood looking out the window, thinking of the wealthy and influential Russian this man worked for.

"For once, I hope this is nothing," he said quietly. But his instinct told him otherwise.

Chapter 14

Fallon was working inside his garage in Bermondsey with the young lad he loosely called his apprentice, when the two men walked in. He recognised them from the breakers yard. One was the owner – he was stocky with plenty of muscle. The other was all muscle and he was big.

"Hello, Gents. What can I do for you?" Fallon knew better than to say names.

"Get rid of him," the owner said, jerking his head towards the lad.

"Danny, go off son. You can finish for the day."

The boy nervously put down his tools and grabbed his jacket and left, not even bothering to clean up. The scrapyard owner pointed to the room Fallon used as an office.

"We need to have a few words. In there."

The big man started pulling down the shutter at the front of the garage, and then joined his boss in Fallon's office.

"I am sure you have read or heard about that Russian who had his head shot off on the golf course."

"Yeah, sure." Fallon tried to hide his nervousness.

"And do you know what car they're looking for in connection with that shooting?"

The boss spoke slowly and calmly.

"No, I didn't see that."

Fallon felt the big man wrench his shoulder back and he yelled in pain.

"Don't give me that, you little shit." The boss stared down at Fallon's contorted face.

"I'll ask you again. What car are they looking for?"

"A…a dark Ford."

Fallon gasped out the words through the pain in his shoulder.

"Yeah, right. A dark Ford. And what car do you bring to my yard just after the shooting? No, I can see you're in pain. Let me tell you. A dark blue bleeding Ford. There's half the fucking police force out there looking for this car and you land it on my doorstep. For five grand! I've had word they're already looking at scrap yards down Guildford way, so you'd better pray no one saw you come near my yard or I'll put you in the bloody crusher. Do you get me?"

Fallon cringed with fear and just nodded.

"I want thirty grand from you and I want it by the end of the week. If I don't get it, well, you certainly won't be walking again. Maybe not even breathing. Right?"

"Yeah. OK. OK." There was nothing else Fallon could say.

"End of the week. We'll be back. And remember Fallon, your card's marked."

The boss leaned forward and poked a finger hard into Fallon's chest. The two men then left. Fallon sat rubbing his shoulder and still shaking from the sheer terror of the encounter. His mind kept conjuring up the image of being dropped into the crusher, and he almost started to vomit. Thirty thousand pounds! Where was he going to get that kind of money. And in cash. He mentally totted up all tangible assets but there was no way he could meet the deadline. And why should he have to pay? It wasn't his car.

All right he got a tidy sum, but only because it was a rush weekend job and he was doing Beck a big favour. No, he thought, this is Beck's problem. I'll have to get hold of him, and quick. He dialled Beck's direct line, his fingers still tingling from the pain in his shoulder.

"Yes, who is it?"

"It's me, Fallon, Mr Beck."

"What do want, Fallon? Why are you phoning me here?"

Beck showed his annoyance at this unwanted call.

"I'm sorry, Mr Beck, but something urgent has come up. I know you're looking for a new car to replace the one you got rid of, and I've heard of a good bargain at a garage in Wimbledon. I wondered if you could meet me there. But we have to be quick."

Beck had stiffened at the mention of "the one you got rid of". What had happened? Fallon was always the weak link. He'd better get down there and meet him.

"OK Fallon, let me have the address. It's gone four now and by the time I get my car out and get through the rush hour, I should get to Wimbledon at about five thirty. This had better be important, messing up my evening like this."

"It is, Mr Beck, very important. I'll read out the address to you."

Beck took down the location of the garage in Wimbledon, told his secretary he was finishing early for the day, and set off along the South Bank to the garage space he had on permanent lease.

Derek Beck was a big man. Over six foot and seventeen stone, but, as with a lot of people his size, he had a lightness of foot and touch that belied his weight. He was now in his forties and had started out in the Army as an Engineer, and eventually ended up in the demolition section where he learned all there was to know about explosives. He had a steady hand, nimble fingers, and a cool head, and he soon became recognised as one of the best in his field. Beck left the Army after twelve years and worked for an international firm of engineers, providing the expertise on demolition. However, his love of whisky and wine led him to a drinking problem and after one particularly bad mishap, he was let go. His severance package was enough for him to start a small business from a one bedroom ground floor flat in Maida Vale dealing in wine. He also attended AA to bring his own demon under control, and after a while, he was doing OK – not a great deal of income, but enough.

It was nearly five years ago that he received the anonymous phone call offering him occasional work using his demolition skills. He would be paid six figure sums for each job, and there could easily be two jobs or more a year. He knew immediately that these would not be legitimate contracts, but he had longed to go up the social ladder, to experience the life of some of his clients, to experience their money world. So, he said yes, and began undertaking contracts for the man he got to know only as Essex, earning upwards of two hundred thousand dollars a time and eventually moving into a smart sixth floor flat on the South Bank. With his new status, his client base grew, and his legitimate income was now covering all his needs, with the burgeoning off-shore account, providing the capital for some ventures outside the UK. His flat was at the back of the building with a Juliet balcony looking towards Stamford Street. He was tempted to switch to the more expensive river view at the front, but on reflection, decided that a small office was the first requirement. He rented an office in a building along the road that had just been completed and employed a secretary to work mornings and take care of his admin and calls.

With the income to move in the right circles, Beck had also met and was now going out with Janice Painter. Janice in her early thirties had a small boutique in Walton Street, propped up by Beck's occasional input of cash. He doubted whether their relationship would have developed had he not been able to provide financial support, but hoped that by now, with all the nights out, summer and winter holidays, and expensive shopping expeditions, they were truly an item. He was even thinking of asking her to move in with him, but that would certainly mean switching to the more expensive river view flat – Janice would not accept anything less. But the biggest problem was that he kept most of his equipment locked away in the spare room with all his old office files and personal things. Janice had already queried this mysterious locked room when she stayed overnight, so it would mean moving the bomb making operation to an outside location which would be very risky. He had started lately to think that he would perhaps stop working for the man. He had enough money and now operated a lucrative business. It would mean that he could leave that life behind and start living with Janice.

Beck found the garage in Wimbledon and pulled in down the road. He could see Fallon on the forecourt of the garage standing alongside what looked like a red E type Jaguar. He flashed his lights. Fallon saw the signal and walked up to the car and got in the front passenger seat.

"What's this all about, Fallon?" Beck made no attempt to hide the irritation in his voice.

"I had a visit, Mr Beck, from some big guys from the car breakers. They want more money."

"What do you mean, more money? You paid them the five thousand, didn't you?"

"Yes, of course, Mr Beck, but they've clocked that the car was the same one the Police are looking for with that shooting on the golf course. I tried to bluff it out, Mr Beck, but they know how to hurt someone."

"Shit Fallon! This was supposed to be a no questions asked deal. My employer will not like this, not at all. They could bring us all down. How much do they want?"

"Thirty grand in cash. And by Friday, or else I get it. They've even threatened to throw me into the crusher, Me Beck."

"What! Who are these animals?" Beck paused and thought for a moment. "Really, Fallon this is your problem. We left it with you to take care of the car and you were paid handsomely for it."

"I can't get that kind of money together. And by Friday! No way! You have to help out, Mr Beck. I'm not going to get done over, or even worse. If you don't help, I'll have to get some protection somewhere."

"What do you mean, protection?"

Beck turned to look Fallon full in the face, and he was not smiling.

"I don't mean anything, honest. I'm......well I'm just bloody shitting myself here."

The boss had said Fallon was the weak link and should be taken care of, and it looks like he was right. But there's not enough time to do anything by Friday. And it would have to be Turan to do it, not me, thought Beck.

"OK. I'll get the money. Meet me here same time Thursday. And this is a one-off, Fallon. I don't want them coming back for more. And you are never to mention my involvement, is that clear?"

"Yes, Mr Beck. And thank you. You've saved my life."

"OK, right now I've got to get back and start sorting out this money. So..."

Fallon took the hint and got out of the car and watched Beck pull away. He breathed a huge sigh of relief.

On the drive back into London, Beck was running two trains of thought. Firstly, thirty thousand pounds in cash is a large sum to draw out of the business account, and his secretary, Mrs Elkin, will need to know how it should be allocated. He had thought of saying it was for the E type Jaguar which would fit neatly, but he didn't think the car would carry that sort of price tag. He was then wondering what the boss will say when they resume contact. It was Beck who had resisted any attempt to eliminate Fallon, and now that decision is coming back to haunt him. Also, the protective wall around the whole operation had been breached. The men at the breakers yard had connected the car with the incident and were now a danger. But only to Fallon. They had no idea who else was involved – Beck had made sure he was never visible. Maybe it would be better for Fallon to be dumped in the crusher. But there was definitely a veiled threat when Fallon mentioned seeking "protection". Did he mean going to the Police?

Although Beck was big and capable of feigned bravado, inside he was unsure of himself. Steady hands and cool head over the explosive device was not matched by his normal temperament. He was now getting agitated over what was happening and wished the boss would come to life again and sort it out. He worried about the situation and the money all the way to the South Bank.

The next morning, Beck left a message for his secretary that he would be out the first part of the morning, although he didn't tell her it was primarily to arrange for the cash for Fallon. He got back to the office late morning. Mrs Elkin was working on the accounts and looked up and smiled when he came in.

"Good morning, Mr Beck. I got your message. I've just

made fresh coffee – shall I get you a cup?"

She was a petite smartly dressed lady in her fifties, happy to have the mornings only job.

"Yes, please, Pat. Coffee would be good."

It still irked Beck that he had just taken thirty thousand pounds from what was effectively his own money.

"Any messages?" he asked making his way to his desk.

"Yes. Mr Pierce and Mr Blackshaw both phoned about more business. Here's your coffee Mr Beck. I'll get back to the accounts."

Beck wasn't in the mood to raise the question of the cash he had arranged to collect the next day. Mrs Elkin would need to know how to account for it and he wasn't ready to answer that just yet. He attended to the two callers, checked his emails and read the market reports. At the end of the morning, Mrs Elkin packed up, gave a cheery goodbye, and left. Beck normally had business lunches with clients, but today he was free and sat through the lunch hour drinking coffee, worrying more and more about Fallon and the car breakers.

Chapter 15

At his desk in the Kremlin, the General was once again peering at photos and fact sheets laid out before him.

"Ivan!"

His aide came hurrying in.

"Yes, Sir?"

"Look at these two photos. Side by side. And tell me - are they the same person, or are my old eyes deceiving me?"

The aide looked at the photos, switching his gaze back and forth between the two.

"No, General, your eyes are not deceiving you. They are I believe the same person."

The General thought for a moment.

"I want this man Neylev brought here. No fuss. Just bring him and take him to the hospital. It says here that he is to marry an English woman. If he resists, make it clear that it would be better for him and his future wife if he cooperated. In fact, I want him to send a message to her saying he has been called away for a few days. I do not want anyone getting alarmed over his absence."

"Yes, General, I will arrange it straight away."

"Oh…and Ivan, get someone to go to his home and bring away a suitcase and some of his clothing. Also, have a quick look around. His desk or wherever he keeps his papers. Bring back anything that looks unusual."

"Yes Sir." Ivan paused for a moment. "Excuse me General, but this Neylev is one of Garnovski's men, I believe."

"Yes, Ivan you are correct. Neylev is one of Garnovski's men."

The aide turned and left the room to carry out the General's orders.

***

The Kurakin Hospital is located on the outskirts of Moscow, in an area bordering the forests, and away from the main road. The hospital specialises in the treatment of mental illness. The main structure is an oblong, three storey block, with bars on the ground floor windows. Some patients stay for only a matter of months whilst the dedicated doctors and nurses deal with their depression, anxiety, self harm and other treatable conditions. The majority are however longer term inmates, unable to confront the realities of the world outside.

Separate from the main block is a small two storey structure with bars on all the windows. This is the retention wing, where the most serious and sometimes violent patients are kept "for their own good". The far side of this building has its own entrance leading into a suite of rooms, comfortably furnished, and with a radio and television. Here, Alexander Neylev sat at the breakfast table, watched over by two guards, wondering what was happening.

He had been brought here from his flat in London with no explanation. He had been told that he was needed in Moscow to assist in an investigation. His protests, and even the mention of his powerful employer, Stepan Garnovski, had little effect. He was warned in no uncertain terms that he would be brought forcibly if need be, and that any trouble he made now would result in much worse trouble for the woman he planned to marry. So, he did as he was told, even phoning Carol, his English fiancee, to explain that he would be away on business for a few days. Neylev had always lived on his wits, working out the odds and swinging whichever way helped him the most. He knew his situation did not look good, but he had followed his old maxim of one step at a time, making sure he survived to take the next one. So here he was, in this place, waiting to see what came next. The door opened and there it was. His confidence dropped immediately he saw General Shepilev walk in with his aide, but he managed to retain his composure. Just. The General sat down opposite him, smiling.

"Ah, I never thought I would ever see you again, Grigor."

"I'm sorry, Sir, you are mistaken. I am Alexander Neylev. There must have been some..."

The General raised his palm to cut him off midsentence.

"Please. Do not go on with this pretence."

The General paused for a moment to still the conversation, before continuing.

"You know Grigor, whilst I am not in love with the West, they do have some good things. And some good sayings. One of my favourites is "Three strikes and you're out". You've had one, and now you only have two left. So, your name is Grigor Zorich and we did want to ask you a few questions back before….what was it….six years ago. But you died in a car crash. In Turkey, I believe?"

Neylev said nothing, but the fear began to show in his eyes.

"No answer counts as strike two."

"Yes. You are right. I am Grigor Zorich. But I had done nothing wrong. I did not know what you wanted to talk to me about and I was afraid. I faked my death. It was foolish, but I didn't know what else to do."

"Good. I'm glad you have spoken some truth, Grigor. I was about to explain what would happen if you used up your three strikes."

The General smiled broadly at Zorich. There was a knock on the door and one of the kitchen staff was let in with a tray with a coffee pot and cups, which was taken by the guard and put down on the breakfast table.

"Coffee. Good. You'll join me, of course, Grigor."

Zorich nodded as the aide poured out the coffee, but didn't drink until after the General had sipped his. The General just smiled at him shaking his head.

"Forever on your guard, eh Grigor? I remember. Now, there is a possibility that we can forget the past. This is after all, a new Russia, and what you were up to six years ago was…well petty in today's light."

Zorich's face brightened up, and he was already sensing a way through this maze.

The General reached down into his briefcase and pulled out a number of documents held together at the top with a large paper clip. He took one sheet and put in front of Zorich. When he saw what was on it, that way through abruptly closed.

"We found the original of this in your flat, together with many other things." The General gestured to the rest of the file. "Can you tell me what it is?"

"I'm not sure. I don't know how it got there. It may be my fiancee's."

"Strike two, Grigor. Only one to go".

The General's voice was very cold and very threatening.

"I….I can't..I.."

Zorich started to stand up almost as a reaction of escape from the corner he was in. He was quickly and roughly pushed back down in his seat by one of the guards. The General's aide stood watching impassively.

"You can, Grigor, and you will. One way or the other. I have tried to make you comfortable here, hoping you will co-operate and we can get this done peacefully, and all return to our business. If you run out of strikes, however, then you will end up somewhere else and we will get the truth the old way. I'm sure you remember the old way, Grigor. Now read out what it says on this paper and explain."

Zorich was crushed but continued working on the basis that he was still alive and now needed to take the next step.

"It says Swiss Metro Bank Zurich and then there is a long

number, and "3M" at the end. It is a numbered bank account into which I had to arrange a payment of three million dollars."

"For what?"

Zorich's instinct was to say "I don't know" but he knew that would be the third strike and a lot of pain would undoubtedly follow.

"For the killing of Andrei Lanskoy in England."

The General sat staring at the man opposite him. Whilst he had a feeling that bank account number that had been found in Zorich's flat could be connected to Lanskoy, the truth was still difficult to take. Finally, the General spoke.

"Three million dollars seems a lot of money to kill someone, Zorich. There are people who would do that for much less."

"I know, Sir, but I was told to find the best and this man is the best. And the price was set high enough to persuade him to take the contract at such short notice."

"I see."

The General breathed in deeply.

"I want you to tell me everything, right from the beginning."

"Yes, Sir. I was asked if I knew of anyone who could take care of someone who was a problem. It would be in England and had to be the best in the field, money no object. I remembered a number I had been given by a contact in Prague of a man who arranged such things."

"Do you have a name?"

"No, just a number."

"Write that number down."

"I don't know that I can remember it."

"Then we will help you remember it."

"No…. I think I can recall most of it…"

Zorich wrote down the number on the piece of paper in front of him.

"Good. Carry on."

"I had to call from a public telephone in London and say that I needed a removal done, and then put down the phone. Which I did. I was then called back and asked what type of removal and from where, and when."

"What was the voice like? English? American?"

"No, it was a computer voice. Er…., strange."

"You mean synthesised." The aide spoke for the first time.

"Yes, synthesised, that's it. When I mentioned that it needed to be done the following week, he refused saying it was too soon to organise. But then I said the fee would be three million dollars, and he agreed to think about it. I also told him that I had an envelope to pass on which had details that would help with the job. He was very hesitant about meeting and would only do so if I gave him my name and address. He said then he would have me checked out and if he wasn't totally satisfied, the deal would be off. If he did go ahead and collected the envelope and it was in anyway a set-up, his associates would kill me and those closest to me."

"What was in the envelope?" the General asked.

"I don't know and that's the truth. I knew already of the meeting at my employer's golf course, but I didn't realise that this would involve any of them."

"And did you meet with this man?"

"Yes. My instructions were to be in Hyde Park at six in the morning with the previous night's Evening Standard.

That's a London newspaper, Sir."

"I know."

"I had to go to a particular bench and sit on the envelope. When I saw one of the early joggers with a blue top stop ten paces away to tie a shoe lace, I was to get up and walk away leaving the envelope on the bench. And that's what happened."

"What did he look like, Zorich?"

"I didn't see him. The instructions were to get up when I saw him tie his lace and move away in the opposite direction and not to look back. All I saw was the blue top and a matching headband. He had one of those masks over his mouth – you know what they wear against the fumes. And dark glasses as well."

"Right. What about this bank account? Why do you have that?"

"I should have destroyed it. I just put it in the drawer. I had to phone again two days later using the same routine, and he confirmed that they would accept the contract and gave me the bank account number. I should have got rid of it once the payment was arranged."

"But you didn't, did you? Always looking for the angle, something that may prove useful in the future."

The General had a forced smile on his face to hide the contempt he felt for the man before him. But, he still needed his co-operation.

"Right, I want you to run through this again, adding anything you've forgotten. My aide will record it. I have to be elsewhere."

The General got up to leave.

"What will happen to me?" asked Zorich.

"You will stay here as our guest for a few more days while we check things out. We may have some more questions for you. And then we might need you to go back to London as if nothing has happened, but you will be working for us."

With that, and a nod to his aide, the General turned and left.

Chapter 16

On Thursday evening, Matteson took a taxi from his flat in Battersea to The Angel Islington. He had at last got hold of Lillian who had that evening off and suggested meeting at the Bella Luna restaurant which she and Jaz used regularly. He walked along Upper Street, and reached the restaurant ten minutes early, so decided to wait outside for Lillian who arrived only a few minutes later. She was dressed casually in a short denim skirt showing off her slim legs, and with little make-up. She kissed him on the cheek and they went into the Bella Luna arm in arm.

It was one of those colourful, bustling places, with waiters moving easily between the tables with that flirtatious banter that the Italians could get away with. Lillian was immediately embraced by the owner with a warm greeting of "Buonasera, dottore!" and a kiss on the cheeks. They were guided to a table by the window, with a glass of prosecco and a plate of olives in front of them before they had barely sat down.

"Grazie, Elio," she smiled at the owner.

"Prego, Signora," he responded, before moving back to his control position by the bar.

"They know you then."

"Yes, Jaz and I often come here. They are so warm and friendly and the food is the best in London. I hope you'll like it?"

"I'm sure I will." He paused looking at her before continuing. "Well, here we are. I've been really looking forward to seeing you again, Lillian."

"Please, call me Lilly. All my friends do. Only my Mum and Dad call me Lillian."

"You didn't get round to telling me about your parents. Where are they?"

"They live in Dorking. My Dad's a doctor there. That's why I went into medicine. When I was growing up, I began to realise how much people loved and respected him and I wanted to be like him. So here I am."

"Do you see them much?"

"Not as often as I would like. The trouble is getting both a Saturday and Sunday off. On the rare occasions when that happens, I go down for the weekend and my sister and her family come over too, and we have a great get-together with a huge Sunday lunch."

Matteson was on the verge of asking about her sister, when the waiter came to take the orders.

The conversation became less formal and more relaxed as the meal went on, with Lilly laughing at some of the tales of his early exploits in Hong Kong. She was obviously enjoying her time off work, and Matteson thought better of bringing up her life at the hospital and stuck more to family and friends. The evening came to a natural end after coffee and Matteson settled the bill and left insisting on escorting Lilly home. She had linked her arm in his and continued to chat for the short walk to her street.

"This is me," she said, stopping outside a terraced house. "Jaz and I have got the top half." Matteson nodded.

"I'd ask you in, John, but Jaz is probably in bed already – we've both got early starts tomorrow."

"I understand. Will I see you again?"

"Yes, I would like to. I know I've got a rare Saturday off next week, but I have to work Sunday, so I won't be going down to Dorking. We could go out Saturday night."

"That would be great. I'll fix something up and give you call."

They both stood looking at each other.

"Thank you for a wonderful evening, John."

Lilly leaned up to kiss him briefly on the lips, but she stayed close, and they embraced again. They were smiling at each other when they pulled away.

"See you Saturday." Lilly said.

"Yes. Saturday. Goodnight."

Matteson waited until the door had closed before turning and heading back to the Angel to get a cab home. He felt light headed. He knew he had met someone special.

Matteson spent most of the week-end thinking about Lillian and their date on the following Saturday, whilst catching up with one or two of his friends who, like him were still single. On the Sunday, his mind wandered to the incident in South Africa and the two men in the wine country and he remembered that his co-traveller on the train, Peter Veldt, owned a restaurant in Amsterdam. Matteson retrieved his card from his desk drawer and phoned the private number that Veldt had written on the back.

"John, how nice to hear from you," said Veldt.

"Peter, I didn't know whether you would be open on a Sunday. And how did you know it was me?"

"Ah, I don't hang about. Your number is already in my system, my friend. Yes, we are open on Sundays, but I am not always here. You're phoning to tell me you're coming to Amsterdam, I hope."

Veldt was pleased to hear from the young Englishman.

"No, I'm sorry, Peter, I'm snowed under with work at the moment."

"Oh, that's too bad. But it is nice to say hello again, even if it is only on the phone."

"Peter, I just wondered if you could help me. I'm getting some information together for a trade article regarding wine brokers in Europe. I wondered if you could tell me anything about wine broking in Holland."

"Wine broking?" Veldt sounded surprised. "Are you sure you mean broking and not wine dealing, John?"

"I think it's broking. What is the difference?"

"Wine brokers never own the wine. They just bring the seller and buyer together. Wine dealers will normally purchase the wine and then sell it on. There's obviously more risk for the dealers, but also more profit if successful."

"Well, I was definitely told brokers, Peter, so I had better stick to that brief."

"In that case, as far as I know, there are hardly any brokers in Holland. Most of that kind of transaction is done elsewhere, particularly in London. I think you will find it's the same in Denmark and probably Belgium. I'm sorry I can't be of more help, John."

"No, Peter. That's a great help. It saves me wasting a lot of time. Thank you so much, and I will definitely come over to see you when I'm not so under pressure."

"OK. Make it soon, yes. Oh, before I go, how is that young lady you met on the train? Did you catch up with her?"

"I didn't know you knew about her?"

"Yes, I did notice you together."

"Her name is Lillian, and I hope to see her again very soon."

"Good. And you must bring her with you when you come to Amsterdam. As my guests, I insist."

"Thank you, Peter. You are very kind. I will arrange something soon. Goodbye and thanks again."

"Goodbye, John. You take care."

Matteson put down the phone and thought about the two men in South Africa whose builds matched those of the two men in the car in Guildford. Frew had definitely said wine brokers, and he was a meticulous enough man not to use the wrong word. The shooting of Lanskoy had obviously been well planned and executed, and if by some remote chance, those two men were involved, then you would expect the same detailed planning to apply to their trip to South Africa. It would not be inconceivable, then, for them to use forged papers to lay a false trail back into Holland. They could easily switch back to their true identities after landing at Schipol and go on to London.

The "ping" signaled his meal was ready, and he took it to the small table in the corner of the lounge and ate with the laptop at the side. He began searching wine brokers on the web. Peter Veldt had been right, there was only one wine broker in Amsterdam, but over seventy in London. The Amsterdam site had photos of the three principals, none of which you could call "big". He started trawling the London sites, but here there were very few photos of individuals. He would have to find some other way of checking each firm. He tried all the angles of approach through the computer, but none were able to show him what anyone looked like.

He concluded that, if he wanted to take this further, he would need to contact each of the brokers listed. This was stepping way beyond his brief and could cause a lot of trouble. He was just getting the unit to where he wanted it, especially with the prospect of more staff, and the last thing he should do is rock the boat. But he just felt that what he had at that moment in time was too flimsy to raise officially, and he needed to put more meat on the bone. Matteson printed off the alphabetical list with their contact details and decided he would start phoning so many at a time from his mobile each afternoon when it was quieter in the office. He knew exactly what he was going to say.

Mrs Elkin had finished as usual at one, and Beck was alone in his office in Stamford Street, when the phone rang.

"Derek Beck," he said.

"Mr Beck?" The voice on the other end still needing confirmation.

"Yes, this is he. Can I help you?"

"My name's Richards. I'm interested in South African wine, and someone told me that you and a colleague were in South Africa last year touring the vineyards, so I wondered if you could help me with an investment."

Beck stiffened.

"Who told you this, Mr Richards, that I was in South Africa last year."

"Just someone I met at a function. I don't remember his name. But it's true then, you were there?"

"No, I was not!" Beck was quite emphatic. "And I don't understand why someone would say it was me. And with another person?"

"Yes. There was supposedly two of you."

Beck stopped to compose himself.

"I'm sorry. You've been misinformed. Your friend or whatever, must have been mistaken. Now, I am rather busy, Mr Richards."

"Yes. Of course. I'm sorry to have bothered you."

"Oh, before you go, Mr Richards, which company are you with?"

"No company. Just a private enquiry. Goodbye."

The call was finished abruptly, and Beck slammed the phone down on the desk.

"Shit, shit, shit!" he said out loud.

What was all that about! Does this man Richards know something? And on top of this Fallon business. Beck groaned. He hadn't had a drink for some years, but right now he would have done anything for a large Scotch. But he knew it wouldn't end there – with just one glass. Or even one bottle. He needed to speak to someone, but it was a lockdown. He had the number of Turan's place in Paris somewhere in the flat. He went back home hunted down the piece of paper and phoned Turan. It rang six times and switched to answer phone, with a message in French and English asking the caller to leave his name and number.

"Turan, this is me in London. You know who. Please give me call as soon as you get this message."

But the man Beck so desperately wanted to speak to was not in his office. Nor in Paris. He was on a plane to Istanbul.

Chapter 17

Turan had settled back into Paris life. All trace of Maurice Beaume had been destroyed, along with the hard drive that had sat for three days in acid in Colombes. He knew that the hunt was on to find the man who shot Lanskoy, and whilst he wasn't bothered about the British investigation, the Russians worried him. There were undoubtedly some people in Moscow who would be seeking revenge, and even those who ordered the hit may want to tie up loose ends. The chance of anyone ending up on his doorstep was slim, but nevertheless, he didn't want his neighbours, if questioned, to say that his shop was closed too often, and he was presumably out of the country. He decided he was going to stay in Clichy and postpone his visit to his sisters in Teheran until later in the year. He would have plenty of time to sort the visa and travel arrangements. He set out to see his neighbours as often as possible, stopping to chat and make his presence known. After normal closing, he went across to the Bar Louis on the other side of the Place to sip a cognac and chat to Oscar behind the bar.

His parents had both died some years earlier and the shop was left to him. He had learned enough from his father to be able to continue to run the business as it provided an ideal front. He bought a lock-up workshop in a unit at Colombes in the northern part of Paris, and then scoured the ads for a classic car in need of repair and found an old Citroen DS 19 in a small town in southern Belgium which he had transported to Colombes. It had no wheels and was on blocks, and Turan was satisfied that no-one would think it worthwhile to break in to steal it. There were parts and tools all over the floor and on the work bench and shelves. His weapons - a Heckler & Koch PDW 4.6 calibre submachine gun, a Glock 17C handgun, and an Arctic sniper's rifle – together with ammunition and spares were wrapped and concealed in sacks in at the back of the garage, directly behind the car. Detector beams inside the garage triggered an alarm on his cellphone when activated.

Three weeks had passed and there had been no suspicious or unusual activity in the area. He was working through an Auction catalogue in his shop, when the door buzzer signaled a visitor. He looked up from the desk to see, dressed in a trouser suit and headscarf, the woman who had been with Simin when she first visited the shop. He came around from the desk and greeted her, arms open and palms up.

"Khosh Amadid," he said, with questioning surprise.

The woman nodded.

"Salam."

Turan spoke in Farsi.

"I am surprised but pleased to see you. Is Simin with you in Paris?"

"No. I need to talk to you about Simin, but someone could be watching. So please show me some things as we talk. It must look like I am here only to buy something."

"Of course."

Turan led her to a display of bronzes, pots, and coins, and gestured to different items, appearing to any observer to be in the process of explaining and hopefully selling to his customer.

"Simin is in great danger," she whispered. "Her husband believes that she was unfaithful, that her visits with you were to be together. He had her watched. He is going to have her killed." Turan stiffened.

"But nothing happened. We just had tea and talked."

"I know, but her husband does not believe her. He would have had her killed openly, but he is in a high position in Teheran and has decided to avoid the scandal and arrange her death as an accident."

"How do you know all this?"

"Her maid and mine talk regularly. Her maid, Parisa, is devoted to her mistress and is very afraid."

"No!" Turan had dropped the pretence for a brief moment. "I cannot let this happen."

"Please. Calm. Someone may be watching."

"What then can I do? Do you come here with a plan......or what?"

"I don't know. But, right or not, it is her meetings with you that have led to this dreadful situation. Can you not somehow tell him. Convince him...I don't know....get him to understand that it was all innocent. Your family were originally from Iran. You know our ways. Can you go and see him?"

She was pleading for her friend. Turan went quiet. He had no immediate answer and needed to think things through. Then he spoke.

"Buy this small stone seal. I will need to make out a bill of sale with your address on. Write down Simin's address at the same time. I will see what I can do. I promise."

They went to the sales desk where he wrapped the seal, and made out the sale document, writing her address on the front. As if to repeat and confirm the details, she gave him Simin's address in Teheran. He gestured that he didn't need paying for the seal, but she insisted, not wanting anything abnormal that could be questioned. After one last look at him almost committing him to help, she gave a slight nod and then left.

Turan went back to his desk, alert to anyone following up the visit to his shop by Simin's friend but saw nothing suspicious outside. Whilst he appeared to be again perusing the Auction list, his mind was in a turmoil following the news about Simin. He knew that if he confronted Simin's husband in Teheran to convince him of the innocence of the meetings in Paris, then he would almost definitely get arrested on some trumped-up charge and end up in prison or worse. He also knew that he could not go to Iran as himself, because if things went wrong, his sisters would be put in danger, and there is no way he could get them involved. But he could not let Simin die. She had come to mean too much to him. He needed to get into Teheran and get her out.

Turan spent the rest of the morning going through in his mind all the options and the dangers involved. He eventually put up the "Ferme" sign and closed for a long lunch. He needed to contact Stils but they were all in lockdown. He knew his work number. Stils was a consultant in IT, with an office in Cologne. He went upstairs to his apartment and phoned Germany.

"Stils Informatik. Kann ich ihnen helfen?" the secretary asked.

"Yes, can I speak to Mr Stils." Turan answered in English.

"Who is calling?"

"Please say it is Philippe from Paris."

Turan waited whilst the secretary conferred and then put him through.

"Philippe? I don't understand. Why are you phoning my office?" asked Stils.

"I am sorry, Rudi. But I need your help. Can I come to Cologne to see you tomorrow?"

"I don't know, Philippe. I thought we were all having a break now. I don't want to get involved in anything at the moment."

"It's personal Rudi, not business. And it is also urgent. Please meet me at the station tomorrow and let me explain."

Stils took his time to think about his answer.

"All right. I'll meet you off the morning train from Paris. But I'm not promising anything, Philippe."

"That's fine. Just hear me out and you can decide. Thanks Rudi."

Turan closed off the call, and then spent the afternoon

on his computer, not bothering to re- open the shop. He researched travel options, routes and times, and a map of Teheran, locating the address which he had been given by Simin's friend. He studied intently the area in District 1 where the house was located. He knew of District 1, the area on the verge of the northern slopes of Teheran where the wealthy and important Iranians lived. He would have preferred Central or Southern Teheran, noisier, busier, and easier to come and go in the crowd, plus there was plenty of everyday transport. Different to the residential area he was going to. He would need a car. Something else to think about.

That evening, he went across to the Bar Louis.

"Ca va?" Oscar said smiling, putting out his hand across the bar to greet Turan, who met the handshake.

"Bien...bien, merci. Et vous, mon ami?"

"Moi, aussi oui."

Oscar gave a slight shrug and then turned to get Turan's usual cognac. The two men conversed amiably in French, interrupted occasionally by a customer needing serving when Oscar's assistant was busy.

"You had a long lunch my friend," Oscar smiled.

"Yes. Family on the phone and things to sort out. I need to go to Istanbul to meet a family friend there. He has some business he wants to discuss. I'd prefer to stay in Paris but my sister is pressing me to go"

"How long will you be gone?"

"Only days. I'm away tomorrow on something else, and then I leave for Turkey on Thursday."

Turan maintained the weary tone to his voice.

"I'll will keep an eye on the shop for you. Though, Phillipe, you should get an assistant. You can lose a lot of business being closed."

Oscar had owned the Bar Louis for twelve years, and Turan was a regular and welcomed customer.

"Yes. You're right Oscar. I think I will start looking when I get back."

Turan left the bar late that evening, satisfied that his movements over the next few days were well covered.

Chapter 18

Early next morning, Turan was at the Gare du Nord to catch the train to Cologne, using the journey time to think through his plans. There were several, but the most difficult to resolve would be getting Simin out. He was going in by plane but it was too risky for Simin to leave that way, under the scrutiny of airport officials. It would have to be car. But it had to be six hours to Tabriz alone, with still a long journey to the Turkish border, and the search for her would probably be well under way by then. But he could think of no other way at this point in time.

Turan came through the platform exit at Cologne to find Stils standing in the station forecourt, looking at the arrivals board. He was, as always, smartly dressed and immaculately groomed, his dark hair swept back from his forehead. They shook hands and chatted for a few moments before Stils led Turan out of the station to his parked car. They had no reason on this trip not to meet openly, but nevertheless Stils drove around for the first five minutes to check that they were not being followed.

"You said it was urgent," Stils queried.

"Yes. I need to get into Iran in the next few days but not on my passport. I don't have a visa anyway."

"And this is nothing to do with the man in London?"

"No, it's private. Someone I care for very much is in danger. In fact, she will be killed unless I can get her out of Iran. I need your help with documents."

Stils was quiet for a moment, and then pulled over.

"Tell me what you need."

"I need a Turkish passport. I have some photos here."

Turan pulled out the packet of ID shots from inside his jacket.

"I need my employment to be a cook, and if possible, I would like my place of birth to be somewhere in Hatay Province."

"Why?"

"It is part of Turkey near the Iran border where they speak Arabic. My Turkish is limited and if I get seriously questioned, I need to explain that I was brought up speaking Arabic. I speak it well enough after six years in the Legion."

Stils nodded.

"I also need a driving licence – international preferably. There are plenty of photos here. Plus, another Turkish passport for a woman. It doesn't matter about name or origin and I don't have photos, but if the woman is mid-thirties to forty, dark hair of course and slim face."

"Whoa…….my friend, that's a lot. And when do want all this by?".

"Thursday. I know its lot to ask. I will pay whatever it

costs. And I will not forget this favour, Rudi."

Stils looked at the pleading face of Turan and shrugged his shoulders.

"I'll see what I can do. There are so many Turks working in Germany, your passport should be no problem. A Turkish woman's passport..........maybe, we could be lucky. But I see little hope of a Turkish driving licence. But I will do my best."

"Thank you. Will you text me?"

"Yes, OK. Thursday's tight. But I'll do what I can. I need to get started right away. What do you want to do now?"

"I could do with some appropriate clothes. Is there some place somewhere where they sell the sort of thing that the Turkish would wear?"

"Yes. Muelheim. You should find what you want there," said Stils, starting up the car. They travelled north along Elieplatz and crossed the Muelheim Bridge into the Turkish quarter of Cologne. Turan suddenly recognised the name.

"Wasn't there some trouble here last year?"

"Yeah, a nail bomb. Really nasty. But it's OK now."

Stils pulled in just short of the main shops and turned to Turan.

"Can you get a taxi back. I need all the time between now and Thursday, and then some."

"Sure."

Turan nodded and got out of the car, and with a hand wave, Stils drove off to head back across the river. Turan was able to mingle easily with the mainly Turkish crowd and set about buying slip on shoes and a selection of clothes, some in dark shades, making sure that they had all been made in Turkey. He then found a taxi and returned to the station, catching the afternoon train back to Paris.

The next day, he booked a business class flight late Thursday with Lufthansa in his own name, Philippe Turan, flying out of Frankfurt to Istanbul, and returning a week later. He also reserved an airport hotel for the Thursday night, and booked and paid for an apartment off Tunel Square for the week starting Friday. Although not making a booking, he also tracked flights from Istanbul to Teheran on the Saturday. There had been some trouble with the newly built Imam Khomeini Airport, and Turkish Airlines were still flying into Mehrabad. He located a suitable hotel, north of Enqelab Avenue, part way between Central and Northern Teheran, and noted the contact details. He also traced a few authentic Iranian restaurants to fit into his cover plan. Finally, he checked the currency in the safe. He would need cash, and knew from past visits to his sisters, that credit cards were not always accepted in Iran. No Rials, and only a few Turkish Lira. He would take Euros and plenty of US dollars and change them in Istanbul.

Turan spent most of that evening studying a Turkish phrase book – this was one of the weak points in his plan. He was to travel into Iran as a chef from Istanbul but knew that he could not sustain a long conversation in Turkish should he be seriously questioned. And even though the birthplace of his alias was Arab speaking, it would obviously arouse suspicion if he couldn't speak any Turkish.

He rose early on Thursday and packed a medium suitcase

with his normal wardrobe, and then the clothes he bought in the Turkish shops in Muelheim He was dressed in the same casual clothes he wore to go Cologne on Tuesday and waited patiently for contact from Stils. The message came through on his mobile just after ten.

"All OK same place"

"3+" Turan texted back.

He grabbed his bag and left in a rush to get the first available taxi to Gard du Nord, arriving just in time to board the 11.15 to Cologne. He had coffee on board, read the newspaper, and mulled over the coming days in his mind. The end aim – to free Simin -somehow seemed surreal.

Turan arrived at Cologne and found Stils waiting in the same spot, near the arrivals information and went out to his car, parked across the way from the main entrance. They sat in the front and Stils passed over a large envelope. Turan took the contents out one piece at a time.

His Turkish passport, complete with his own photo, in the name of Mesut Senal. Occupation Chef. Also a passport of a woman who looked slightly older and broader in the face than Simin. But OK. He nodded. The last piece of paper appeared to be a Turkish driving licence but it was smudged in parts.

Stils spoke for the first time.

"That one was a problem. My contact had an old one and we had to doctor it as best we could. If you use it, avoid any of the big reputable hire companies. Go for someone who will be happy to get the money and not ask too many questions."

"They're all fine. Really good. How much do I owe you?"

"Well, it cost me over two thousand dollars, "said Stils, "but listen.........let's sort it out when you get back. I sense you have enough to think about for now."

"Thanks. I'll contact you as soon as."

The two men shook hands and Turan got out of the car and walked back to the station, and Stils drove off into Cologne. Turan caught the train to Frankfurt airport where he checked in the suitcase and, with the Turkish passports and driving licence secure in the button-down inside pocket of his jacket, he was soon settled into the business class section of the Lufthansa evening flight to Istanbul. The arrival time was too late for him to get access to the apartment in town, and he spent a restless night at the airport hotel before making his way to Tunel Square and collecting the keys from the management company. Speaking in French and English, he made a point of telling them that he was looking for antiques for his business and could be away overnight during the week. The accommodation was a large three bedroom apartment on the third floor, with plenty of room for Simin to relax in her own space. He would need time in the flat after the escape to work out how to get her into Germany and then on into France.

Turan spent most of Friday scouring the antiques markets of Istanbul, purchasing three items from different outlets with supporting bills of sale. He doubted whether they would sell in his own shop in Clichy but suited his cover at this time. In the afternoon, he booked the morning flight from Istanbul to Mehrabad in the name of Mesut Sunal, arranging to collect and pay for his ticket at the airport. He also telephoned the Varzesh hotel in Teheran and booked a room for three nights, asking specifically for a booking reference to confirm his stay.

He was awake early the next morning, dressed in the light clothes and shoes bought in Muelheim, and packed for the journey. The darker clothes, and personal items in the hold-all with Simin's Turkish passport concealed between the layers of clothing. He was now Mesut Sunal and left any reference to Philippe Turan locked away in the Istanbul apartment. Having paid for his ticket at the airline desk, and by noon he was flying southeast over the changing landscape of Turkey, heading towards Iran.

Chapter 19

Turan passed easily through immigration, able to show his booking reference for the Varzesh Hotel, his return ticket to Istanbul, and a convincing explanation that he was a chef in Teheran to learn how better to cook Iranian dishes. He thought his holdall might be opened with the possibility that Simin's fake passport would be found and queried. But that didn't happen, and he was soon outside in the rising heat and noise of Mehrabad airport. He had, and would throughout his stay in Teheran, speak in broken Farsi, interjected with a few Turkish phrases when he ostensibly stumbled with a word. He had been looked at with a mixture of disdain and amusement.

He could find no low cost car rental at the airport, the only hire firm appearing to be too officious not to question his driving licence. He opted to get a taxi to the hotel and see what was available in the city. The Varzesh was quite happy to take cash as an upfront payment for the three nights until Tuesday, and also gave him the number of Auto Robat where they said he should have no trouble renting a car with his Turkish licence. He phoned and booked the car for the following day, Sunday.

Turan was always alert and careful about his movements, whichever country he was in. But he knew that in Teheran, perhaps more than any other city, you always assume that you are being watched. So, the first thing was to cement his cover. He took a taxi to the best dizi restaurant in Teheran. He knew the dish – his mother had made it in the early days in Paris - but he was here to learn how to perfect Iranian dishes and dizi was number one. Even though the lunch time rush was over, and it was early afternoon, he still had to queue before he was shown inside to a small table, one of many in a row. Around him, the tables were full of customers at various stages through their meal. The food arrived. He drained the lamb broth from the dizi into the bowl and mashed in some rock bread and ate through the first stage of the meal. He then went back to the pot still containing the meat, and used the pestle provided to mash up everything, including the lamb fat, which he then ate, with more bread, and the pickles and condiments provided. He believed that no one could cook like his mother, but this dizi was exceptional. He stopped a passing waiter.

"Could I speak to the owner, please?"

"No. He is busy," came the curt reply.

"Please ask. I have come a long way to eat here," Turan pleaded.

The waiter looked at him, annoyed to be interrupted in his busy day, but grunted some sort of agreement and went off to the kitchen. A few minutes later, a tall elegant man in his fifties came to his table.

"I am sorry. We are very busy. What did you want?"

The man was smiling but with little warmth. Turan stood up.

"I am a chef in Istanbul and I am here for a few days to learn of Iranian cooking. I love this dish – it is wonderful. I would like to be able to cook it in my restaurant. I wondered if I could see how you made it."

The owner looked at him, with his hands out in a gesture of disbelief.

"No, no! This is a family secret. No one is allowed in my kitchen. I am sorry."

He turned and walked away, with Turan calling his thanks after him. Turan then paid for his food and left, satisfied that the display at the table would be enough to convince anyone watching that the reason for him being in Iran was just food. He returned to Enquelab Avenue and stayed in and around his hotel. Although his sisters lived in the suburbs, his whole plan would obviously be blown if they or any of their families came across him in Teheran, so from now on, he would stay clear of Central and would also travel around by car.

The next morning, he took a taxi to Auto Robat, although after some time in the Teheran traffic, he figured he could have walked there quicker. It was a small outfit with only six cars on display, all looking a little worse for wear. But, with just a cursory glance at his Turkish licence, they willingly took his money in cash including a substantial deposit. He chose a Saipa Caravan 701. Whilst working on the Citroen in Colombes, he had learnt enough about cars to be able to satisfy himself that the Saipa was roadworthy and would be able to make the journey to Tabriz and on out of Iran. It was also spacious for Simin to travel, and easy to cover an area inside should she need to be hidden from view at any time during the journey. The documents provided with the car were limited and there was no map. After some discussion with the rental office and the offer of more cash, they managed to find a suitable street map and Turan was soon working his way through the chaotic traffic to pick up the road to Tajrish.

He found the house off Sadabad Street and did an initial drive pass. It was a two storey corner building with a double wooden gate at the front drive entrance, and a small pedestrian gate round the side. It was a reasonable size but not anything grand, certainly not as imposing as some of the houses in District 1. Turan parked two streets away and walked back past the house. There were close planted trees in both roads that made up the corner, and the traffic and pavements were busy, but nothing as crowded as Central. He noted a video wired entry keypad at the side entrance and another by the front gates. There happened to be movement in and out of some of the other houses he passed, and they were all controlled by armed guards, so he had to assume that this would be the case at the Hamani house. He walked back round from the front to the side road looking for a likely point of entry. He could not be sure that the gates were not alarmed so it had to be over the wall. Trees were an integral part of Teheran gardens, and he soon found what he was looking for. A large old Eucalyptus in the garden that partly overhung the boundary wall; and the nearby tree lining the avenue had a protruding stump where a major branch had been cut near the base crown. This had to be it, but getting up and across to the Eucalyptus unnoticed would be difficult. Turan returned to the car, not wanting to linger too long in the area, and drove to a restaurant near Tajrish square where he again adopted the guise of a visiting Turkish chef interested in Iranian specialities. It was Sunday, and he would need to come back at night to check that his plan could work.

Turan waited in his hotel until well after dusk, and then drove back to the house, doing a pass- by and noting the floodlight above the entrance, primarily illuminating the inside driveway. Again, he could see no sign of any CCTV cameras. He found a side road where a number of cars were already parked and slid the Saipa into a space. Walking back past the house, he was relieved to see that the area of road around the tree with the protruding stump was not directly lit. However, there was a glow of uplights in the garden, but not too close to the eucalyptus. He then went around the corner past the main entrance of the house on the opposite side of the road. He saw nothing unusual and walked away for a block and then back again along the same route. This time, as he passed the house on the other side, a large Mercedes drew up in front of the gates, with a driver and passenger. The driver beeped the horn and the gates were opened inwards manually from inside. Turan had a glimpse of the armed guard before the car drove in and the gates were closed.

Turan spent most of Monday morning in his hotel room, his mind going back and forth over the computations of what he might have to confront and how to handle it. He came to the conclusion that there was no point in waiting another day carrying on the pretence of being a Turkish chef which always had the risk of being exposed. He would go in that night. Who knows when Hamani planned to murder Simin, and the sooner she was out of that house, the better.

Chapter 20

Turan checked out of the hotel in the evening, saying that he was heading North out of Teheran to look at some traditional restaurants in the hills. He parked the car off Sadabad put on some latex gloves and waited until sunset when the roads were quieter. He walked on the other side of the road until he was beyond the side gate, and making certain that no one was around, swiftly crossed the road and hauled himself up on to the protruding limb of the tree and over the wall to the eucalyptus. The upper branch swayed a little under his weight and he climbed down to a sturdier section and remained still for several minutes. He was listening for any sign that he had been seen either inside or outside the wall. All was quiet.

From the tree top vantage point, he could see through the foliage to the lit drive-in and the closed gates. There was a small hut just by the gates with a figure moving around inside. There was no sign of the Mercedes nor any other guards or servants. Turan dropped onto the ground, and avoiding the large palm that was underlit, moved silently to a tree just by the driveway. After a few minutes, the guard appeared and started to walk up the drive to the front entrance of the house. He was small and overweight, wearing a military style flak jacket with what looked like a revolver strapped to his side. The guard went a few steps into the front hall and called out to someone. The reply was muffled but it sounded like a young woman's voice. The man then closed the front door and started walking back up the drive to his hut. Turan stepped out from the shadows behind the guard, clasped the man's nose and mouth from behind with his left hand, whilst using his right to put a strangle hold round the man's throat. The guard struggled briefly before slipping into unconsciousness and dropping to the ground. Turan dragged him into the dark area of the garden, put on the guard's flak jacket and strapped on the revolver. The gun would have to be a last resort. Too much noise.

He approached the front entrance but could see no sign of any cameras. There was an alarm box above the front door, but the guard had entered freely so it was obviously not yet switched on. There may be other guards somewhere on duty. He pushed open the ornate front door into the coolness of the marble floored hall. He could hear noise down stairs and followed the sound to a kitchen area, where he saw a young woman preparing food, with some soft music in the background. Simin's maid? He padded silently up behind her, cupped her mouth and nose, and pressed his other hand into her carotid, gently dropping her to the floor. She could not be party to what was going to happen. He used a knife to cut up a cloth into strips, and bound and gagged the maid, making sure she could still breathe. He carried her to a storeroom, positioned her sitting against the wall, and locked the storeroom door.

Turan checked that the remainder of the downstairs rooms were empty, and then went up the open staircase to the first floor. Again, all was quiet. He opened each bedroom door, the revolver at the ready, but encountered no-one. One door was locked, and he knew instinctively that he had found Simin. He did one tap on the door and said softly.

"Simin?"

He heard someone move inside the room. She then spoke in Farsi.

"Who are you? What do you want?" Her voice registered alarm.

"It is me, Simin. Philippe. From Paris."

"Philippe! No, I do not believe you. Have you come....from my husband!?"

"No...no, Simin. It is I, Philippe. I am here to help you. I will tell you the last thing you said to me. It was "we will meet again in the garden". Do you remember? Please open the door. I am not here to harm you."

"Philippe! Yes, I remember. But why are you here? I don't understand."

"Open the door and I will explain everything."

"I cannot. I am locked in. But there is a key somewhere on the table in the passage. The one with the large vase."

Turan went along the passage and found the key on the table. He put the gun back in the holster and unlocked the door. Simin still not completely accepting what was happening, had retreated to the back of the bedroom, her hands crossed in front of her body in symbolic defence.

"Philippe! It is you," she said with astonishment and relief.

He moved towards her. He wanted so much to hold her and to comfort her.

"Your friend......I still don't know her name. The one you came to Paris with?"

"Noushin?"

"Yes, I think so. She came to tell me that you are in danger. That your husband intends to have you killed because of your visits to me."

Simin put her hand to her mouth and then touched his arm as she spoke.

"She is a good friend. But she should not have told you. You can do nothing and now you are in danger."

"No. I can get you away from here. To Turkey and then on to France. I have a passport for you, and a car to get to Tabriz and then on to the border. But we must hurry."

"A passport? Car? I don't understand, Philippe." Simin pulled back and stared him.

"And why are you wearing the guard's uniform?"

Before he could answer, she said in alarm.

"And Parisa! What has happened to my maid?!"

"Please Simin. Nothing has happened to her She is locked in the storeroom and no harm will come to her. And the guard is just unconscious, but he will wake soon. What about your husband? I presume he will be back tonight. We have to go. Please trust me."

Simin looked at him for a few moments, and then calmly sat on the end of the bed and gestured Turan to sit alongside her. He removed his glove and took her hand in his.

"My Philippe. You came here to rescue me. But I must stay."

Turan shook his head.

"No, no Philippe, I cannot go with you. I have a son. He is at University and does not live here. He is the best thing to come from my marriage and I will do nothing to harm him. I cannot bring disgrace to him. It will ruin his life."

"But your death at the hands of your husband will surely harm him a thousand times more."

"No. It will be sad, but it will look like an accident. My son will never know the truth. I am resigned to my fate, Philippe, but I must implore you to leave and save yourself. Please do this for me."

"I cannot leave you to die, Simin. I cannot do that."

She touched his face with her hand and smiled softly.

"Remember, we will meet again in the garden. Now you must go. Lock the bedroom and leave things as they are. My husband will believe we had burglars."

Turan did not move.

"I understand about your son. But your husband.........if something happened to your husband, how would you feel?"

Simin pulled her hand back from his and looked at him in shock.

"What are you saying Philippe? Are you Hashashin!"

Turan took back her hand to calm her.

"No, I am what you know me to be – a dealer in antiques

144

in Paris who wishes to save the woman that he cares for. But I was in the Legion for many years as a young man and I learned things that you don't forget. So, I ask you again, Simin, what would you do if something happened to your husband?"

She looked at his face for a long time before saying flatly, "I would mourn the way a devoted and loyal wife would mourn."

"I understand. Where is your husband and when will he return?"

"He is out. I know not where. But he will back any time now. He has a driver who is also his bodyguard."

Turan could see the contempt in her eyes.

"Is that look for your husband or the guard?"

"Both. What my husband will arrange for me, I do not know, but I do know that…. that man, the guard, will be one to do it."

"I see. I must move quickly, Simin."Turan pulled the blue glove back on. "I will have to lock you back in. Who else works here."

"The cook and gardener come at six each morning."

"They will find what awaits downstairs. They will also be able to release the maid – she will be all right. You could help by delaying any call to the police for as long as you can. But, Simin, do not do or say anything that could arouse suspicion for you. Please."

She nodded and walked with him to the door. He gently kissed her hand.

"Until I see again one day in Paris."

She smiled and went to close the door, but Turan stopped for a moment.

"You must wash your hands, Simin. You held my hand without my glove on, and I kissed yours. Just to be safe."

Simin nodded and then closed the door, which Turan locked from the outside before replacing the key on the small table on the landing.

He then went downstairs and into the kitchen and checked all the cooking knives, eventually choosing a 5" blade, double edged part way at the front, well used and sharpened, and with a reasonable balance. He wrapped the knife in a small toweling cloth and put it in his pocket.

He then went back into the garden to the prostrate guard, who was beginning to move, moaning slightly. He knew he now had no choice, and went down on his knees and hoisted the man up from behind into a sitting position. He contra-gripped his neck back and front with both arms and jerked the head sideways. The guard slumped dead. He then went into the hut and located and severed the wires controlling the two video entry phones. He also took the stool out and clambered up to remove the bulb from the light that illuminated the entrance area inside the gate. Turan then thought for a moment, and went back into the house, took a stuffed cushion from the chair in the hall, and returned to the guard hut and waited.

The wait lasted nearly forty minutes, and then a car horn beeped twice outside the gate. Turan slid the bolts back and pulled open the gates, hiding as much of his body from the car headlights as he could. The silver Mercedes drove in and stopped on the driveway, whilst Turan closed the gates and stood with his back to the car, knife in the right hand and gesturing up with his left at "the stupid light".

"Hey, what's happened to the light?" said the driver, as he got out of the car and started to open the rear passenger door.

Turan turned and threw the knife with a powerful jerk. The driver staggered back, stumbling as he clutched at the knife buried into his chest. Turan then grabbed the cushion and strode quickly to the car drawing the revolver from its holster. He pushed back the partly open door and shot through the cushion hitting Hamani in the side as he scrambled to open the other rear door in a desperate attempt to escape. The man clutched his side, groaning in pain. Turan leaned in and placed the cushion against Hamani's temple and fired again. This time, Simin's husband slumped dead. He then turned back to the guard who lay in the driveway. Not wishing to risk the sound of a shot in the open, he took the cushion and smothered the injured man until he stopped breathing. He then dragged the body off the driveway and in amongst the garden bushes and trees.

Turan waited until he was satisfied that the shots inside the car had been muffled enough by the cushion not to attract attention. He then threw the gun, gloves, and flak jacket inside the Mercedes. He still had the cloth used to wrap the knife and, with one last glance at the house, he slipped out of the side gate using the cloth to wipe the handle. He made his way back to the car and drove off to the airport, thinking about Simin and what would happen when the bodies were discovered. It could not obviously be a burglary gone wrong, so he had made it look like a professional hit. Hamani must have enemies. Either way, Simin will be free of the death threat, and hopefully one day, will join him in Paris. But first, he must get out of Iran as soon as possible – it was already getting late.

Chapter 21

Without Simin, Turan could see no point in driving to Tabriz. It would make more sense to fly straight back to Turkey. He had to get to the airport as quickly as possible. He might still need the car if he couldn't get a flight and not spend the night at Mehrabad, which would probably be the first place to go on alert in the morning as soon as the bodies were found. He headed west and took the outer route south down to Mehrabad and drove two blocks back in towards the city and parked the Saipa in the street. He closed up the car, putting the keys on the rear offside tyre, and set off with his bag to walk the short distance to the airport, knowing that he could get back to the car if there were no flights, and would hopefully still have ten hours of driving until the alarm was raised back at the Hamani house. He would certainly make Tabriz, and possibly the Turkish border.

Only one terminal was open at the airport, and the only desk staffed was that of Air Iran. Turan again used broken Farsi as he explained to the Air Iran ground hostess that he needed to return urgently to Istanbul since his mother had

149

been taken gravely ill.

"I am sorry, "she said, "but it is too late for flights to Istanbul. You will have to wait until the morning."

Turan pleaded.

"Please. I need to get home quickly."

The young woman shook her head. Then she thought and gestured Turan to wait whilst she went off to speak her colleague in the back office. Turan could see the two women talking but could not hear what was being said. The ground hostess came back to the desk smiling.

"I think we can help. There is a last flight going in thirty minutes to Tabriz, and a Turkish Airline flight out of Tabriz to Istanbul at 5.30am. This will get you back several hours before the first flight out of here tomorrow."

Turan thanked the woman profusely.

"Please," she said, still needing his attention, "you must pay here for your flight to Tabriz and then speak to Turkish Airlines about using your ticket for the flight to Istanbul. And you have to hurry, the plane goes from the other terminal."

He nodded, paid the required amount in cash, and was quickly ushered through the security check and escorted out of the building to the next terminal, and onto the waiting Fokker plane. After a short flight north, he arrived at Tabriz, and spent the night at the airport until Turkish Airlines opened when he exchanged his ticket from Merhabad to Istanbul for the flight out of Tabriz. The plane took off almost on time at 5.45am, climbing swiftly away from Tabriz on a clear, fresh Tuesday morning, and was soon crossing the border into Turkish airspace. He was a mixture of emotions. Relief at having escaped Iran, but with a sadness that Simin was not with him. He was also cold from the night in the airport, and suddenly very hungry, unable to remember when he last ate.

At that same time, shortly after dawn, the elderly cook arrived at the side gate of the Hamani household. The woman rang the entry phone bell and knocked on the door but nothing happened. She waited patiently for nearly twenty minutes until the young gardener arrived. He also failed to arouse anyone inside. They both went round to the front entrance, and the gardener banged on the gates. Finally, he put one foot on the base of the pillar and was able to push himself up and grab the top of the gates and haul himself over. The car was in the driveway but the gatehouse was empty. He opened the gate and the two servants walked up the drive past the car towards the house. Then the cook screamed as she caught sight of the dead body of Hamani lying across the back seat of the Mercedes.

The gardener looked inside the car, and then peered around the grounds, catching sight of the bodies of the two guards, lying partly hidden amidst the trees.

"Stay near the gate whilst I check the house," he said, trying to calm her.

The man went into the house, treading softly and pausing every few steps, alert for any sudden attack from an assailant. But there was no one there on the ground floor. He heard a muffled banging and traced it to the storeroom in the kitchen. The key was in the lock and when he opened the door, he found the bound and gagged maid, Parisa, who had been kicking against the inside wall. He took off her gag and untied her. She had been crying and the tears had dried on her cheeks. She gasped for breath through her mouth, and then, with a terrified look in her eyes, she said,

"My Mistress? Is she......where is she?"

"I don't know. Things have happened outside, but I have not seen Mistress Hamani. I have not gone upstairs. I am not allowed upstairs, but I will look if you wish."

"Yes, please come with me."

They climbed the stairs, the gardener looking out for any danger. The maid took the key from the passage table and went straight to Simin's bedroom. She knocked and unlocked the door, speaking at the same time.

"Mistress. Mistress. It is me Parisa."

Simin opened the door and the maid fell on her knees in front of her.

"You are safe!"

The relief was evident in the young girl's voice and Simin gently brought her up off her knees.

"What has happened?" she asked.

"I was attacked last night and tied up and locked in the kitchen storeroom. I thought that....".

Simin looked at the gardener, questioning why he was there. The young man, head slightly bowed, explained what had happened that morning, but left out the gruesome details, simply that they had found three bodies.

"We must contact the police," Simin said. "But first, I need to see what has happened outside."

"Please, Madame, please no. You should not see."

But Simin ushered them out of the bedroom and downstairs to the front of the house. The gardener opened the rear door of the car. Simin gasped and held her hands to her face. Although she knew what to expect, the sight of her dead husband shocked her immensely. Much of the grief and horror she showed in her face was real. Although this man had intended to kill her, he had been her husband for over twenty years and the only man she had known. They had been good together in the early days and he was the father of her beloved son. She whispered to herself. "Oh, my son, my son, you have lost your father." Simin collapsed on the ground sobbing.

***

Turan landed at Attaturk airport shortly before seven and was soon through passport and baggage control and in a taxi on his way to the apartment in Tunel Square. Once inside, he checked that his French passport was still where he had hidden it and then showered and changed, bundling the more simple clothes of the Turkish chef into a waste disposal bag. He cut up the passport and driving licence of Menet Sunel and burnt the pieces in a pot on the kitchen stove. He kept Simin's alias passport just in case it was ever needed. He also phoned the hire car company in Teheran explaining he had to leave in a hurry because of family illness, and the car had stalled on the way to the airport. Yes, of course they must keep the substantial cash deposit he paid, to help retrieve the car.

He was still pumped up. He did not want to languish any longer in Istanbul, so he booked the first flight that he could get back to Paris. He would catch up with Rudi sometime in the next few weeks.

Turan was back home in his apartment at Clichy by early evening. He knew he had to mentally put Teheran and Simin to one side. She was no longer in danger from her husband, and hopefully it would all work out and she would one day arrive at his front door. But the mourning was a long process, and it would be many months before there was any chance of her coming to Paris. Right now, he needed some relief. He phoned the house at Moulin. Sophie had not yet started so he booked her out for the evening from eight onwards. He arranged for her to come to his place, and after a first hour together, he would take her to dinner and on to the Club Dauphin.

Chapter 22

Matteson had used his cell phone to make the calls, working through the long list of wine brokers five at a time during his breaks at work. He had not told anyone else about this, not even Frew Douglas, and thought it safer at this stage to use the name Richards. He realised he was linking a supposedly legitimate wine merchant from Amsterdam in South Africa on business when an explosion occurred at the titanium plant, with an unknown man sitting in a car in Guildford. Still too far-fetched to make it official He would work through the list first and see what comes up. And he did it alphabetically and Beck's name had come in the first batch.

He sat in his office after the call to Beck, with a frown on his face. A strange response. The man was agitated, for sure, but he could be having a bad day. I've had days when I've been annoyed with time wasters on the phone, he thought. Nevertheless, I'll put a question mark against his name. A sort of short list to go into in more detail later.

He had managed to get two good seats at Drury Lane,

paying a hefty premium for the Saturday tickets, but he wanted the evening to be really special. He also booked a pre- theatre supper at Rules, requesting a booth, but with no promises from the receptionist.

Matteson picked Lilly up at just after five and they continued by taxi to Covent Garden in time for their early meal at Rules. No booth, but they were given a good table away from the restaurant traffic. They were both at ease and happy to be together.

After the show, Matteson suggested a drink in one of the bars in Convent Garden, but Lilly wasn't keen, so they got a taxi back to Islington. He walked Lilly to her door, with the taxi idling, waiting to take him on to Battersea.

"That was a wonderful night, Lilly. I really enjoyed it."

"Me too. But it's still early, why don't you come in for coffee?"

Matteson gestured towards the taxi.

"You can get another one, John. There's always plenty at the Angel."

"Ok. That would be great."

With that, Matteson paid the taxi off, and followed Lilly upstairs to her flat.

She showed him into the lounge with two big, comfortable settees and a small dining table in the corner.

"Make yourself at home. I'll put the coffee on."

Lilly came back out of the kitchenette and sat down next to him.

"It won't be long," she said smiling warmly.

"Where's Jaz tonight?" he asked. "I won't stay too long if

she's due back soon. She won't want me here if she's come in from one of those long shifts you do."

"No, she's got the weekend off, lucky thing. She's gone off for a romantic break with her boyfriend, Steve. I think it's Paris. She didn't really know where – it's supposed to be a surprise."

"Right."

Matteson couldn't think what else to say, his mind taking in the fact that it was just the two of them there. Lilly got up and brought in the coffee. They looked at each other and then moved together for their first long, passionate kiss. The coffee was forgotten as Lilly led him to her bedroom, and stumbling, kissing, panting, they were soon undressed and naked together on the bed. It had been a while for both of them, and the sex was all consuming. Afterwards he stayed inside her, not moving other than to plant gentle kisses on her cheeks, her eyelids, her forehead and her lips. He then rolled away, and they snuggled up close, with Lilly's head on his chest.

"Am I staying the night? I'd like to."

"I don't have to leave until ten tomorrow, so yes. I would like you to."

Lilly got up and brought the coffee through to the bedroom. It was lukewarm, but they drank it anyway. They chatted through the next forty minutes before making love again. Afterwards, they cuddled up together, murmured and whispered for a while before drifting off into a very contented sleep. It was well past eight when they awoke, with a thin streak of the morning sun getting through the closed curtains of the bedroom. Matteson particularly enjoyed lazy, morning sex, but there was no time for that. Lilly had to be out the door by nine thirty, so it was showers, with a finger tooth clean for Matteson, coffee and toast, and away. Lilly to St Barts, looking very clean and smart; and Matteson unshaven and in his clothes from the previous evening, getting the first taxi he could find back to Battersea to get changed for work. Over the next few weeks they met as often as they could, ending up either at Lilly's, or at Matteson's flat in Battersea.

"You seem happy," Jaz said to Lilly. They had both finished late and were sitting together on one of the sofas, feet up, sipping a glass of wine.

"Yes, I am. I like him a lot."

"I'm so pleased for you. It's nice to see you smiling after that last business."

"Oh James. No, that's all behind me now."

"Good."

Jaz leant over and gave her friend a hug.

"Has he met your parents yet?"

"No, but I'm going to ask Dad to get a ticket for John to accompany me to the Summer Ball in Dorking. It will be a nice way to meet them."

"That's a great idea. Do you think your mother will be OK?"

"Yes, she'll be fine. John's a great guy – really charming. He'll win her over."

Chapter 23

Nothing much on the golf course shooting had come across Matteson's desk. He went to a meeting with Andrew Trivett who had asked if his team had uncovered anything, but Matteson said they had drawn a blank even though he was still working through his list of wine brokers. He was still waiting to get something tangible before he raised it officially.

"By the way, I hear you've got a new girlfriend. About time."

Matteson groaned. Lindsay, his secretary, had noticed a change in him and had teased out of him that he had met someone. How on earth it had got as far as Andrew Trivett, he just couldn't figure out.

"Yes, Andrew, I have met someone. Her name's Lilly and she's a Doctor at St Barts."

"Great. You must bring her down one weekend and have Sunday lunch with us. Dawn and the kids always love to see you."

"I will. Thank you."

Matteson had narrowed down his list to six people, wine brokers who, for one reason or another, could be the person he was looking for. There were no photographs available of any of them, so the first thing he had to do was get a look at these individuals and see which ones, if any, fitted the description of "large". Derek Beck was first on the list, and Matteson brought back into his mind their conversation on the phone and the somewhat unusual response of Beck to his questions. He finished early that Monday afternoon, and got the tube to Blackfriars, walked across the bridge and down Stamford Street until he found Becks office. The door was locked so he rang the bell. He heard someone approaching, and the door opened to reveal a big man in a pinstripe suit.

"Mr Beck?" Matteson said, trying to keep his voice calm. "I wondered if I could speak to you about a wine investment?"

"Yes, come in. Please sit down."

Beck was polite and courteous to his potential new customer.

"Do you know what you're interested in, Mr.......I'm sorry I didn't get your name."

"Logan. David Logan. Well anything really. I don't know much about wine as an investment."

"Well, that's what I'm here for. Let me give you a brief run down and then we can discuss the best options for you."

Beck very efficiently outlined how the wine industry operates, going to a cabinet once or twice to take out some brochures for his potential client. Matteson took those opportunities to look around Beck's office for anything distinctive. And he saw something.

"Were you in the services, Mr Beck?"

Beck paused at this unusual question.

"Yes, I was. How do you know?"

"The photograph on the shelf over there. It looks like the Army? What were you in? I only ask because I thought of a career in the services once."

"Yes, I was in the Army. Royal Engineers. Now, I've got some figures for you here of actual returns I have achieved for some of my clients."

Beck laid out some graphs in front of Matteson.

"You weren't in bomb disposal, by any chance, Mr Beck?"

Beck gathered up the papers on the desk, his face turning red in annoyance.

"I don't know what this is about Mr Logan, but it obviously isn't wine."

"Oh, it is, I can assure you. My friend, Mr Richards, told me about your knowledge of South African wines and I am just following this up."

"Please leave my office now!" Beck's annoyance had turned to anger.

"Of course. I think I have all I need."

Matteson turned and left. Once outside and away from the building, he let out a huge sigh of relief. He knew he had pushed his luck and crossed boundaries, but he also knew he was on to something. What he didn't know was that Beck, although alarmed and unnerved by the encounter, was determined to find out who this man was and what he was up to. He followed Matteson as he walked down Stamford Street to Waterloo Station. The rush hour had begun and there was already a stream of people on the route providing Beck with cover. He got on the same train as Matteson but almost lost his quarry when Matteson got off after only one stop. Beck followed him along Battersea Park Road until he turned into Alexandra Avenue, and then entered the front of a residential block. Beck waited well back out of sight for several minutes until he was satisfied that Matteson must have gone inside and then walked past the building and saw what he thought was a doorman at the front entrance and a drive that swept down under the building leading to what was obviously underground parking. He carried on into Prince of Wales Drive, walked round to the station and got the train back to Waterloo.

The first thing Beck did when he got back to his flat was to phone Turan again. This time he got an answer.

"What do you want? What is so urgent that you have to phone me here?"

Turan was annoyed. He had listened to Beck's original message when he got back from Turkey, but chose to ignore it. He didn't want to talk to the man. But here he was phoning again.

"I know. I know. I wouldn't have phoned you if there was any other way. I can't get hold of Essex."

"No names! What is wrong with you! And not on this phone. I'll call you back in five minutes."

With that, Turan shut off the call and got a new pay-as-you-go cell phone with pre-loaded time, and phoned Beck back, hoping that the mobile Beck was using was also safe.

"Right, what has happened?"

"There's a guy come in here wanting to invest in wine. But I think he is the same guy who phoned me earlier saying I had been in South Africa last year, which I said no. But he came back here under another name asking about my Army service and was I in the bomb squad. He must know something. I'm really worried."

Turan went quiet for a moment. This was not what he wanted to hear.

"Do you know where he's from?" he asked.

"I don't know. He may be something to do with the Police."

"If it was the Police, they would be searching your place now. No, something else. Government maybe. But again, they would have taken you in by now if they had the slightest suspicion you were involved with explosives. It could be a reporter who's got wind of something somehow."

"I don't know what to do. Can you come over and sort it?"

"No, I can't! I cannot come to England again at this time and you know why. It is too soon. Things have not quietened down enough. You will have to take care of it. I suggest you take no chances and get rid of this problem."

"How? That's not what I do. I'm not you!" Becks voice had risen noticeably.

"Really? What do you think happens when one of your bombs explode? No one gets hurt? No one dies? Take care of it Beck before someone takes care of you. Don't phone me again."

The line went dead. Beck could still feel the menace in Turan's voice. He paced up and down, breathing heavily and talking to himself. He then left, went down to the off licence in Waterloo Road, and came back with a bottle of Scotch, and spent the rest of the evening getting blind drunk, ignoring even the calls from Janice Painter.

The next morning, he cursed himself for slipping, but inside he knew how much he had enjoyed that drink and was pleased that all he had was a mild hangover that some coffee soon put right. He had also found some new determination, and having told Mrs Elkins he wasn't available that day, Beck opened up the spare room and set about making a surprise package for Mr Richards. He cleared the small table and covered it with a plastic sheet. He then unlocked the metal filing cabinet, took out a large glass jar, and a bowl containing two bags of crystals from the lower drawer; and the heavy-duty apron, latex gloves and protective goggles kept in the upper drawer. Beck then went out to the kitchen and came back with the bottle of vegetable oil, a large serving spoon, a wooden spoon, and a rolling pin. He put on the protective clothing and started making the explosive. He took a break part way through, made some more coffee, and phoned Janice to say that something urgent had come up and he wouldn't be able to see her for the next few days. Janice was in fact relieved. She had lunch meetings and cocktails to show off the new lines – box cut jackets and gypsy styles – and Beck stood out in the wrong way amongst the gathering of fashionistas.

Beck spent a long time rolling the crystals, slowly and without too much pressure, until he had the powder form he needed to start the mixing. He took another short break before assembling the bomb and was eventually finished by mid-afternoon. The metal box containing the bomb was resting on top a polystyrene square with a cut out in the middle to cushion the switch protruding from the base. He had used up practically all his stock of crystals, but that fitted in with what he had planned. Beck had concluded that the whole bomb making set up would have to go. He would have absolutely no defence if anyone did raid his flat and find the equipment there. He placed the metal box in a large polystyrene carton and packed the sides to keep it from moving in transit. The lid was put on the carton which was then sealed. Stickers on the outside said "Medical Supplies – Urgent". Beck shuffled through his collection of ID cards until he found the one proclaiming him to be a volunteer driver to transport medical supplies. All he needed now was to find Logan…Richards…or whatever he called himself.

Matteson was in fact phoning Andrew Trivett to ask to meet informally so he could see what he thought about Beck and the possible link as "the big man" seen in the car.

"Mr Trivett's office."

"Oh, Sarah. It's John Matteson. Is he in?"

"No, I'm sorry Mr Matteson, he's away at the moment and won't be back until Monday."

"Oh. Is he at home?"

"No, he's in Scotland. Shall I put you through to Mr Stokes?"

"No. No that's fine. I'll catch up with Mr Trivett when he gets back. Thanks Sarah."

The last person Matteson wanted to raise this issue with

was Graham Stokes. He would probably get reprimanded for going way outside his brief and restricted to trade work from then on. No, it can wait until Andrew gets back. He'll understand why Matteson did what he did and would also know how to look deeper into Beck and his Army career. In the meantime, Matteson had the Summer Ball to look forward to on Friday. He had explained to Lilly that he had meetings and interviews all Friday and wouldn't be able to get away until late, but he would make sure that he arrived in time for the dinner. Lilly was finishing early and going down in the afternoon.

On that Tuesday evening, Beck put the polystyrene box in a large holdall which took along to the garage that he leased and put it in the spares cabinet behind the Saab. Janice had been pushing him to get something more dashing, but he was happy with his Saab for the moment. He then spent the rest of the evening, clearing up the spare room. The mechanical bits and pieces from the bomb making drawers he put in two large bin bags immersed in old files, clothes, travel brochures and general tat that he didn't need any more. Those he would take to a recycling plant on the outskirts of Hanworth that he had been to before and which still used a crusher for non-recyclable waste. The few crystals he had left he distributed between some paper food bags which he would weigh down with sand and drop into the Thames. Fortunately, he had used the last of the caps which would have been more difficult to get rid of.

On the next day, Wednesday, Beck carried the bin bags to the garage and having checked that the cabinet was still securely locked, he drove off to Hanworth and dumped the bags in the crusher. On the way back, he stopped at a builder's merchants and bought a small bag of sand and returned to London. Late afternoon, Beck got into his car again and drove to Battersea to watch and wait. He had to move the car around from time to time but was always back in sight of Alexandra Avenue. He had been there over two hours when Matteson appeared, walking up from Battersea Park Road. Beck watched him go into the building, greet the concierge, and then disappear down the corridor.

"Does he have a car?" Beck thought. He must have. He wouldn't be paying the premium of a covered parking space if he didn't have one, surely. He waited until eight, but Matteson did not reappear, and Beck wary that some busybody could be noting his loitering, decided to head back to the South Bank. Back at his flat, he filled the paper bags containing the crystals with sand and bunched up the tops. He was feeling thirsty and hadn't had a drink all day. And he wouldn't, not when he was "working". But it was only nine and he had to wait over an hour before it would be dark enough. He made some coffee and kept the craving at bay until it was time to go out. Beck took the two paper bags inside a carrier and walked along to Waterloo Bridge. Halfway over, he stopped to admire the view towards Westminster, and upended the carrier bag letting the two paper bags plop into the water. No one was close enough to see what he had done. Beck went into the pub opposite Waterloo station and had three doubles in quick succession before going home.

Chapter 24

Beck waited until five on Thursday, and then took the container from the cabinet and put it in the boot of the Saab, and went back to Battersea . Matteson didn't arrive home until almost nine and Beck waited only for a further hour until he gave up the vigil and returned to his flat, this time accompanied by a large bottle of Scotch. He was getting anxious. If he couldn't nail the man in his car soon, he would have to find some other way. But what? If Beck had stopped to think rationally, he would perhaps have wondered why no one had come knocking at his door, and possibly Matteson was not the danger he thought he was. But Beck was not thinking rationally. The drink and the recurring final threatening words of Turan drove him on. No, he had eyed his prey, and would keep chasing until he brought him down.

So, Friday late afternoon, Beck was once again prowling the Battersea Bridge area and this time he struck lucky. He saw Matteson arrive just after seven, but in a taxi this time. He seemed in a hurry. Forty minutes later, Beck saw an Audi coming out of the underground drive with the man he thought to be Richards at the wheel. He was wearing a bow tie and what was probably a white dress shirt. Beck realised he was off to some function. He frowned. London venues are too crowded for what he had planned, but the fact that Matteson was using his car, could well mean that he was heading out of town. And he was right. The Audi went along Battersea Park Road and turned left at Latchmere Road heading towards Clapham Common. Beck followed a discreet distance behind, driving as smoothly as possible, conscious of the package in the boot. But it was well protected, and he had taken the precaution of loading some of the boxes of unwanted clothes from the spare room into the boot to keep the polystyrene container safely in position.

The Audi turned west through Wandsworth, then past Kingston before picking up the south bound Leatherhead Road and then on to Dorking. It then headed east along the A25. Beck didn't find it easy to keep two or three cars behind the Audi, but at the same time be ready to turn with it at a moment's notice. And he had no idea how much further they were going. He was therefore relieved when the Audi started slowing at a place called Brockham. His quarry was obviously looking for somewhere and rather than mimic his stop and start, Beck thought it safer to pull some way back and drive slow. He then saw the car ahead turn into a wide pillared opening and driveway. The board at the entrance showed it to be The Wenlock Country Hotel, and Beck could see the lit-up building set well back from the road. He drove on, pulling in at a lay-by some four hundred metres down the A25. He couldn't see many cars turning into the hotel grounds and suspected that most of the other guests were already there. He would wait until everyone was settled in for their evening, when hopefully, the sun would have dipped a little. At least there were some clouds building up in the sky to mask the brightness. He didn't want to wait for too long at the lay-by, so after twenty minutes, he slowly drove a measured distance of ten miles and then turned back at the next roundabout, watching ten miles clock up until he saw the lay-by again on the opposite side of the road, and was ready for the turn in to the Wenlock hotel.

Beck drove up the winding approach road, past the hotel building where he could see waiters moving around a large chandeliered ballroom and a band setting up at one end. He followed the signs to the parking, some two hundred metres from the house, and drove around the car park ostensibly looking for a space, but more on the alert to find Matteson's car. He spotted the Audi, and then squeezed in six vehicles down, and sat doing a visual sweep of the car park for any sign of life. But there was none. All the guests must now be sitting down to their dinner before the music would start. He reckoned this function would go on into the night.

Matteson had hurried into the hotel, past the large sign indicating that there was a private function in progress, the Staunton Hospital Summer Ball. He was annoyed with himself for running late. Lilly's father had a standing invitation to the Summer Ball because of the consultancy work he did at Staunton and had arranged a table for four with his wife, Lilly and Matteson. The ballroom was full, with everyone already seated at their tables. Lilly had been watching the door and gave a wave when she saw him. He worked his way through to their table near the front.

"I am so sorry for being late," he said, kissing Lilly on the cheek and shaking hands with Dr Culver and his wife. Whilst Lilly's father had been totally warm and welcoming to him, her mother remained a little reserved, perhaps still wishing her daughter had made a go of it with the budding surgeon, James.

"That's all right," said William Culver, smiling amiably, "they're only just serving the starters."

Lilly squeezed Matteson's hand under the table.

"Did you get held up at work, John?"

"Yes, a little, and then the traffic out of London. I should have left earlier, but I just couldn't get away."

He smiled lovingly at her. He wanted to tell her how beautiful she looked but not at the table in front of her parents, so he settled for another kiss on the cheek.

"Yes, I'm sorry about it being a Friday," said Dr Culver. "It would normally have been tomorrow, but someone slipped up and a wedding party got in first. But we're all here now, and it's really good to have you with us, John."

"Thank you. I'm pleased to be here. It looks like a good gathering. The car park is pretty full."

"We came by taxi," said Lilly.

"Really?"

Lilly's father answered.

"Yes, I just didn't want to drive. Although I don't drink, I've still got to stay alert if I'm to drive us home. I wanted to be able to relax tonight. The four of us together. I've been looking forward to it."

"Thanks, Dad."

Lilly smiled sweetly at her father, and then turned to Matteson.

"Did you manage to get somewhere to stay tonight, John?"

"Yes, thanks. I'd left a bit late, I'm afraid, but I found a place eventually - on the Guildford Bypass."

They settled into the evening, chatting amiably through the dinner. Although not drinking himself, Dr Culver had generously ordered the wine for each of the three courses. Matteson stuck to water except for the main course, when he allowed himself one glass. Lilly drank moderately, her mother more copiously. It was after the last course had been cleared away, that Heather Culver started her questioning of Matteson.

"John, I still don't know what exactly it is that you do?"

Her husband gave her a slightly disapproving sideways glance.

"Well, I work for the government as a trade analyst, Heather. I have a small team of people and we try to project how current and future events will affect Britain's trade worldwide. Not very exciting, I'm afraid."

Heather Culver resumed her inquisition.

"But how do you progress. I mean, do you rise in the ranks? Is there a knighthood at the end of it all?"

"Oh, Heather, please," interjected her husband in exasperation.

"No….I know that may sound silly, but you know what I mean."

"Yes of course, I do know what you mean. It's fine. There is ample scope to go up the ladder. But, as for a Knighthood….", he smiled broadly, switching his gaze from Heather Culver to Lilly.

"Enough questions," said William Culver, closing the conversation. "Ah, the music is just starting."

Chapter 25

Beck got out of the Saab and carefully took out the polystyrene box and placed it on the ground whilst he locked up. Making sure he had his pencil torch in his pocket, he carried the box and an old raincoat along to the Audi, and with one last look around, got down at the side of the car. He took the lid off the box, and very gently lifted out the metal encased bomb. It had a magnetised lid, and Beck had fitted a tilt fuse, sitting on top of a spring, with a locking rod to hold the fuse still during transport. The locking rod screwed through the side casing, and on the end was a burr wheel to move the rod. There was also a built -in fail safe delay timer which set at 30 minutes, long enough for him to get away, not only from the blast, but also well out of the area when the Police arrive. He laid out the raincoat, put the pencil torch in his mouth and went down under the car and slowly brought the bomb towards him until he was able to lift and clamp it on the underside of the engine block. Satisfied it was secure, he very slowly turned the burr wheel and removed the bar from the spring. Finally, he flicked the switch on the underside to activate the battery power and start the timer. He preferred the solid feel of the switch to any press buttons, especially when working blind. He slid out under the car and peered over the bonnet of the Audi to make certain there was still no one around and walked back to his Saab. He put the polystyrene box and raincoat back in the boot and drove off, keeping revs at a minimum to silence his exit.

A waiter on a quick smoking break at the side of the front portico entrance stubbed out his cigarette and turned to go back to work, paying little attention to the Saab quietly driving out of the hotel.

The band were playing "Wonderful Tonight", and Matteson and Lilly were dancing a slow foxtrot, her head nestled into his shoulder.

"You like beautiful," he whispered. "I wanted to tell you as soon as I saw you, but......well, not in front of your parents."

"Not in front of my mother you mean. I'm sorry, but she is warming to you. She always wanted me to marry a doctor, a surgeon preferably, but she will accept that I'm with you. It will just take time."

At the table, the Culvers had sat this dance out and were watching their daughter and her new man. William Culver turned to his wife,

"They make a lovely couple. It's nice to see Lillian happy again."

"Yes, it is, I give you that."

The evening was drawing to a close, and a few guests were

already saying their goodbyes. Dr Culver had settled the bill and was back at the table. Lilly and her mother had gone to the cloak room.

"I'll drive you home," Matteson said when he was alone with Dr Culver. "No need to worry about taxis."

"No, you don't have to do that."

"I insist. It's not a problem."

"That's good of you." Culver paused. "Look, John, why don't stay the night with us. We've got a spare room and it will be a lot better than some lonely hotel. Also, there's half a bottle of good wine there. You can sit awhile and enjoy a glass or two. You've had hardly anything all evening. I'll drive your car to our house."

"I don't want to put you out."

"No, we'd be pleased to have you."

At which point the two women returned and sat down.

"John's staying with us the night. I'm going to drive us all home so he can sit and enjoy the rest of the wine." Lilly beamed. Heather frowned and said.

"But you didn't want to drive. That's why we got a taxi. And you've ordered one to pick us up."

"That's being cancelled. And I'm fine. I think it will be wonderful. John, give me the keys and I'll phone and cancel the taxi and bring your car up front.">

A slightly embarrassed Matteson handed over his car keys. "It's a grey Audi, sort of over the back on the right." Lillian stood up with her father.

"I know the car. I'll come with you, Dad." Turning to Matteson, she continued, "You and Mum can get to know each other better over a nice glass of wine."

Lillian and her father exchanged conspiratorial smiles, and left arm in arm, leaving Matteson to start the charm offensive with Lillian's mother.

Dr Culver and his daughter walked out of the hotel, and were heading across to the car park, when the first drops of rain fell from the dark clouds above.

"You'd better get under that tree Lillian or you'll get wet through. I'll find the car and bring it up."

She nodded in agreement. She only had a shoulder wrap and the rain was getting heavier, so she sheltered under the old oak and watched her father walk along the row of cars until he came to John's Audi. Fortunately, the car alongside the driver's door had already left and there was plenty of room for her father to get in. Another car, further down the line had its headlights on, preparing to depart, otherwise there was no one else in that section of the car park.

Dr Culver fumbled a little until he got the key into the ignition and started the car. The engine block on the Audi moved hardly at all, and he engaged the first gear to drive out but stalled the car part way. He turned the key in the ignition again but forgot to take the car out of gear. There was clunking shudder, and a split second later the car blew, the violent explosion lifting the vehicle initially off the ground at the front until it fell back, shattered and on fire.

Lilly saw the first few seconds of the blast, before she was blown off her feet and lay on the floor concussed and injured by flying debris.

The majority of the party goers were crowding out of the

front of the hotel readying to leave when they stopped en masse in shock at the noise and inferno in the car park. Matteson was talking to Heather when he heard the explosion, and they rushed out of the hotel, jostling with the hotel staff and other guests anxious to see what had happened. When he saw where the flames were coming from, he knew instinctively that it was his Audi and pushed frantically through the crowd followed by Heather. He found Lilly lying on the ground. Heather was screaming, having to be held back from the burning car by two of waiters who had rushed to the scene. Matteson's face reflected the full horror of what was unfolding before him.

Chapter 26

The next twenty-four hours were the worst Matteson had ever known. Police, ambulances, bomb squad, reporters – all converged on this small hotel near Dorking. He had stayed with Lilly until she was taken away to Guildford hospital in an ambulance, drifting in and out of consciousness. Her mother, Heather, had been heavily sedated and also taken away in an ambulance. Other guests in the vicinity when the car exploded were treated at the scene for minor injuries. All guests and staff were kept at the hotel to be questioned. Red tape looped around the outer perimeter of the explosion zone, whilst the ominous white tent was erected over the remains of the Audi and the shattered body within.

Matteson, as the owner of the car, was questioned at length and by different officers. No, he knew no one who could possibly have done this, and as far as he knew, he had no enemies who would wish him dead. All the while he was answering their questions, the name Beck was at the front of his mind. But still he held back, wanting to speak to Andrew Trivett first.

At long last, he was free to leave. The hotel had offered him and the rest of the guests the use of the rooms whilst they were waiting to make their statements. Matteson just wanted to get to Guildford and be with Lilly, but now he had no car and had to wait for the police to give him a lift.

He arrived at Guildford hospital at seven in the morning, tired, dishevelled, and worried, and went straight to the room where they had put Lilly, under the watchful eye of a WPC. Like her mother, she had been sedated but not so heavily, and was lying in bed half awake, her faced marked in numerous places by the small splinters of glass that the nurses had removed, and one large plaster patch on her cheek.

Matteson gently took her hand.

"Lilly. It's me, John."

Lilly turned a sleepy gaze towards him.

"John......are you all right....John.......what happened. My Dad...."

Lilly's voice began to choke up.

"I know, Lilly. I'm so sorry."

"Where am I? This is not real, is it John?"

"Just rest, please Lilly. We can talk later when you're better. Just remember ...I love you so much."

Lilly tried to smile at those last words but drifted off again. Matteson was not going to leave her and sat holding her hand wondering how he would ever be able to make it up to her.

The WPC came into the room.

"Excuse me, Sir, you are needed outside."

Matteson reluctantly let go of Lilly's hand and went out into the corridor where Andrew Trivett stood waiting.

"John, what on earth is going on. Special Branch got a message to me about you and a bomb!?"

"Yes. I'm sorry, Andrew. It's been a nightmare. But I thought you were away?"

"I was. In Scotland with the family. But that doesn't matter. We need to go somewhere and talk."

Trivett looked through the window into the room where Lilly lay.

"Is that your young lady?"

"Yes."

"Will she be OK?"

"Her leg is damaged. And there are a lot of cuts. But it's her father, Andrew. He was blown to pieces. I just…"

"Come on, John, let's not talk here. They don't have an office we can use, so we'll have to sit in my car. Let's get some coffee."

With one last look through the window at Lilly, Matteson left to follow Trivett to the hospital cafeteria. Matteson couldn't face any food at that time and they both settled for just coffee, which they took out to Trivett's car.

"Now, start from the beginning. And don't leave anything out."

Matteson just nodded, and then began to relate how he connected the incident in South Africa with the description of the two men seen in the car in the Yvonne Arnaud car park, followed by his on-line investigations leading up to the list of London wine brokers. He did not see any reason to involve his friend Peter Veldt in this conversation with Trivett. The last part of his story was the phone call and subsequent meeting with Derek Beck.

"For Heaven's sake, John! Why on earth didn't you tell me about this?"

Trivett was both angry and exasperated at his friend's actions.

"If it was this Beck, all of this could have been avoided. That poor man would still be alive!"

"I know, Andrew. Don't you think I know that. I feel devastated...awful...and so guilty. I did try to get you on Wednesday, but you had left. I decided to leave it until you got back. Your secretary asked if I wanted to speak to Graham Stokes, but.........I should have and taken the consequences."

"You're in a lot of trouble, John"

Trivett thought for a moment, then spoke again.

"Look, I'm not going to rush to speak to Stokes. We have until Monday, possibly even Tuesday and I can use that time to find out whether Beck was the bomber or not. I can get some people to check him out and if it looks like him, then the Police will have to go in, and Stokes will have to be told about everything. After all, this could indeed be connected to the shooting in Surrey. But if it turns out not to be him, then maybe we can just forget your dealings with Mr Beck and put all our efforts into finding out who did target your car."

"Thanks, Andrew. I suppose if it was Beck, then I lose my job. But if it was some other unknown, then, well perhaps there's a lot more at stake."

"We will sort it one way or the other. In the meantime, you are going to have the Police guarding you round the clock. I shall arrange that immediately. Stay in, and also don't come to work on Monday. Say you have a chill or something."

"Yes. Thank you, Andrew."

"We're not there yet. And I can only go so far, you understand that don't you."

"Yes. Of course."

"Now get back to that girl friend of yours. Lilly isn't it. She's going to need all the love and comforting she can get. I'll talk to you soon."

Matteson watched his friend drive off. His thoughts went back to Hong Kong and the Suen Ling affair which ended in a tragic shooting. Matteson could have been jailed or at the very least sent back from Hong Kong in disgrace. It was Trivett who had saved him then, and here he was doing his best to save him again.

Matteson returned to the hospital and Lilly's bedside. She was still sleeping. He wondered what to do and then realised that he had no car, no clothes other than the evening wear he was standing in, and he was a long way from his flat in Battersea. He set about booking into a hotel at the top of the High Street and getting through to his car Insurers to arrange a temporary vehicle. He then toured the men's clothes shops in Guildford to assemble some sort of minimal wardrobe, and emerged from his hotel in the early afternoon, refreshed and ready to go back to the hospital.

Lilly was sitting up in the hospital bed when he arrived. Some of the minor cuts on her face and arms were starting to retreat, but she still had a nasty looking gash on her cheek. She smiled when she saw him, but she it wasn't her usual warm smile.

"You look so much better," said Matteson sitting alongside her and holding her hand.

"I feel better. This one still hurts, and it looks awful". Lilly gently touching her gashed cheek.

"And my leg is troublesome, but they done all they can and it's just a matter of letting it heal."

"Yes, plenty of rest and TLC."

Lilly looked into Matteson's eyes.

"What happened at the hotel, John? Why did someone put a bomb under your car? I need to know what's going on. My Dad…."

Her voice trailed off and her eyes began to fill up. She wiped away the tears and waited for his answer.

"I don't know, Lilly, that's the truth. The Police believe it may have been mistaken identity. I just feel so dreadfully guilty. Mistake or not, it should have been me in that car and not your Dad."

"You are just a civil servant, aren't you John? You're not mixed up in other things?"

"No, I swear. There was absolutely no reason to put a bomb under my car. I don't understand it."

Lilly turned away.

"They're letting me go home today. And my mother, too. My sister's coming to get us."

"I could run you home, Lilly. The insurers are getting me another car and it should be here within the hour."

"No, I have to go home with the family. We need to sort out Dad's funeral. Oh God, my poor Dad."

She couldn't stop the tears this time and Matteson leaned forward to comfort her. She dried her eyes again and turned to face him.

"I'm sorry John, but things are going to be difficult. I have to be there to support my Mother through this, and the truth is that she blames you for what happened to Dad. I know it wasn't directly your fault, but it would be better if you stayed away for a while. I am sorry, really."

"No, I understand. I hoped somehow to make amends, but yes……I see what you mean."

"They will be here to collect me soon, so……."

"Of course. I'll get out of the way. Will you phone me when you can?"

"Yes, I promise."

She kissed him on the cheek, and Matteson left with his heart breaking.

He didn't know how he got through the rest of the week-end. The loan car was delivered to his hotel and he checked out, not even having spent the night there, and drove back to his flat in Battersea. As he drove in, he glimpsed the patrol car stationed along the road. Andrew Trivett had been quick to act. He stayed in all day Sunday, dejected at what had happened – feeling angry and vengeful towards this man Beck, and drinking more than he should. He also kept going to the phone every twenty minutes or so, imagining a missed call or message from Lilly. He slept badly and was still in bed at nine on the Monday morning when the phone did ring. It was Andrew Trivett.

"John, it's Andrew. Things have happened. Are you OK?"

"Yes. What's happened Andrew?"

"Beck is dead."

"What!"

"Yes, he was found dead this morning in the yard at the back of Trinkers, the shop on the ground floor of the flats where he lived. It's looks like he had been drinking heavily and fell off the balcony, probably sometime last night."

"That's incredible, Andrew. And, it's a bit of a coincidence, isn't it?"

"Yes, I thought so at first, but I had checked up on him and he lost his job some years ago because of his drinking. He was also seen by neighbours swaying around and leaning on the balcony rail. But you were right about one thing– he was in the Army and connected to explosives, so I did think at first that we had our man. But I got the Police to check his flat and they found no trace of any bomb making equipment. Nothing suspicious at all. We've still got to look at his car which is garaged nearby, but so far, nothing has been found to connect him to the Hotel explosion."

"Right, I see. But it still seems odd. And if he's not responsible, then who was?"

"We're still looking at that. The Police do believe it could be mistaken identity – it does happen, but in the meantime, you still take it easy and be careful."

"I will."

"How's your girlfriend doing? No permanent damage, I hope."

"Well, she's on the mend, but she doesn't want to see me at the moment. The family still think it was my fault that Dr Culver was killed."

"That's a bit unfair, John. It will work out I'm sure." Trivett paused for a moment and then continued. "Look, now that Beck is dead, I will be informing Graham Stokes today about the bomb under your car, and no doubt he will phone you. But I am not going to mention Beck, so you haven't told me anything about what you were doing before, do you understand?"

"Yes, I appreciate it, Andrew, I really do."

"I'm putting my job on the line here, John, so do not mention a word about Beck to anyone, please."

"No, I won't, I promise."

"Why don't you get away for a while until things blow over. Let Lilly have some space. When you come back, you can start afresh. I'll clear it with Stokes."

"Yes, you're probably right. I don't think I'm in any useful state to work at the moment. I'll go up to Yorkshire, to my Aunt's."

"Good. The Police patrol will stay around until you leave. Do take care of yourself and we'll speak again when you get back."

With that Trivett finished the call, and Matteson sat back contemplating what to do. All he really wanted was to be with Lilly, but Andrew was right – he should give Lilly some space, and he should get away from London. But he felt uncomfortable. What he had considered as an adventure – tracking down "the big man"- had exposed him to the other side of that world where death seemed never to be very far away. He realised he was totally unprepared for such danger and needed to do something about it. He dialed Peter Veldt's number.

"Hello John. How are you?"

"Hello Peter. I wondered if I could come over to see you?"

"Yes, of course. You sound very serious. Has anything happened?"

"Well, yes, but I'd rather explain when we meet. Can I come over tomorrow?"

"I'm sure that will be fine. Let me look….Tuesday….no, I have nothing that can't be rescheduled. How long will you be here?"

"I was hoping to stay one or two days."

"Make it two. I can show you Amsterdam then. And I'll arrange a room for you in the American Hotel. It's only a short walk to my restaurant. Will you be coming on your own, John?"

"Yes. Just me."

"I see. Well, give me a call when you arrive. I must go. I'll see you tomorrow, my friend."

Chapter 27

Matteson flew into Schipol on Tuesday morning and checked into the American Hotel. There was a note from Peter Veldt waiting for him at reception giving the directions to the restaurant which was a fifteen minute walk away. He walked into the Paleis Restaurant before the lunch time rush and was met by Veldt who greeted him warmly and took to him to his office in the back, ordering coffee on the way.

"Well, John, what do you think of my restaurant?"

"It's very impressive. And large. Do you get very busy?"

"Yes, we are packed most lunch times and nights. I have spent most of my life building up the reputation of this restaurant. My wife too. She used to put in a lot of hours here when we started, but now I am pleased she can take it easy and do all the other things she has always wanted to do."

"And you? Are you able to take it easy, Peter?"

Veldt laughed.

"No, I wouldn't know how." Veldt paused for a moment. "But you said you wanted to ask me something….and you sounded serious."

"I wondered if you could teach me how to shoot a gun?"

The smile went from Veldt's face.

"Why would you want me to do that? And why not learn in England? Why here?"

"Someone tried to blow me up, Peter."

"Gad verdamme!" Veldt looked shocked. "How? Why would someone want to blow you up?"

"The Police think it was mistaken identity. Someone had put a bomb under my car, and the worst thing is that someone else got in the car and started it. Lilly's father, Dr Culver."

"Oh, no!" Veldt shook his head.

"He was killed instantly. Lilly was nearby and injured. It all happened on Friday and I've been in a nightmare ever since."

"Did they find out who did it?"

"No. That's the trouble. They think it was mistaken identity but at this stage, nobody really knows. My relationship with Lilly is…well, it's not good now which is hard for me, Peter, really hard."

"Yes, I can see that. Forgive me, but I still don't understand why you have come to me to learn to shoot?"

"I don't want anyone to know. I am still pursued by reporters, and I would not want my learning to shoot a gun ending up in newspapers. My employers most certainly would not approve. I've come to you, hoping you would help. A bit of a cheek I know, but…."

"There are two sides to guns, John. The sport – controlled and designed to harm no one.

And the other side, which I want no part of. I am sorry, but I just could not be responsible for you learning to handle a gun so you can go and avenge your friend's death."

"I wouldn't do that Peter, believe me. I am not planning to get a gun. It is all controlled in England anyway, and as I say, my boss would almost definitely not allow it. I just feel so vulnerable. I would like to know that, if I ever find myself in a situation involving guns, I won't freeze. I won't be like a rabbit in the headlights."

Veldt sat tapping his fingers on his desk and looking at Matteson. He then spoke.

"Wait a minute. Let me make a phone call."

For the next five minutes, Veldt was on the phone speaking Dutch to someone, with Matteson not understanding a word of the conversation.

"I have spoken to the people at my club," said Veldt putting down the phone. "They have agreed to let me take you there for two hours this afternoon. They only agreed because of my standing at the club, do you understand John?"

"Yes, Peter. I am very grateful."

"Fine. It's over an hour's drive so we need to leave straight after lunch. This means that I will have to do some things now. Plus, I had hoped to show you around this afternoon, but that will have to wait. Why don't you go and have a walk around the main square – it is very interesting, and then come back for something to eat and then we will go."

"Yes, I'll do that. And thanks again Peter."

Veldt waved acknowledgement of the thanks and started on his paperwork.

It was mid-afternoon when they finally arrived at gun club. Nearly everyone nodded, smiled or spoke to Veldt, and it was obvious that he was a much liked and respected member. Matteson had to complete and sign a guest visitor's form, which Veldt explained also included a waiver of liability. He was then kitted out with goggles and ear muffs, Veldt having already checked that his shoes were appropriate – no open toe footwear allowed. They finally made their way to the end station.

The first thing Veldt did was to show Matteson the gun.

"This is a .22 semi-automatic. Lighter than some handguns but perfect to learn with. The first thing I want you to do is handle this gun and get the feel of it. The safety catch is on and it is not loaded. But that does not mean you can wave it about. Always, but always, point the gun down the range. Try it."

Veldt handed the pistol sideways to Matteson, with the muzzle pointing towards the target. Matteson did find it lighter than he expected and moved it around in front of him.

"Now, John, hold it up as to how you think you would shoot the target, and keep it in position for a count of thirty. There, now it's feeling a bit heavier, yes? Remember that. And also, that is without ammunition."

"Now try the classic two-handed grip aiming at the target and hold it."

Veldt waited a few moments before shouting as loud as he can.

"John!!"

Matteson turned towards him in alarm, to see Veldt standing there looking at him, gently shaking his head.

"Do not move the gun round with you. Keep it pointing down target at all times, even if someone shouts at you. Have you got that?"

"Yes, Peter. I'm sorry."

"That's OK. You are doing well for your first time. Right I am going to load the weapon. You will be able to shoot three bullets. Slide on the ear muffs. Take the same two-handed grip, look down the sight to the target, and squeeze the trigger, OK?"

Matteson nodded. Veldt then loaded the pistol and passed it carefully to Matteson, making sure it was always pointing away. When it was in Matteson's hands, Veldt leaned over and slipped the safety catch. Matteson did as instructed and fired his first shot at the bullseye target. It was wildly off, just clipping the outside edge. Veldt leaned in to yell in Matteson's ear, whilst at the same time putting his hand on Matteson's forearm to make sure that the gun stayed where it should.

"Don't snatch the trigger. Squeeze."

Matteson nodded and tried again, this time ready for the noise and the slight recoil of the 22. It was a better shot, hitting the outer. The third attempt also plugged into the outer. Veldt then leaned across again and took the gun from Matteson and slid on the safety catch. They both pulled back their ear muffs.

"That was quite good for a first time. You must remember

that although you are looking down the sight, the end game is the target and make sure you follow through, keeping position until you see that bullet hit the target. That way, you not only have a better shot, but you also know where it has hit and you can adjust accordingly if you need to rapid fire. But it was fine. Let's do another three shots."

The afternoon seemed to pass quite quickly, and Matteson was surprised how much he enjoyed it. Although he asked Peter Veldt if he could watch him shoot, the Dutchman refused, saying he was here for Matteson's lesson only. They were soon on their way back to Amsterdam, with Veldt giving little pointers on gun handling throughout the journey.

The rest of his trip to Amsterdam was very much more relaxing, with discussions about guns and shooting now left aside. Peter Veldt's wife came to the restaurant that evening to join them for dinner; and Veldt arranged for one of his staff, Marja, to take Matteson around the sights the next day. Although Lilly was never too far from his mind, Marja was good company. She was also very pretty.

Matteson graciously declined a second evening at the restaurant, opting to sit in the hotel bar and think through what he should do and how to get Lilly back. The next morning, he walked to the Paleis to say goodbye to Peter Veldt.

"So, you're on your way back to London."

"Yes, I am Peter. Thank you so much for being so hospitable. I really enjoyed Amsterdam and of course your wonderful restaurant."

"I'm glad. Look, I hope you can find some way through this dreadful business and do not do anything… well, you know what I mean."

"Yes, of course. It will work out. And I'm not going to do anything silly Peter. I do feel less vulnerable though. It's strange."

"Not the rabbit……..how did you say it?"

"The rabbit in the headlights. No, not like that if the situation ever does arise, which I hope it does not".

"I hope not too. Take care of yourself, John."

"Thank you, I will. And please thank your wife and Marja. And also, please come to London soon so I can be host and you my guest."

With that, Matteson left and returned to his hotel to take the taxi to Schipol and the early flight back to London.

Chapter 28

Ed Barrow and his wife had also flown into London, from Geneva. Veronique loved to go to theatre whenever possible and as it would soon be her birthday, Barrow booked ahead to get two good seats for the Billy Elliot musical at the Victoria Palace. They were now settled into their hotel off Piccadilly with a few days of birthday shopping before the show at the end of the week.

Barrow was reading a selection of papers, catching up on the news, noting that Mikhael Khodorkovski had started a nine year prison sentence, and New Labour had laid out its plans for the next five years. He also read the inside page follow up on a possible terrorist car bomb explosion in Dorking, which now identified the dead man as Dr Ross Culver, and the car owner as John Matteson. He then spotted the small item at the bottom of the page.

"Man Found Dead After Balcony Fall".

He would have glanced past the report had he not caught the name in the first line.

"The man now identified as Derek Beck......."

Derek Beck? Derek Beck? I know that name, he thought. He read through the complete article, which reported that Beck had fallen off the balcony of his South Bank flat sometime over the week-end and had not been found until staff at Trinkers opened the ground floor shop on Monday morning and discovered the dead body in their rear yard. It was believed that Beck had been drunk at the time and had accidentally toppled over the balcony rail. Beck and drink! Yes, I remember him now. He looked at his watch. It was still the middle of the night on the West Coast and he would have to phone later.

They returned from shopping late afternoon, with Veronique's new dress laid out on the bed. She went downstairs to have her hair done at the hotel's hairdressing salon ready for dinner that evening, and Ed Barrow took the opportunity to phone California.

"Mel Carter" the voice answered.

"Mel, it's me. Ed."

"Ed! It's good to hear you my old friend. It's been a long time."

"Yes, it has, and that's my fault, Mel. I've been meaning to call you for the last year, but you know how it slips by."

"Yeah, I do. But that's no excuse. I want you and the lovely Veronique to come out here and see us. And soon, like you promised."

"We will, just as soon as I've sorted some business out."

"You still working? I thought you were taking it easy now like me. And where are those kids you were planning?"

"No, that didn't happen. But we're looking to adopt, and

hopefully real soon. I needed to ask you something, Mel."

"Fire away, I'm all ears."

"Do you remember a guy called Beck? Derek Beck? He was looking to work for us"

"Beck? Let me think. Derek Beck. Was he the English guy? Big fella?"

"Yes, that's him."

"Yeah, I remember him. He came to us wondering whether we could use him in the business as an explosives expert. If I remember rightly, we didn't take him 'cos we found out he had a drink problem. He was let go by Parkes Demolition. Why are you interested in this guy, Ed?"

"Well it's not so much him. It's just that an old friend who I owe a favour has asked me to look at a shooting in England and see if I can help identify who the shooter was."

"Oh, shit, you don't want to get mixed up in all that business."

"I'm not Mel. I've made it clear that I will only go as far as I can without treading on anyone's toes. And the guy I owe this favour to knows and accepts that."

"I hope so Ed, I hope so."

"Anyway, I seem to remember some years after we rejected this guy – it must have been close to when we were selling the business – his name cropped up in connection with some suspect incidents."

"Yeah, I remember. Very suspect. Just rumours but yes."

"I recall there was another guy associated with him. A shooter. Do you remember who it was?"

"I don't Ed....oh, let me think. It was some years

now.........hang on....the Legionnaire! I am sure it was the Legionnaire."

"You're right Mel! That was him! The Legionnaire."

"What are you going to do with this name, Ed?"

"Just pass it on. That's all, and I think that will be me finished."

"Yeah, good. Get shot of it and get yourself out here for some Californian sunshine. Deb and the kids would love to see you both. Hang on Ed........."

Barrow heard shouts in the background.

"Breakfast is on the table, Ed. It's one of my great pleasures now – eating breakfast with my wife and children. You'll be doing that soon, I know. The yelling's getting louder, Ed, I gotta go. Come soon, buddy. And love to Veronique."

Barrow put the phone down and sat smiling. Mel – his old friend and partner. Still the same. Yes, he would take Veronique out to see them. Just as soon as he's done with the General. He would phone him when he got back to Geneva. The Legionnaire! – he just had a feeling that this could be the man who killed Lanskoy. In the meantime, he had two more days to enjoy London with Veronique, and the theatre to look forward to.

Beck's death had prompted action in other quarters. Fallon had read with alarm the report of Beck's fall from his balcony, and like Matteson was not entirely convinced that it was an accident. Following the incident with the car breakers, he now knew that the Ford he had arranged for Beck was used for something much more sinister than he had first realised. Shooting Russians, and powerful ones at that, was treading on dangerous ground, very dangerous ground. What with that and the constant fear that the heavy mob from the breakers yard could come back for more, Fallon decided it was about time he disappeared, before someone arranges it on a permanent basis. He started by getting his lad to continue his apprenticeship at a mate's garage, and then got on to an agent to sell his business and flat. He insisted that no boards should be put up outside – he didn't want anyone to get wind of what he was up to. He also arranged the transfer of his bank accounts to Ireland. He then locked up and said goodbye to the garage that had been his home for over eighteen years, and after depositing the keys with the agent, Reginald Patrick Fallon left London for good.

***

Having spent a pleasant few days with his wife in London, Ed Barrow was back in Geneva on Monday morning, ready to phone Moscow. After the usual clicks and switches, the call reached the General.

"Good morning, Edward. Do you have any news for me?"

"Yes, I do, General. I think I've tracked down our man – the one who carried out the shooting. I don't have his actual name, but he is known as the Legionnaire."

"The Legionnaire. I see. That is good Edward. What makes you think this is our man?"

"Purely by chance when I was in London last week, I read

about the death of a man called Beck whom I remembered from the time I was running the security firm. This man Beck was an explosives expert who we turned down for work because of his drink problem. But later, I heard through some old contacts that he had teamed up with others who were hired out for any type of job. It was said that one of the other people he worked with a shooter known as the Legionnaire. Now with a name like that, he must be ex-military and associated with France in some way or other which puts him right in the profile that I gave you."

"Yes, it would fit. And also, I have advanced at this end and it does appear that Lanskoy's killing was arranged through someone based in London which may be where this group is controlled from. Strangely, my breakthrough came also with a name from the past. It must be the science of meaningful coincidences."

"Excuse me?"

"Oh, it's nothing. Just something I read. I will get my people to track anything we have on the Legionnaire. You have done more than enough, Edward, but if you wish, I will let you know what we find."

"Yes, I would like to know. Oh, General, you might also look at the name John Matteson. Mid thirties and lives and works in London. The reason I mention him is that I also read of a bomb that destroyed a car belonging to Matteson. This happened on a Friday, and only two days later, Beck, the explosives expert, is found dead."

"I will have this man Matteson checked out as well and call you when I have some news. Goodbye Edward."

Chapter 29

In London, Matteson had also read the newspaper report of Beck's death, and still had his misgivings. He noted that the article also mentioned "his partner, Janice Painter, the owner of Kudos in Knightsbridge, who was too distraught to comment and is being comforted by friends". He looked up the name and found it to be a ladies' fashion boutique in Walton Street, and decided to call on Janice Painter.

He arrived outside the shop to find it closed, but he could see a woman moving around inside, so he rang the bell. The woman gestured that they were closed but he persisted with the bell, and eventually she came to the door, opening it just sufficiently to say, "We're closed. I'm sorry."

The voice sounded fractured and the woman had obviously been crying.

"Miss Painter, I'm a friend of Derek's. Could you just give me a minute?"

She hesitated, but eventually pulled open the door and gestured for him to come in.

"I'm Alan Richards. Derek and I were in the Army

together. I know this is a dreadful time for you, but I wondered if you would mind if I came to the funeral?"

"No, of course…do come. But I don't have a date at the moment. I don't know when they will release the….the body… You know……all these things they need to do." Her voice descended into a whisper.

"Yes, of course. I don't remember Derek mentioning relatives? Did he have any?"

"His Mother. But she's senile and in a home. Derek paid for it. I don't know what will happen to her or to the shop – Derek sort of helped finance the business. I'm sorry I need to sit down."

"Yes please. Here let me get this chair for you."

After Janice had sat down, Matteson said gently, "I'm sure Derek will have taken care of you and his Mother in his will. It will be all right."

Matteson then continued, speaking as sympathetically as he could.

"The report said he was drunk. I didn't know he drank that much."

"He had a problem a long time ago, but he only started again in the last few days."

"Did anything unusual happen? And please don't trouble yourself if it's too much, it's just…well, difficult to understand."

"Yes, very hard to understand. No, nothing I know of. The only odd thing was his phone. The Police came to my flat -it's above the shop here – to ask if I knew where his mobile phone was, but I said it wasn't there. He had it when he was with me on Saturday evening. He had drunk too much and was shouting why he couldn't get to Essex. He also kept phoning France. I think it was Paris ....and kept on about.... oh, somewhere in Italy. I'm sorry, I can't really do this."

She put her head in her hands.

"No, you don't have to go through this. I'm sorry Janice. Can I get you a glass of water or something?"

She shook her head.

"Is there no one that can be with you for a while?"

Janice recovered her composure a little.

"Yes, I have friends who are coming over. I shall be OK, but I would like to rest now if you don't mind."

"Of course. Thank you for speaking to me. Can I have your number and phone you next week to see if anything has been arranged?"

"Yes, I might know by then. Here it is."

She handed him a card with her details on.

"I'll leave you then. I am really sorry about what happened."

Janice just nodded thanks as she closed the door after him.

Matteson walked back down towards Knightsbridge, feeling somewhat ashamed that he had deceived this woman in the midst of her grief. However, his thoughts were more dominated by what she had said about Beck's last evening with her. He had been drinking obviously and had been trying to phone France and going on about Essex and somewhere in Italy.

What was that all about? He would like to have

questioned Janice more on exactly what Beck had said, but this was obviously not the right time.

The visit to Janice Painter had been a brief respite from his constant wondering about Lilly. He had called her mobile several times each day, but it was always a dead line. He had also phoned St Barts but no one would tell him anything about Dr Culver except that she was on sick leave. Somehow, he had never got her friend's last name, only knowing her as Jaz. He had even thought of driving down to Dorking but knew that he could not just arrive at the door of her mother's house......not after what had happened. He was aching inside for Lilly but there seemed nothing he could do about it. He suddenly decided to get a taxi to Islington before going back to the office and was dropped off outside Lilly's house. He rang the bell for several minutes, but as with last time he called, there was no response from the upstairs flat. He walked down to the nearest newsagents and bought as packet of envelopes, returning to the house where he wrote a note to Jaz on one envelope, imploring with her to get Lilly to phone him. He folded up the message and put it in a separate envelope, marked "To Jaz Urgent and Personal" and put it through the letterbox. And with a somewhat heavy heart, he returned to his office in Whitehall.

In typical civil service style, only the very urgent work had been looked at during his time off, even though the sick leave immediately after the explosion in Dorking had been officially sanctioned. It was now a matter of catching up, especially in his own region of expertise, the Far East, and most importantly, choosing which candidate would be offered a job with the unit. The final two short listed were both exceptional. But Russ Sterne, although older than anyone else, spoke fluent Arabic and had years of experience in the Middle East, North Africa, and Pakistan. He liked Rebecca Hart, the other short-listed candidate, but knew that, at this moment in time, he would have to choose Russ Sterne. He set about dictating the appropriate letters to them both.

Chapter 30

It was a warm summer morning and the sun was shining down onto Lake Geneva, scattering specks of colour through the shroud of water falling from the majestic fountain. Ed Barrow sat in his office with his coffee, reading a selection of newspapers. He had his morning routine – breakfast with his wife, Veronique, who then left him whilst he worked through anything on his computer, and go through the newspapers, catching up on events, and also checking on his investments, whilst she tended to their garden looking out onto the lake. From lunch onwards, they would spend the rest of the day together.

The phone rang. It was the land line he had secured for any calls with the General, so he knew immediately who was phoning.

"Good morning General."

"Good morning Edward. Are you able to talk?"

"Yes, all secure."

"Good. I thought I would let you know my news. My people were able to trace in our records a Legionnaire living in Marseilles, but he is not the shooter. He is one of the Marseilles criminals, who happened to strike lucky and get hold of a large stock of plastic explosives out of Libya."

"Not our man then." Barrow was disappointed.

"No, but we did get something useful from him after a little persuasion. He has had some dealings with another man from the Legion. He supplied him with some Semtex a couple of years back. This man was from Paris and he knew him only as Sammy. They never served together but Sammy apparently had a reputation as being a good shot."

"That sounds more promising. Did he describe this Sammy?"

"In his forties, not very tall, and sort of swarthy. Possibly Arab descent."

"That would certainly fit the profile and the description of the man who worked with Beck. And of course, Beck was an explosives man, so there's another link there. The trouble is, General, there are hundreds of men of that description living in the suburb estates around Paris."

"No, I don't think he comes from any of those places. The man this other Legionnaire described was sharply dressed, wore expensively tailored clothes, and a had gold Rolex. He believed our man lived in central Paris and had some sort of business there."

"OK. Did you want me to do anything with this information?"

"Well, my men don't operate as freely in Paris as they can in London, so it would be good if you could see what you can find out. But only if you want to. You have helped enough already, so it would be OK if you would prefer to leave it to us."

"No, I'll look into it. I'm intrigued by this guy. But what if the Legionnaire from Marseilles tips him off?"

"He won't be doing that, Edward. I can guarantee you that."

Barrett paused, taking in the full implication of the General's remark.

"All right. I'll get on to it. How are things going at your end?"

"Fine. Sort of. I know now who instructed the killing of Andrei Lanskoy. The door is open, but for some reason, I do not want to step through it. Something isn't right. But that is my problem, Edward. Oh, there are two other things I needed to mention and then I will let you get on with your day. Do you have anything planned?"

"Yes. After lunch, my wife and I are going sailing on the lake."

"I didn't know you sailed."

"No, it's sort of new. Now I'm retired, I can try all these things."

"Ah, retired. I need to do that soon, I really do. I grow a little more weary with each year."

"Yes, I understand."

"But back to business. The other two things I wanted to tell you about. First, this man Matteson. He seems to be a British trade expert only, who occasionally crosses our radar as a courier for some people in the British secret service who we do know very well. But nothing sinister, and I have no idea why someone would want to blow up his car. The other thing is however more sinister. It appears that the man who shot Lanskoy was part of an organisation that undertakes these contracts, possibly based in London. Maybe this ties in with this explosives man Beck."

"That is interesting and explains a lot. Someone had to be organising this hit, and I suspect, many others before as well. Are you going to track him down?"

"I have really nothing to go on. Whoever he is, he is very clever and very careful. And he could be based anywhere for all I know. We do have a Swiss numbered account but it would be impossible to get his identity from the bank. I do……."

The General started to cough, taking over a minute to recover, and then speaking even more hoarsely than before.

"Forgive me. This cough plagues me now. I'll just get some water."

Barrett waited patiently for the General to return. For whatever reason, he liked the man and was concerned for his health.

"I'm OK now Edward. Yes, as I was saying, I have some people trying to hack into the account and who knows? We may at least get a print out of the money in and out. If I get anything, I will let you know. I must rest now. Please take care in Paris. We will speak soon."

With that the call ended. Barrett pictured the General's lumbering frame going to lie down somewhere. He must be nearly seventy, he thought. Time for the old man to call it a day and spend the rest of his years with his family. But would he ever?

Barrett needed to arrange his trip. Veronique would obviously jump at a chance to shop in Paris, but there was undoubtedly an element of danger especially if he finds this Sammy. He would have to make a suitable excuse why she couldn't go with him. But first, there was a lot to do on the computer, looking for any link between the Legion, Sammy, Paris, a business, and Beck. He also planned to track down a contact number for John Matteson.

The General had sat in the armchair in the corner of his office, with his legs stretched out onto the coffee table. The doctors had told him that he had a shadow on his lung that would only get worse if he did not start treatment. He knew they were right and he would have to speak to the President about stepping down for good. But first, he had one last puzzle to solve. He should be instigating action against Stepan Garnovski, who instructed Zorich to arrange the shooting. But he had thought of the man as a friend and it did not sit easily. And what did Garnovski hope to gain? Control of Interlansk and the metals market? A major industry, yes, but Garnovski did not need it. He already had immense wealth and power in the industrial world. Why would he arrange to kill someone he looked upon almost as a son just to get more money? No, there was something more, and there was only one thing that Garnovski could not buy – the Presidency. The General suddenly realised that this must be the opening move to get to the Presidency, when it becomes vacant at the end of 2007. But how?

He switched his thoughts to the other question that

troubled him, Grigor Zorich's actions. This is a man who never does anything for nothing. And yet he wants the General to believe that he would risk the comfortable life he had built up in London where he was about to marry an English woman, and walk into a dangerous situation, for no apparent gain? No, not possible, the General thought. What is Gorich getting out of this? "

"Ivan!" the General shouted as he rose from the armchair and walked back to his desk. The aide came in quickly.

"Yes, Sir?"

"We need to go back and speak to Zorich again. Did your men find any bank statements, cash savings, anything that might show a recent payment?"

"I think there were some things, Sir. I will get whatever we have straight away."

"Good. As soon as you have them, arrange the car to go back to the hospital."

"Yes, General." Ivan hesitated. "Should we question Zorich's woman?"

"No, Ivan, definitely not. The fingers are pointing at Moscow already over this killing, and we need to avoid any more trouble at this time. If it got out that we had interrogated a British citizen......well..., No, we leave her alone."

"Yes, Sir. Understood."

Chapter 31

Matteson was sitting in his office on Thursday morning working through the lengthy list of emails on his computer, when his mobile rang. He immediately thought it could be Lilly and hastily answered.

"Hello."

"John Matteson?"

It wasn't her. The voice was male with a slight American drawl.

"Yes, this is John Matteson. Can I help you?"

"Yes, we have, or should I say had, a mutual friend, Derek Beck."

Matteson sat up immediately at the mention of Beck's name.

"Who is this speaking?"

"No, I'm not giving you my name. Not at this stage at any rate. I wanted to know if you would be interested in meeting and looking at the other aspects of Beck's death and his associates."

"What do you mean, associates?"

"Well, Beck did not work alone. For starters, he worked with another man who I believe was responsible for the shooting of Lanskoy last month."

Matteson was startled to hear a complete stranger virtually corroborate what he had been thinking all along. He thought for a moment what best to do with this caller.

"I think you should be speaking to someone more senior about this. I just deal with trade issues. My involvement with Beck was........."

The man on the other end cut him short.

"No. Just you. I want to talk to you. What you do after is your business."

"I can't do that, I'm sorry."

"I am going to hang up in a minute. I've been on this call too long already. If you want to meet, be at the Cafe de Flore in Paris tomorrow at eleven. Be alone and make sure you get a seat inside and bring this phone you're using."

"Paris tomorrow! But I............."

Matteson's voice trailed off as he realised that the stranger had ended the call. He was both alarmed and curious at what had been said. His first thoughts were that he should phone Andrew Trivett and tell him what had happened, but he suspected that the meeting would not happen if anyone other than Matteson appeared at the Cafe de Flore. He was also sure that the call would prove untraceable. But did he want to go back into the murky waters that had led to Beck blowing up his car and destroying so much with it. His dilemma was that if he acted alone and got found out, it would definitely be the end of his career, and maybe even his freedom. Andrew Trivett could not step in and cover for him again. But if he passed it upstairs, the whole thing could collapse and the chance of finding Beck's partner, the smaller man, would be gone. Matteson made up his mind. He couldn't let this opportunity be lost. He would go to the meeting in Paris, and depending on what came of it, he would decide how to go forward.

The first thing he did was to tell Lindsay, his secretary, that he was taking a long week- end in Yorkshire and would not be in the office on Friday. Lindsay was fond of Matteson and was concerned that perhaps he had not fully dealt with the trauma of that day in Dorking. She smiled encouragingly at his decision to go to his Aunt for the week-end.

That lunchtime, Matteson walked to Victoria Street to a travel agent and booked the earliest flight available ensuring that he could get into Paris by mid-morning. He also purchased a guide to Paris with a comprehensive street map attached and looked up the Cafe de Flore. He had heard of it but had never been there. He found it in the guide on the Boulevard de St Germain. It had been a famous venue for the academics and writers of Paris, and still attracted celebrities to this day.

Ed Barrow was already in Paris. He had driven down the day before and checked into a hotel off the Champs Elysee, one of the few that had parking. He had been thinking about Veronique during the journey down, and the conversation they had before he left.

"I'm sorry, I can't take you with me on this trip. I have got to stop at a few places on the way, and then cut up to Reims.

The meeting in Paris is on Saturday, so unfortunately, it will take up most of the weekend."

"That's all right, dear. I'll come with you next time."

Veronique smiled understandingly, but he knew that she was disappointed, not only about Paris, but also that he would be away at the weekend.

"Why don't you spend the time at your mother's? You haven't been to Lucerne for a while and you can catch up with some of your old friends."

"Yes, I will. You're right, Ed, we always have mother here. It will be good to go to the old house for a few days. I'll go and call her now."

He gave his wife a hug and a kiss. He loved her so much and knew how much it hurt her that they couldn't start a family. They had tried everything going, whatever the cost, but it just hadn't happened. He brushed a strand of hair off her face, looked at her intently and made up his mind.

"Veronique, this is going to be my last bit of business. When it's done, I promise you that, apart from managing the funds, I will finish with work completely. No more consultancy, no more trips away without you."

Her face lit up.

"Really?"

"Yes, really."

Giving him a big squeeze, Veronique went off a lot happier to phone her mother and arrange her visit to Lucerne.

Barrow had booked an early wake up, and after a quick coffee, he was out of the hotel just after six thirty walking briskly to the Place de La Concorde, across the river, and down the Boulevard St Germain. He spent the next thirty minutes walking around the area of the Cafe de Flore, mingling with the early morning workers and commuters, stopping to buy a newspaper, and going into a small cafe near the Flore corner, where he sat lingering over his second coffee of the day.

He had chosen Paris over London since he knew that any official action by the British to set up a surveillance op in Paris would need French approval and setting the meeting for the very next morning put pressure on that to be arranged. This also meant that the likely time for them to move in and multi-locate sight points would be first thing Friday morning before the crowds appear. He had walked up and down the roads around the Flore, scanning the buildings and windows but could see nothing out of place. It seemed that Matteson could possibly be coming on his own, or it was going to be a low key unofficial op with just one or two trailing him. Either way, it was all handleable and now he was feeling hungry. He had over two hours before he needed to be back in position, so he returned to his hotel for a leisurely breakfast with the morning papers and check the mail on his laptop.

The day was warming up in the June sun when Barrow left the hotel and made his way back across the river to the Boulevard St Germain. The popular district was already filling with tourists mingling with the students, and he noted the outside seats on both corners of the Flore were already full. He stayed on the Flore side of the tree lined boulevard, browsing the shops, for something special to take back to his wife, but always with one eye on the cafe entrance. At ten minutes to eleven, he saw Matteson get out of a taxi a hundred metres along the Boulevard. He had a backpack loose over one shoulder. He was different to the photograph in the newspaper, not old, but not as boyish as the picture had shown. He watched Matteson go into the cafe and saw his tallish figure standing around for several minutes before he was shown to a table inside. Barrow left the shop he was in and walked to another on the other side of the Boulevard where he spent a good fifteen minutes buying a book on Paris and the history of the Cafe Flore. He emerged with the wrapped parcel in view, looking every bit like the regular tourist in the area. He pulled out his phone as if to answer a call and phoned Matteson's cell phone.

"Mr Matteson, I need you to leave the cafe now and walk down the Boulevard to the Musee de Cluny on the right-hand side. I will meet you there."

Barrow stood there as if still on the phone and talking, and watched, as some minutes later, a confused Matteson emerged from the Cafe Flore, looked around, and started hesitantly walking down the Boulevard St Germain. Barrow waited for a full five minutes to make sure that no one else suddenly left the cafe or the surrounding area to trail Matteson, before following and catching up with a waiting Matteson at the Musee de Cluny.

"Mr Matteson?"

Matteson turned around to at last confront his mysterious caller.

"I'm sorry about the subterfuge. I had to be sure you had

come alone. Let's walk down to the gardens and talk on the way."

Barrow directed the younger man across to Rue Racine and then towards the Jardin du Luxembourg.

"Do I get to know your name?" Matteson asked.

"Perhaps later. Let's see how it goes. It's difficult to talk over the traffic, so let's get into the gardens and sit somewhere."

When they had found an empty bench, Barrow turned to Matteson who was waiting impatiently for an explanation for this bizarre meeting.

"Firstly, I do not work for any government organisation, or any private company. I am in fact retired, but I was asked by a friend to look at the shooting of Andrei Lanskoy on that golf course in England."

"Why? What kind of friend would ask that?"

Matteson was still feeling annoyed about the morning's charade and was not going to give any leeway to this American.

"An important friend. Don't fight me, John – I hope I can call you that – you will get more out of this meeting than I will, I'm pretty sure."

Matteson just nodded.

"Right," continued Barrow, "I now believe that the shooter was French of Arab descent and lives and works here in Paris. I also know that he was part of a group organised by someone probably based in England."

"What!" exclaimed Matteson.

"Yes, incredible as it may sound. And Beck was almost

certainly another member of that group, and as I think you already believe, it was probably Beck who planted the bomb under your car."

"Yes, I knew it was him! And I was also pretty sure that he worked with another smaller man at times, which fits in with what you are saying."

"What I want to know is why Beck would blow up your car? You are supposed to be just a trade expert. Why were you a target for these people?"

Matteson put his hands to his face for a moment and groaned.

"It was because I did something stupid. I do just run a commercial and trade section, and purely routine, I had reports on an explosion in South Africa that mentioned two men in a car – one large and one small. If you have researched the Surrey incident which I'm sure you have, you'll know that it is the same description given by a witness who saw a car parked in Guildford around the time of the shooting. I should have just passed this on to whoever, but I got carried away and worked through other leads to reach Beck. I didn't think for one moment that he would be shaken enough to do what he did. I will never forgive myself for what happened. And I am paying for it, believe me."

"There isn't a 'no-war' zone between Beck's world and yours. You cross the line and you are straight into it. Killing is what these people do. I'm sorry you had to learn that the hard way. Right now, Beck's gone, although his suicide did seem very convenient, and we are left with two known members of the ring – the shooter here in Paris and the head man possibly in London. My client wants me to find the guy here in Paris. I thought we could leave the man in England to you."

"Look, after what I told you about Beck, do you think I want to walk into another minefield on my own?"

"No, but you do have friends along the road in Whitehall."

Barrow ignored Matteson's look of surprise and continued.

"I need to know anything you've uncovered to see if it will to help me locate my man. In return, I will get you all the information we have on the head man in London. What you do with it is up to you. The proviso is that you don't mention me to anyone. The information for you will be managed in such a way that it will seem that it was sent to you because of your connection with Beck."

"I understand," said Matteson. "What you said about the man being here in Paris fits in with what Beck's girl friend told me. Beck went to her flat on the night he died. He was very drunk and shouting about various things. He was also trying to get someone on his mobile and Janice – that's his partner's name – believes he was calling Paris. He also said something about a place in Italy, but when I spoke to her she couldn't remember where. She was understandably shocked by his death and was feeling it, so I didn't want to press her too much at the time."

"This is good, John. What happened to his phone?"

"I don't know. The Police apparently couldn't find it at Beck's flat. They even came to Janice's place to ask if it was there, but she hadn't seen it since he left, and presumed he took it with him."

"That's a shame. It could have really helped us." Barrow looked disappointed. "All I have on this man is that he was in the Foreign Legion, around forty, Middle Eastern descent and was known as Sammy. Oh, plus he dresses well and is believed to have a business here in Paris. But you've probably passed a dozen people who fit that description since you left the Flore."

Both men went quiet for a moment, before Barrow spoke again.

"How did you get to speak to Beck's woman?"

"Janice? I pretended to be an old Army colleague of Beck's, and said I wanted to pay my respects and attend his funeral. It was really deceitful, and I wasn't happy about it."

"You have to get back to her, John. We need to know more about this phone call. It's our only real lead."

"OK. I've put her number in my phone. I'll call her now."

Matteson took out his mobile and phoned Janice's number. She answered almost immediately.

"Hello, who is that?"

"It's me Janice, Alan Richards. How are you?"

"Oh, Alan. Well, it's not much better. I'm still trying to sort things out."

"Is anyone helping you?"

"A couple of my friends come by. But I've heard nothing from Derek's friends or his clients. It seems none of them want to know. Except you, of course and I'm grateful you phoned, Alan."

"It's the least I can do. Derek was a good mate. Talking

about mates, Janice, I'm actually in France on business at the moment, and thought that while I'm here, I might try to locate another guy who served with Derek, who I believed moved to France. I recall you mentioned Derek had tried to phone Paris, and I was just wondering if he was trying to get hold of the same bloke?"

"I don't know, Alan, but I did find his phone. I remembered he had gone into the spare room where I keep a lot of stock. I had a good look last night and it was inside an opened box with some shorts and things. The lid was closed but loose. He must have put it on top and not realised it had slid down between the flaps. I was just wondering whether the Police would still need it. It's not going to change their findings. It is officially accidental........".

Janice paused, obviously beginning to feel emotional again, and Matteson stepped in.

"Don't worry about that now Janice. You have enough on your plate. But could you possibly just check the last number Derek called. It would help me, if it's not too much for you."

"No. I'll go and get it."

"Matteson heard her moving around before coming back to her phone.

"Here it is. It's a long number. It's 0-0-3-3-42-93-61-38."

Matteson repeated the digits out loud as Barrow wrote them down.

"That's great Janice, thanks. Look, I would just leave the phone if I were you. As you say, it's not going to make any difference now. The Police have concluded their investigation."

"Yes, you're probably right."

"Oh Janice, while I'm on, do you have a date for the service?"

"Yes. It's Friday, June Twenty Fourth at three in the afternoon. It's at the Highfield Crematorium."

"I've got it. I shall be there without fail. But I should be back before then, so perhaps I can give you a call and see if there is anything I can do to help."

"Yes. That's kind of you. Thanks Alan."

"Bye then Janice. I'll see you soon."

"Good work," said Barrow. "This could be it. I need to get back to my hotel and find an address for this number."

"I presume it's too risky just to phone it?" Matteson asked.

"Yes, it certainly is. This man is a professional and dangerous. Some strange call out of the blue is going to make him suspicious and on the alert, and that is the last thing we want. No, I'll get the address and phone you. It will probably be late afternoon. Have you got a room booked?"

"No. I didn't know how long I would be here. But I brought a change of clothes just in case," said Matteson nodding towards his backpack.

"Well, you'd better get something before the evening. There's a hotel along Boulevard Haussman near the Opera. Try there. You should be OK. Let me go first and wait a while before you leave. I'll phone you later."

With that, Barrow rose and walked back towards St

Germain. Matteson waited for ten minutes before following across the river, up to Place de l'Opera, and along Haussman until he found the hotel, and booked in for two nights. Since he couldn't be sure when Barrow would phone, he thought it best to stay around the hotel, have something to eat, and rest up in his room.

Chapter 32

It was well past seven when Matteson's phone rang.

"John, it's me, Ed."

"Ed?" Matteson was surprised at being given a name at last.

"Yes, it's Ed. Now listen, I've tracked the address for this number. It's a shop in Place Clichy called Turans, specialising in Persian artefacts. Note the name, John – Turan. That's the place in Italy your friend heard– Turin? Except it wasn't Turin Beck was talking about but this man Turan, his partner. I've walked past it once and it looks closed. I want you to do the same to make sure. Walk back along Haussman, turn right at the Galeries Lafayette and keep walking straight and then along Rue de Clichy to the Place. Keep left going around the square and you'll pass a cafe and then shortly after is Turans. Just walk casually by and see if it is still shut. Then come on up and meet me outside the Moulin Rouge."

Matteson hastily put on a clean shirt and then started down Haussman, following the instructions and eventually reaching Place Clichy where he worked his way round past Turans. He glanced at the entrance long enough to catch the "Ferme" sign, and then walked on to the meeting outside the Moulin Rouge. Barrow had changed into darker clothes and was now wearing a cotton bomber jacket.

"How did it look?"

"It was definitely closed."

"Right. You saw that cafe, Oscars, nearby. Well I'm going to go and see what I can dig up there. I want you to stay here – two people asking questions looks too official. I should be back in under thirty minutes. Have a drink somewhere – there's plenty of bars around but be back here in thirty minutes whether I phone or not. OK?"

"Yeah, sure."

Ed Barrow walked back to Clichy and into Oscars, sitting down at a table by the window. He noticed that there were only two young men working at that time, one behind the bar and the other serving and clearing the tables. Barrow's French was near fluent and he had no trouble conversing with the young waiter as he came to his table. He ordered a Pastis and as his drink was being put down, he asked the young man about Turans.

"You know the place over there, Turans, I was hoping to speak to the owner about some important artefacts I was looking for. Will he back tonight?"

The young man shrugged.

"I don't know, Monsieur."

"Listen, I really need to meet him tonight. I'm leaving first thing in the morning. I would appreciate your help."

Barrow had taken out a roll of money which he kept hidden from view on his lap. He peeled a twenty Euro note and put it on the table, with his hand covering most of it. The waiter looked at the money, obviously interested, but said in a low voice.

"I am sorry Monsieur, le Patron forbids us to talk about anything like this."

Barrow peeled off another twenty Euro note. The young man glanced around to make sure no one was watching.

"I do not think Monsieur Turan will be back until late. I think he has gone to Colombes. He has a workshop there."

"Do you have an address?" Barrow asked, sliding yet a third note out from the bundle.`

"All I know is that it is next to the DF Electrique factory. I must go now."

Barrow palmed the three notes onto the tray where they were quickly scooped up and into the waiter's pocket. The young man moved away to tend other tables, and Barrow took his time enjoying his Pastis before settling the tab with more than the usual few coins tip on the side. He decided to play safe with the waiter and told him that he wouldn't bother to go all the way to Colombes that night but would go to Turans on his next visit to Paris. He then left and walked up to the Moulin Rouge to find Matteson.

"The waiter thinks our man is at a workshop he uses in a place called Colombes, which I believe is north of here. We need to get back to my hotel and get my car. It's probably quicker to walk than try to get a taxi at this time of the evening. I'll get on the phone and arrange for the car to be ready, and then see if I can find out about this place."

Matteson nodded his agreement and the two men started walking down towards the Champs Elysees. Barrow had phoned ahead and by the time they turned into the hotel forecourt, the car was waiting for them. He had also tracked a post code for DF Electrique, and they were soon moving slowly along the Champs Elysees, with the SatNav voice now switched to English for Matteson's benefit, directing them towards Colombes. They went along the Avenue Charles de Gaulle, then headed to Courlevoie, and onto Colombes, eventually arriving outside the large, imposing factory building of DF Electrique. It was now late evening and the factory had ceased working for the day, with just a few lights still on in the upper floors. They drove slowly along the road, and immediately after the end of the factory perimeter, they passed a small open compound with about eight to ten individual workshop units. Barrow carried on past the opening and pulled in ahead of a lorry parked overnight in the road. He reached across Matteson and took pair of compact binoculars out of the glove compartment. He worked steadily along the row of workshops, pausing with the binoculars at each one.

"They seem to be mostly small businesses. Some have converted their fronts to have an office, but most are just drop-down shutters with access doors. You can see there are just three cars there and it looks like, apart from those three, the rest have packed up for the day. One of them at the far end has got a trade name......it looks like Chow Lat....something like that. Anyway, it's obviously a Chinese food importer so he's not our man. The other two are near each other but I can't see any names or trade descriptions. Here, take a look."

He handed the binoculars to Matteson who followed the line of units along. Suddenly, the door of one of two unmarked workshops opened, and a man walked out to one of the cars. Matteson immediately passed the glasses to Barrow.

"Look, Ed, that guy certainly fits the description of the man we're looking for."

Barrow had seen the movement and, looking through the binoculars, started nodding his head.

"Yeah, that's him for sure. That's the Legionaire."

Just then the neighbouring workshop door also opened, and a young man in overalls came out locking up behind him. The two men spoke for a while before getting into their cars to leave. They both automatically glanced up and down at the exit for any moving traffic, and Matteson was thankful Barrow had parked ahead of the lorry and out of sight. The cars turned right into the service road and on to the main route leading into Colombes. Barrow waited for a further ten minutes, before going to the car boot and taking out a small canvas bag.

"You stay here, John. I'm going to take a look inside the workshop."

Matteson's mind was voicing "How will you get in? What about the Chinese unit at the end?", but he just nodded. He was beginning to realise that this man Ed knew what he was doing.

Barrow walked quickly to the shutter door, put on some gloves, pulled out his picks and started working on the lock. He had it open in under three minutes. He kept the door slightly ajar listening for any hidden alarm but there was none. He then took out his torch and shone it sideways through the door opening to the far wall and saw the infrared beam receptor. Barrow moved inside closing the door behind him, stepped over the beam, and started searching the workshop with his torch. An old Citroen car was to the left of him, on blocks, and close to the side wall. To the right, was a work bench with tools, oil, a large glass jar with a piece of slate on top, car spares, a pack of blue gloves, and a cluster of small boxes of nuts, bolts, and washers. The wheels were hung up on hooks above the bench. He moved over to the car and tried to go around to the back, but found his way blocked by a load of empty boxes, tyres, rags, and discarded bits and pieces. It seemed to contrast with the tidy set up on the bench opposite, and Barrow decided to look closer. He pushed one of the tyres and some of the boxes away and found the edge of the ground sheet which he yanked up to reveal what was obviously a wrapped up rifle.

Matteson had been watching from Barrow's car and had seen the lights go out in the far end unit and the owner of the Chinese food importers leave. The compound was now deserted, with just a faint glow reaching the area from the perimeter lights of the DF Electrique factory. Barrow had been inside for ten minutes when Matteson saw a car approaching in the wing mirror. The car came up the road past the factory and turned into the compound, cutting the engine to coast up, stopping outside the adjoining workshop. It was Turan's Peugeot! He had come back. Matteson grabbed his phone and started to dial Barrow to warn him, but by that time Turan had unlocked the door and gone inside. Matteson knew he couldn't just leave Barrow, so he hurried out of the car and searched the boot for any kind of weapon.

Turan had not long been into his journey back to Clichy when his phone sounded the distinctive siren sound that told him someone had broken into his unit which had triggered the alarm to his cell phone. He immediately turned around and sped back to the compound, ignoring the lorry which had been parked there most of the day and which now hid Barrow's car. Turan cut the Peugeot's engine and coasted in. He stopped short of his unit to make sure whoever was inside would not hear the car approaching, or the doors opening and closing. Turan took out a switch blade knife from the glove compartment, and stepped swiftly inside his workshop, switching on the lights just inside the door.

Barrow turned, startled at the sudden flood of light, and saw Turan coming through the door, the knife in his hand, and with a look on his face that told Barrow that this man was going to kill him. He scrambled across the boxes round to the front of the car and across to the bench, grabbing the first thing to hand, a large spanner, as Turan came for him.

Barrow tried to ward off the arc of the knife, but it cut through his bomber jacket, and he felt the sudden pain as blood spurted from his arm. He dropped the spanner and reached back, grabbing the slate off the glass jar and throwing it at Turan. He knew he was going to die any second now, but he saw a slight flicker in Turan's eyes when he reached for the slate. The smell that now came from the glass jar told him it was acid, and Turan obviously knew this. Barrow picked the jar up with both hands, threatening to throw it over Turan, who quickly backed off and dived under the car, working his way to the other side. He was going for the guns! Barrow knew he couldn't clamber over the boxes with the jar of acid, which had already spilt and burnt through his glove onto his hand. He put the jar down and started kicking at the blocks supporting the far corner of the car until the blocks gave way, and the car dropped at that end catching the edge of Turan's right arm. But Barrow didn't move quickly enough, and the falling car struck his shin as he pulled his leg away.

At this point, Matteson burst into the garage with the metal rod from the car jack, to find Barrow on the floor holding his shin, blood flooding his sleeve, and in obvious pain. He looked down the far side of the car to see Turan, with the Glock in his limp right hand, having wrenched the arm from under the rim of the fallen car. He was pulling out a magazine with his left hand, ready to load the Glock. From under the car, he could still get a good shot at Barrow lying on the ground, and also shoot at Matteson's legs to bring him down.

Barrow screamed through his pain.

"Kick the blocks! Kick the blocks!"

Matteson began hammering at the blocks supporting the other corner, with the jack rod. Turan was scrambling to get the magazine loaded but had trouble gripping the gun steady in his other hand. Just then the car started to tilt. Matteson went around to the other side of the car to give it a final push over.

Turan realised he wasn't going to make it and he stopped for those last seconds of his life, his mind trying to reach Simin. Then there was the sudden pain and blackness as the whole far side of the car fell on him, crushing his neck. Matteson took one look to make sure Turan was dead. He grimaced at the sight he saw. He then went over to Barrow.

"You look bad, Ed."

"I feel bad. This arm won't stop bleeding and my leg....uuh". His face contorted in pain. "I may have done something to my shin. That bloody car caught it."

"Let me see if I can fix you up and get you out of here. What's that smell?"

"It's acid. In that jar. It's lethal – look, this was just a droplet that spilt onto my hand."

Barrow showed Matteson the burn through his glove and onto the back of his left hand.

"Put that bit of slate back on, John, as soon as."

Matteson found the slate and quickly put it back on the jar.

"Now, you have to clear up everything, and make it look like an accident". Barrow was talking between gasps of pain.

"After I've seen to you."

Matteson looked around, saw nothing to help, so took off his jacket and shirt.

"I need a knife".

"Turan's is under the car somewhere but put on some gloves before you touch anything."

Matteson pulled a pair of blues from the box, and then very carefully stretched his arm under the still upended front side of the car and brought out the knife. He cut off both sleeves of his shirt, and then cut the back of the shirt into two squares which he folded up into pads.

He then as gently as possible took off Barrow's bomber jacket and undid the sleeve of his shirt to get at the knife wound. Matteson put a pad over the cut and bandaged the arm with one of the shirt sleeves. After carefully slitting open Barrows right trouser leg, he did the same for the damaged shin.

"There, that's the best I can do for now. Right, I'll get this cleared up and get you out of here and get some proper treatment."

"No, John. No hospitals, no doctors. Once Turan is found, people might start putting two and two together and we can't risk that. Get me back to the hotel. Just along the Champs is an all-night pharmacy. You can get some stuff there."

"OK, as you wish."

Matteson put his jacket back on, and started clearing up, trying to guess where things should be, checking with Barrow when he was unsure. He cleaned up the blood splatter from the wound with some petrol out of a can. Finally, he went to the back of the car to put the gun and magazine out of sight again, trying not to look at Turan's dead body. He held the Glock up and stopped for a few moments.

"What are you doing with that gun, John?"

"I was just thinking. You've found your man, but I still have to face what may be in London. If Beck was sent to kill me, the head of this gang whoever he is, may get someone else to finish the job. I'd feel a lot happier with one of these beside me."

"No. That gun has history. If you get caught with it, you will be in really serious trouble. And how would you get it back to England? Just waltz on the plane with a Glock in your backpack. Forget it. Put it back and get me out of here, please! This arm is going numb, and my leg is killing me."

Matteson nodded. Of course, Ed was right. He put the gun and magazine back under the tarpaulin and spread some of the tyres and boxes over the top. He then went out and drove Barrows car up to outside the unit. When he went back inside, Barrow was pointing up to the wheels hanging on the wall over the bench.

"I wondered what triggered the alarm. Look up there – second wheel from the left. See that shiny plastic. That's another detector. A PIR. Limited field, but enough to pick me up crossing the workshop floor. Very clever of him, very stupid of me."

"OK Ed, let me help you out to the car."

The two men moved slowly out to the car, Matteson taking all of Barrow's weight on his right side. It was a painful trip for the older man, but he was eventually settled in the back with the front passenger seat as far forward as it could go. Matteson went back into the workshop for one last check and get Barrow's canvas bag. He left the lights on as if

Turan had been working in the night, pulled the door shut, and set off back to Paris.

Matteson could almost see La Defense, and virtually every sign pointed to the centre of Paris. He could hear little gasps coming from the back as Barrow fought to control the pain, so he drove as fast as he felt comfortable with, and they were soon moving along the Champs Elysee, albeit at a much slower pace. When they reached the hotel, Matteson went straight down to the basement garage, preferring to take Barrow up from there in the state he was in, rather than through the hotel's front entrance. Once in the room, he settled Barrow in an armchair with a whisky from the mini bar to help with the pain.

"I'll go and find the pharmacy, but I need a shirt or something, Ed. I can't walk through the hotel like this." Matteson pointed to his bare chest under his jacket.

"The shirts will all be too small. But there's a large sloppy kind of sweatshirt in that drawer."

Matteson found the sweatshirt which was still a little snug but would do.

He was soon back laden with bandages, lint pads, antiseptic ointments, and the strongest pain killers the pharmacist, who fortunately spoke good English, would allow without a prescription. The first thing Matteson did was give Barrow some painkillers, and then set about cleaning and dressing the wounds, including some ointment on the acid burn.

"Thanks, John. In a way I hope this little spot stays," he said looking at the back of his hand. "If that acid hadn't been in reach, Turan would have got me for sure. I really thought it was the end of the line."

"What are you going to do? I mean, you have to get these wounds properly treated. This is just an emergency dressing."

"When those pain killers really take hold and I can talk better, I shall phone my wife to come and get me in the morning. She'll be able to drive us back to......well, back home, and I can get it sorted then."

"What will you tell her?"

"Oh, I don't know. I don't want her upset. I shall say that I fell down some concrete steps. It will be OK. But you have to go John. You need to get back to what you were supposed to be doing this weekend and cover your tracks."

"I've got a room at the hotel, so I can stay here for a while. I'll get an early flight back tomorrow morning after I know that you are going to be OK."

"No, I appreciate it, but I need to be alone. I shall probably be on the phone some time. You go. If I hit trouble, I'll call you".

"If you're sure......." Matteson got up and walked to the door, turning back to Barrow before he left.

"But the slightest problem, anything you can't handle, you phone me, Ed. Even if it is the middle of the night."

Matteson slowly strolled along to his hotel on Boulevard Haussman, going back over the day from his arrival at the Cafe de Flore through to that dreadful scene in Turan's workshop, and Barrow sitting injured in his hotel room. He knew he would never forget this Friday. Not just for the actual events, but also because he sensed a change in himself. The academic with the almost boyish charm, which he knew he played to when it suited, was hardening around the edges. But did he want that? Could he stop it? He didn't know the answer to either of those questions.

The next day he was up early and had packed and checked out of the hotel by the time he phoned Barrow.

"Hi, Ed, how are you? Did you get any sleep?"

"A little, John, a little. I've been munching on those pain killers – they really do work. My wife is arriving in about two hours, and then I'll be on my way. I want to thank you for all you did yesterday – I wouldn't have survived without you."

"No, forget it. As long as you're OK, that's the main thing. I'll get going then, back to London. Take care of yourself, Ed."

"And you, John, and you."

Matteson flew back into Heathrow, collected his car, and drove straight up to Yorkshire and his Aunt's cottage on the outskirts of Netherton. He spent the day with her before checking into his room at the Nether Inn. He was concerned that his Aunt Mary seemed to be losing the plot, and drove over to Leeds that evening for a drink and chat with cousin Ruby and her husband, Vic. She too had noticed her mother's deterioration and had already started looking at carers, and even nursing homes. She promised to let him know if things got worse; and having spent a few more hours with his Aunt Mary on Sunday morning, Matteson drove back down to London, less concerned about covering his tracks and more about the health of his Aunt. She was the only real link with his parents and, in particular, his mother. He looked forward to his visits and hearing the tales of his mother's early life, even if many of them were regular repeats. When he got back to his flat in Battersea, he immediately checked his land line for messages, but there was nothing from Lilly.

Chapter 33

That week in June had also been an important time in the life of Grigor Zorich. His stay at the Kurakin hospital was not unpleasant. Good food and drink, TV, radio and newspapers – he could have been in a hotel if it wasn't for the fact of the bars on the windows and the guards at the door. But he knew he was in a very precarious position. The part he played in the killing of Andrei Lanskoy would almost certainly bring a death sentence, or at the least life imprisonment with hard labour which might even be worse. There had been talk of a possible reprieve if he switched allegiance to General Shepilev, and he had to be ready to play the game to get back to London where he and Carol could disappear. He had already put those plans in place immediately after the shooting.

He had been told that the General wished to talk to him again that Wednesday morning and he was seated at the table waiting, when the General came in with his aide, Ivan, and sat down opposite Zorich, whilst one of the guards fetched coffee.

"Well, Grigor, I am sorry you have had to wait here for so long, but it has taken some time to get what I needed. I hope you have been comfortable?"

"Yes, I have been, thank you General."

"Good. You know of course that you should be standing in front of a firing squad for what you have done, but I need someone in London with access to the group of industrialists that are active there. I need to know what is going on, and I am prepared to consider forgetting your part in this business and sending you back to London reporting to me. Secretly, of course."

"I would be eternally grateful for this chance to make amends, and I would do whatever you ask, General."

"I am pleased to hear that Zorich."

The General sipped his coffee before continuing. "The problem is – can I trust you? How can........."

"You can trust me, Sir, you can!"

"I haven't finished.........How can I be sure that you are telling me the truth about the killing of Lanskoy. After all there is no way of corroborating what you say, and Garnovski would naturally deny any involvement."

"It's all true, General, every bit of it."

"Yes, perhaps, but let's run through a few things again shall we, and see if you remember anything else that would help with your story. Ivan, record this please."

The aide had set up a camera on a tripod, and started filming the meeting, focusing mainly on Zorich.

"The first question is the contact in Prague. Do you remember anything else that was said about the man you arranged the contract with?"

"No, I don't......." Zorich was ferreting around in his mind trying to get something to appease the General "......no, now I think about it, I do remember something. He said that he was told the man originally used two letters...S and X. SX. But he said he heard he had dropped that now and has no identity at all."

"SX......what is that? What does it stand for?"

"I don't know, General, I really don't."

"All right. Moving on. This man never spoke except through a machine?"

"Yes."

"And you only had a glimpse of the him running in the park. I find it hard to believe that you just left it at that, Grigor. You didn't follow him at all?"

"He had warned me not to, but I did wait around out of sight and saw him run out the entrance and down the road to the museums, but it was just his back view."

"Museums? What museums?"

"The road leads down to the Natural History Museum and another one opposite."

"I see. And the package you left for him, where did that come from?"

"It was put through my letter box. I didn't see anyone. I presumed it was someone else who worked for Mr K...arnovski."

Zorich tried to rescue the split-second slip of the tongue, but it did not go unnoticed, even though the General continued in the same relaxed voice. Zorich however felt a surge of anxiety at his mistake.

"What about the money, how did you arrange payment?"

"I didn't. That was done by someone else."

"Who?" The General's tone was hardening.

"I….I don't know who, Sir. I don't."

"Then who did you give the bank account number to."

"I just phoned it through to….a….a…." Zorich was starting to panic.

The General leaned forward looked hard into Zorich's face.

"You are lying and I have no place for liars!"

"I'm not…."

"My man could put a bullet in the back of your head now, and no one would give a shit! But I need to know about this set up. I will arrange for you to be tortured in manners you could not imagine and get the truth out of you. And then you will be shot - if you are still alive."

Zorich started wailing like a wounded animal, tears beginning to stream down his cheeks. The thought of endless brutal torture and pain had broken him. The General, his aide Ivan, and the two guards waited, their faces showing no expression.

"Please, General, please. I will tell you everything, but please, no torture. Please let me go. All I want is to go back to London."

"Then start talking. I want the truth and then we will see what we will do."

"Everything I have told you about the man in London is true. There is nothing more there, but….but the person who

I gave the bank number to and who paid for the contract was Fyodor Krupin."

"Krupin!! Not Garnovski!" The General slammed his fist down on the table, making Zorich cower even more. "I could have had my friend Garnovski killed over this!"

The General's anger brought on a coughing fit, and he hurriedly got up from his chair and went into the bathroom and closed the door. The rest of the room sat in silence listening to the racking cough which went on for several minutes. That is except Ivan, his aide, who stood by the door ready to help if needed. The coughing ceased, and the General came out of the bathroom, patting Ivan on the shoulder in appreciation of his concern; and went back to the table to resume his interrogation, his voice sounding even more growly than before.

"Now, Zorich, tell me why would you do this for Krupin when you work for Garnovski? What were you going to get out of this betrayal."

"A new life in Canada for my wife and me after we get married. Canadian passports and enough money be comfortable. I hated working for Mr Garnovski. He treated me like dirt."

"But why Andrei Lanskoy? Why him? He was such a good man."

"Yes, Sir. I'm sorry. I don't know. I just wanted to get away to a new start. What will happen to me now?"

"I will think about that. If what you have told me this time is the truth, then you might be spared. Ivan, we must go. There are things to attend to."

The General left Zorich slumped at the table and walked out to his car with his aide carrying the camera and equipment.

"You have all that recorded?"

"Yes Sir. What do you want done with Zorich."

"Send him back to where he came from."

"I'm sorry, Sir, do you mean London?"

"No, Ivan, I mean his grave. Get rid of that bastard."

Ed Barrow was back in his house on Lake Geneva. His wife had driven him home from Paris on that Saturday. She was distraught at the state she had found him in when she got to the hotel and was insisting that he go to hospital in Paris for treatment. In the end she reluctantly agreed to his wishes to get him home as soon as possible and have their own doctor tend his wounds. It was now Monday morning, and after spending all day Sunday in bed, he was sitting at his desk ready to phone the General to tell him what had happened and get closure on the whole business of the Legionnaire as quickly as possible. Veronique had put a new dressing on his arm that morning, as instructed by the doctor. His shin bone was badly bruised and had a hairline crack; and was now heavily bandaged and in a splint.

Barrow hobbled around the house with the aid of a crutch.

The General answered immediately.

"Edward, do you have news?"

"Yes, I do. The Legionnaire is dead."

"You got him! That is good. But how? Tell me what happened?"

"I got hold of that Englishman, Matteson, who was able to track a phone call from the explosives man, Beck, to a number in Paris which led us to a man called Turan. French but with, I believe, Iranian parents. He ran a Persian antiques shop in the centre of Paris. But he also had a workshop on the outskirts which we were able to find and where he kept his weapons. Glocks, an Arctic rifle, ammunition. He was definitely our sniper. No question."

"So, what happened to him? Are you telling me he's dead or what?"

"He's dead. But we've made it look like an accident."

"Are you all right, Edward?"

"Some wounds, General. I'll live. But I am pleased it is all over now. I want to get back to my quiet life here in Switzerland."

"Of course. And I shall not forget what you did to help me. But, what about this man Matteson? Can he be trusted?"

"Yes, completely. I wouldn't have made it without him. I believe his promise not to tell anyone. And, you were not mentioned at all, General. As far as Matteson is concerned, I am the end stop of this business."

"Good. You may be interested to know that I have now put together all the pieces to my puzzle. But I am still not sure what the picture is saying to me. I must spend more time on it before I make my move. Oh yes, also, Edward, there is the information on the London man who heads up this gang of assassins. Do you still want to look at that, or have you had enough?"

"Well, I sort of promised John Matteson that I would let

him have that and leave him to decide what to do with it. You know he has connections up the line. I don't want to take it any further. I've had enough now."

"Yes, I understand. I too do not want to get involved in any action in England. The waters have not yet calmed following this shooting in their country. And to be honest, Edward, I have my man, and you've killed the bastard who shot poor Lanskoy. I am not really interested in hunting down the head of this gang at this time. Tell me, do you have a fax?"

"Yes, somewhere. I don't use it so much these days."

"No one here knows of our conversations or that you have been involved in any way. I do not want to send this information to you by post or courier and have your address showing. I know you would prefer to have that remain private. I myself will send you some papers by fax."

"I appreciate that, General. Here I've found the number."

Barrow read out the number over the phone.

"I will get that to you today. This is goodbye then, Edward. You can always get me on the number you have if ever you need me. Thank you again, and as they say in your old country, have a good life. Goodbye."

"Goodbye, Sir."

As Barrow put down the phone, his wife, Veronique, put her head round the office door.

"You are supposed to be resting!" she admonished him.

"I am really."

He beckoned her over and put his arm round her waist.

"Last few things, and then as I said before I went to Paris, that will be it. No more work, I promise."

He went quiet for a moment thinking about the documents that would come through on the fax later that day and getting them to Matteson.

"Could you get the fax machine out of the cupboard, honey, and help me set it up here. And there is something I need today so I wondered if you could go into town and get it for me."

Chapter 34

Matteson spent the first two days back assuring everyone in the office who asked that it had indeed been an enjoyable week-end in Yorkshire. He was also busy on his workload and setting up the small office and desk for the arrival of Russ Sterne on the first of July. The evenings went slowly, waiting and hoping for contact from Lilly.

The events of the previous Friday kept flooding back, and in some bizarre way, part of his mind kept wanting to dismiss the whole episode as something he'd read or seen in a film. A book that he had now finished and put back on the shelf. But he knew it had been real, that he had become involved in a dangerous game that ended with one man injured, and the other dead in the most gruesome way. He also knew that there was still another man out there who had run the operation, sending Beck and Turan and whoever else out to destroy and to kill. Was he still in danger? Probably so, he thought.

On Wednesday morning he was summoned to a meeting in the conference room in Graham Stokes' building along

Whitehall. There were seven people present. Stokes and Andrew Trivett, a man called Mortimer from one of Services whom he'd met before, Marjorie Oliver from the Ministry, and two other men who were introduced to him as Curtis and Wick. Together, their names sounded like a firm of solicitors, but they obviously weren't. Matteson was not told what they did. The meeting was called to discuss developments on the assassination of Andrei Lanskoy, and any impact it had on Anglo-Russian relations. Matteson, of course, was in no position to add anything useful to the discussions and his contribution lasted less than ten minutes. The rest of the time, he sat there trying to look interested, nodding where appropriate, but all the while churning inside with the knowledge of Turan, the shooter, and his death, and the yet to be uncovered head of the group. He was glad when the meeting ended, with little resolution other than to log an update conference call for a month's time. Andrew Trivett walked him out.

"That was a bit of an uphill struggle. I don't think we're going to get anywhere with this, you know. But how are you John? Are you managing to put that awful business behind you?"

"Yes and no, Andrew. I'm getting stuck into work, but I've heard nothing from Lilly."

"Why don't you drive down there. I'm sure she must know by now that it was nothing to do with you."

"I would but she's moved back home now, and I don't think her mother's ready to welcome me in".

"Oh, I see. Look, why don't you come down to mine for

a break. We would love to have you. We've got family next week-end, but what about towards the end of the month? Stop over and relax. You'll probably have to do battle with the kids, but it will be great."

"That's really good of you. I would love to if it's not too much trouble for Dawn."

"No, she loves to see you, you know that. So that's a date."

They had reached the exit gate.

"Everything will work out, John, I'm sure."

With that, they parted, and Matteson headed back to his office, disturbed that he was deceiving his old friend and wondering whether to fall on his sword and confess everything.

When he got back to Battersea in the evening, the concierge had a parcel waiting for him. An oblong box, no sender's address, no clear sign of postage. Matteson thanked the concierge and took the parcel up to his apartment and put it on the kitchen worktop. He was naturally curious, but also wary. He took his Stanley knife from the work box in the cupboard and slit a flap in the top of the box, making sure he didn't cut too deep. He then very carefully ran his finger along the underneath of the flap but could feel nothing. He pulled the flap back, revealing what appeared to be the front of a shirt. Matteson smiled, feeling pretty sure that he knew what it was and where it had come from. When he opened the box, he found a gleaming white silk shirt with a card on top.

"Hope it fits. Make sure you have something underneath".

Matteson opened the shirt out, smiling and shaking his head. But, Ed, why should I wear something underneath such a stylish shirt? He looked at the box, thought for a moment, and then carefully cut the inside edges of the bottom of the box. It was a false base, under which he found a slim file that had been sandwiched between the two layers of cardboard. There was another card from Ed.

"This is the info I promised. It comes from an irrefutable source. It's yours to do with as you wish. If you would still be happier with something to hold, phone the number on the back. He is David, you are Alistair. He is expecting your call. Burn these cards after reading. Thanks for everything. Remember our agreement. Forever Anonymous."

Matteson looked at the number on the back and decided to call "David" straight away and check out the file afterwards.

"Hello".

"This is Alistair. Is that David?"

"Yes, it is, Alistair. A friend has asked me to help you out. Can we meet first? Do you know the Grapes?"

"Yes, I do."

"Say, One thirty tomorrow? I have a grey suit, reddish tie, dark horn rims and fair hair. See you then."

End of call. Slightly whirlwind! Matteson pondered what the meeting with this man David would lead to. He then poured a glass of wine and settled down in his armchair to read the file from the shirt box. The pages were all copies of faxed documents that had been cut top and bottom, presumably by Ed Barrow, to remove any details of the fax number, dates, and origin.

Ten minutes later, Matteson sat staring at the wall in disbelief. He had read the first three pages which were headed up - "Confession of Person responsible for arranging Assassination of Andrei Lanskoy"

The pages were a transcript of the sessions the General had with Grigor Zorich, except that all names had been removed, leaving numerous blank spaces in the text. Furthermore, the General had not wanted to show in any way where the document originated from. Since he was editing and sending the fax himself, this meant that he avoided writing any sequence numbers or Q & A symbols in the margins that might point to it coming from a Russian hand. This made the document difficult to understand at the very beginning, but Matteson was soon able to work out which were the questions, and which were the answers. The sessions were shocking enough, confirming that there was indeed a ring operating in Europe headed up by someone in England, and it had been responsible for Lanskoy's murder. The description of the jogger in the early session brought a questioning frown to Matteson's face, but it was the later session that sent a shock wave through him. The man being interrogated was asked to describe again the jogger he saw and repeated his initial description with one addition.

"You said he wore a sweat band around his forehead, but you could see the top of his head. What colour was his hair."

"Reddish, I think."

"You think. Was it red or ginger, what colour."

"It was lighter than ginger. Sort of straw or sand. And thick. Yes, I remember it was very thick and I wondered if that's why he didn't wear a cap."

Andrew Trivett! That man has described Andrew Trivett. His age, build, and that very distinctive shock of hair, still thick and rough even in his forties. Plus, Matteson knew that Trivett jogged in Hyde Park early on the mornings that he stayed up in London, and his flat was in South Kensington where the jogger was seen heading towards. But this can't be! There's something wrong here. This could be a very neat Russian set up to get rid of Trivett from the Security Service. But Ed Barrow had vouched for the source.

Matteson tried to clear his troubled mind and concentrate on the other document, which appeared to be a printout of movements over the last eighteen months of a bank account with simply a number at the top, no names or addresses mentioned. There were only a handful of entries and the one that Matteson noticed first was the transactions in May shortly after the assassination in Surrey. It showed three million dollars paid in, and two payments out to different account numbers of one million and two hundred thousand. Barrow had penciled on the side "T & B "- meaning Turan and Beck! There was also a payment in of one million dollars, with two payments out to the same accounts of two hundred and fifty thousand each, in April 2004, which tallied with the explosion at the titanium plant in South Africa. There was no notation at the side, but Matteson knew from Frew's investigations into the incident that this must again have been Turan and Beck. The only other significant entry was a further payment of one million into the account in June 2004, with nothing going out.

Matteson had no idea what that related to.

The net balance in was nearly three and a half million dollars, but there must have been numerous payments before 2004 because the total balance carried forward at the bottom of the page was over fourteen million dollars plus. If this was Andrew Trivett's numbered account, he had certainly accumulated a substantial amount of money running this operation. Matteson could not recall in the ten years he had known him, any outward evidence of wealth, and had presumed that the house in Oxford had been inherited.

He put down the papers and sat back wondering what to do. He would have to confront Andrew, but in private and disclose the information he had received without directly accusing him. But if he was the ringleader, which Matteson still could not accept, then he could be putting himself in danger. He knew he had to meet this David and get himself a weapon.

Chapter 35

Matteson found it hard to concentrate on work the next morning.

"Is everything all right JP?" asked Lindsay, putting a large mug of coffee on his desk. Matteson replied without looking up from his computer.

"Yes, fine thanks, Lindsay."

But she didn't leave and just stood there in front of his desk.

Matteson sighed, looked at her and smiled. He knew she cared about him and he needed to tell her something.

"I'm OK, really. It's just….well….I really liked Lillian Culver. Even imagined a future together. But now, I don't know if it will ever get back to the way it was."

That was the truth. He did feel that way, but on that particular morning there were other things troubling him.

"I'm sure it will work out. That was a truly dreadful thing for her to see – her father being blown up. You need to give her plenty of time, but still be there for her when she needs you."

"Yes. Yes, you're right, Lindsay. That's exactly what I must do. Thank you."

She gave him a warm smile and left him alone with his coffee and his thoughts.

***

When Matteson walked into the Grapes, he had no difficulty in finding David who looked exactly as he had described himself and was sitting just inside the bar sipping a pint and reading the newspaper.

"David?"

"Yes. Alistair, I presume. Have a seat."

Matteson sat down and noticed how young David was. Early to mid-thirties, certainly no older than himself.

"Tell me Alistair, what on earth happened to our friend's right hand?" David's voice was full of concern.

"Some acid spilt on it. Went through his glove and left a nasty burn. And it was his left hand actually, David."

David smiled.

"Yes, it was, wasn't it. Let me get you a drink. Pint?"

"Yes, a pint will be great."

David returned to the table with Matteson's beer.

"Right, our American friend explained things to me. I deal in bulk, Alistair. Really major orders, and all above board. Well most of it. But I do have some odds and ends knocking around. Are we talking heavy or light?"

"I don't really know."

"If you're new to it, I think light to begin with. Yes, I've got something that I think will suit. Are you free Saturday?"

"I can be."

"Good."

David handed him a slip of paper.

"This is the name and Satnav of a sports club just above the North Circular. Meet me at eleven on Saturday. What car do you drive?"

"At the moment I have a hire car. A dark blue Ford Mondeo."

"Right. Park opposite the entrance to the building, or as close as you can get. I shall come out, recognise you, and come over for a chat, getting in the front passenger seat next to you. Act as if we are old friends. Got it?"

"Yes, I've got it. Thanks. But what about payment?"

"Well, I don't really deal in singles. I'm doing this as a favour. But cover my costs plus maybe a good dinner somewhere, shall we say five hundred? Cash of course."

"Yes, I'll have it all ready."

"Last thing. Look as if you are playing yourself...you know, shorts or tracksuit. And carry a suitable small sports bag with the cash wrapped up in something."

"OK. I'll make sure I've got that together."

"Good. Have you been following Wimbledon Alistair?"

Matteson was initially taken aback by the sudden switch in subject.

"Er….Yes, I have."

"Henman looks as if he's struggling a bit, don't you think?"

The next ten minutes of conversation was all about the tennis and who was likely to be the 2005 champion. Then

David swigged down the last of his beer and got up to go.

"See you Saturday, Alistair. Cheerio."

Matteson was home Friday evening, anticipating his meeting with David the next day. He played tennis when he could, so already had suitable clothing and a sports holdall. The five hundred pounds in twenties was in a plastic bag, wrapped around itself to form a small flat parcel. He didn't know which gun he was getting and went back going over everything Peter Veldt had taught him at the shooting club in Holland. He was also thinking all the time about the confession and the letters "SX". He then remembered that there was another thing that Janice had mentioned. Beck kept shouting about getting "Essex" which he naturally thought was the place, but now knew he was referring to the man in London. But he could think of no link to Andrew whatsoever, either in the name or the initials, SX.

The thoughts churning around in his mind were interrupted by his phone ringing.

"Hello John."

It was Lilly!

"Lilly! Oh, you don't know how pleased I am to hear your voice. I've being trying everywhere to speak to you."

"I know, John. I am sorry, but things have been difficult."

Her voice sounded fragile. Not the strong, confident woman he knew. But he remembered Lindsay's words.

"I understand. It was a terrible thing for you to go through. But I just couldn't find you. Your phone seemed disconnected. And St Barts – no one would tell me anything."

"I've left St Barts. I'm taking up a post at Guildford Hospital so I can be with my Mum and my sister. And we've all changed our phones. There were so many calls from people, all wanting to know this and that. It was too much. I wanted to call you, but I didn't know what to say. When I got the message you left for Jaz, I realised I was being unfair. I know it wasn't your fault. The Police have explained everything. Just a stupid, tragic case of mistaken identity."

Matteson could sense she was getting close to tears.

"Oh Lilly, I wish I could be there to hold you."

"I know. I wish that too. But that's the reason for the call – well one of the reasons. I'm free tomorrow until early evening, so I wondered if I should come up to London and see you?"

Matteson's mind raced. He had to see David in the morning. And he didn't want Lilly in any danger. He had already been responsible for the loss of her father, and London with this Andrew business unresolved and the possibility of someone still out to get him – no, he needed to make the meeting as safe as humanly possible.

"Listen, Lilly, I have a meeting in the morning that I can't cancel. But I should be finished by twelve, so what if I come down and meet you in Guildford. We can have lunch, get a boat up the river, walk in the countryside. Just have a nice day together."

"OK, that sounds great. Shall I meet you at the station at say, one?"

He was pleased to hear her more upbeat.

"Yes, I'll be there by one. I am so looking forward to

seeing you. You know how much you mean to me, Lilly."

"Yes. Yes, I do. I'm looking forward to seeing you too, John. I have to go now. Until tomorrow. Bye."

He heard what sounded like a door opening and someone calling her name. It could have been her mother, Heather, which would explain the hasty end to their conversation. Matteson had no doubt that, despite Lilly's belief that it wasn't his fault, it would be a very long time before Mrs Culver felt the same way.

On Saturday morning, Matteson was sitting in his blue Ford hire car, parked almost opposite the entrance to the sports club building. He wore his tennis whites and had his arm leaning casually on the open car window. At his feet was a sports bag containing amongst other things the bundle of twenty pound notes. He was anything but calm.

At last he saw David coming out of the entrance and gave him a wave. David feigned initial surprise and then burst into a grin and came over to the car.

"Alistair! How good to see you again. How are you?"

"I'm fine, David. It's been a long time."

"Let me get in and we can have a chat."

David made his way round to the front and got into the passenger seat, putting his bag on the floor.

"Good, Alistair. Just keep smiling and all that while we talk. You'll like what I've got for you. It's a Walther. No bad history. It's old, but still works really well. It's been adapted for a silencer, and I've given you a full mag. Completely clean, and with a dead-end trail."

David removed the bundle from his bag and passed it

over to Matteson, who slipped it into his own bag and then retrieved the package of cash for David.

"Our friend said you could be trusted, Alistair. So, from now on, we've never met, and you got the gun from a guy in a pub somewhere. But not my pub, not the Grapes!" David roared at his joke.

"I hope you never have to use it in anger, but if you do, the best advice I can give you is to leave the gun there at the scene. Obviously without your fingerprints, but that way, there is nothing to connect you. As I say, the gun is completely clean and untainted. If you hang on to it and for some reason it gets discovered, you will find yourself in one shit load of trouble. Lecture over. Take care Alistair, and you know the drill – forget everything about me, there's a good chap."

They shook hands and David got out of the car, waited until Matteson had driven off, and then walked out of the club car park, round to a side road to his parked Jaguar and drove away.

Matteson in the meanwhile headed back to his flat in Battersea. He was in a hurry to get down to Guildford in time to meet Lilly. When he got home, he had a quick look at the gun and ammunition and then put them back in the sports bag which he then hid in the bottom of his wardrobe.

Chapter 36

General Leonid Shepilev was sitting in his favourite armchair in his office, sipping his morning coffee, trying to solve the conundrum of Lanskoy's death. It came in two parts. The first was the framing of Garnovski, and the second, what did Krupin hope to get out of all this. He would concentrate his mind on the first part to begin with.

Krupin had used an employee of Garnovski to arrange the killing of Lanskoy. But his plan to frame the other man would only work if the powers that be had evidence of Garnovski's involvement. That evidence could only be provided by Zorich – or Neylev as they knew him, who would then be known to have been implicated in the assassination of Lanskoy and would be tried and imprisoned or shot. But Krupun was arranging for Zorich and his partner to disappear into a new life in Canada with new identities as part of the deal. So how would that much needed evidence come to light?

The General suddenly shouted out loud. "What an idiot I am! Ivan! Come quickly."

The aide came hurrying in.

"Ivan, has Zorich been disposed of?"

"No, Sir, we are still arranging it."

"Good! Go back to the hospital and speak to him. He has made a written or recorded confession implicating Garnovski. We have to find it. Use any means you wish but get him to tell us where he has hidden that confession. It was intended to be found so I think it will probably be somewhere in his apartment in London. If so, get someone there immediately and bring it back here."

"Yes, Sir. Straight away."

"Oh, and Ivan, if he has hidden it in the home of his woman, go there and get it, preferably when she is not there. But whatever, get me that confession."

"Yes, General."

"And ask someone to bring me some more coffee."

Zorich, you are a fool, thought the General. Krupin would not have left you and your woman alive in Canada. Probably weeks at the most. And of course, with the false confession public, Zorich's disappearance would have been construed as Garnovski having him killed to tie up any loose ends.

So, what was this man Krupin after? Like the others, he didn't need money, but they all craved power. And power meant the Presidency. The General knew that Krupin had privately phoned the President offering his services to help run Lanskoy's business until something could be arranged. He had wondered about this offer but didn't think anything sinister was behind it, believing at that time that Garnovski was responsible for the shooting. Now he knew different. Would Krupin make the same gesture with Garnovski's empire when he fell? The President was no fool and would surely ask himself what was behind these actions. On the other hand, two major props of the Russian economy would be leaderless, and Krupin had a good and experienced team who could keep things running in the interim. The President may just go for it. Therefore, what would be Krupin's long term aim? Accumulate power to challenge President Putin? That would be a foolish move, and Krupin has shown that he is no fool. No, he is trying to get close to the President, to prove himself, and may in a couple of years have ingratiated himself enough to be in the running as the President's choice to replace him for the next term. It was generally accepted that Putin would still be the power behind the throne, but it could be Krupin sitting on that throne, and who knows where that could lead?

What do I do with you, Krupin? I need to think this through some more, thought the General, but first, I need to make sure that we find Zorich's confession.

***

The plan had been for Matteson to catch the train to Guildford and be picked up by Lilly. But he was running late after his meeting with David, and drove down, parking in the station car park and walking up to find Lilly waiting in the forecourt. She was wearing a white cotton dress, and Matteson could see that she had lost weight. She turned to greet him, and they held each other for several moments.

"It's so good to be with you again, John. But I thought you were coming on the train."

"No, my meeting overran so I drove down."

He looked at her face. The scar on her cheek left by the flying debris was still there but fading.

"I've missed you so much. I keep wondering if you're OK, just wanting to be there for you."

"I know. It's been hard for us all."

"Where would you like to go? On the river or outside somewhere? "

"I'd like to go to that pub on Shamley Green. You know, where we went one Sunday. I'll drive. My car's just here."

On the way down to Shamley Green, Lilly told Matteson about her move to Guildford Hospital, getting to know her new colleagues, and the sadness at leaving behind all her old friends in London, especially Jaz who she had started out with. When they arrived at the pub, they opted to stay in the bar rather than go into the dining area.

"We held a service for Dad, last week."

Matteson was surprised. "I didn't know. I thought it would be a long time yet."

"No. Apparently there was no point in waiting. We couldn't do anything. Well, you know…"

Lilly looked down at the table, the sadness etched in her face.

"Of course. I'm sorry Lilly, I wasn't thinking."

She looked up at him.

"I still have nightmares about that night, John. I still see my Dad and that awful explosion. I don't know if it will ever leave me."

Matteson put a comforting arm around her. He had always seen the bomb blast from his point of view – arriving after the explosion, concerned about the physical injuries Lilly had suffered. He now began to realise the real horror of that night. Lilly having to watch her father being blown to pieces. He felt the anger swell up inside. Beck was dead, and he would see to it that whoever else was involved would also pay for what they did.

They lingered for the early part of the afternoon at the pub in Shamley Green, getting closer and more comfortable again in each other's company, and then went back to Guildford and walked down by the river. By five, they were making their way back to the station to get their cars and go their separate ways – Lilly home to change for work, and Matteson back to his flat and the challenge of Andrew Trivett. Matteson walked Lilly to her car and they kissed for the first time that afternoon. Lilly clung to him, not wanting to let go.

"Thank you for this afternoon, John. Being with you….well,it's what I needed."

"I'm always here. Shall we meet up again. When you're free, that is."

"Yes, I really want to. I'll call you, promise."

Chapter 37

Matteson stayed in Saturday night and most of Sunday, still unsure what to do. The description in the confession certainly fitted Trivett, but was that enough? He needed more before confronting Andrew, and felt that the key was in the code name the man in London had used in the early years, SX. There was something. Something at the back of his mind, but he just couldn't bring it up.

He left the problem for the moment and spent some time examining the Walther pistol. He soon identified the safety catch on the side of the gun which could be pushed up and down with the thumb whilst holding the grip. He worked the weapon a few times, using both single and double hand holds, pulling the trigger with both the safety catch on and off, satisfied that it was effective. He then loaded the magazine, and with the safety catch on, he again tried different holds to get used to the new weight of a loaded gun. Finally, he practiced putting the silencer on the gun barrel. He wished he could somehow fire the Walther, but he knew that was impossible. He also thought of phoning Peter Veldt for some advice, but he couldn't bring anyone else into the loop.

It was now late afternoon, and Matteson went back to the part of the puzzle he had yet to solve. SX. He decided to take a walk through Battersea Park and get some fresh air, and think it through again.

The bank statement balance showed that the operation was ongoing for some years. Working on three million dollars plus as the average annual net input, then it should be at least four years to get a balance of fourteen million dollars. Possibly longer if it took some time to start up a successful business. If he worked on five to six years back from 2005, it takes it to some time before the millenium. But code names usually have a link with something before an operation is put into practice, therefore it could be more the mid to late nineties, if not earlier. Trivett was in Hong Kong for most of that time, a Major in the Army. Matteson started to go back to those days and his life in Hong Kong. But nothing came to him. Then he remembered the car journey to Heathrow with Suen Ling.

It was in 2003, by which time Matteson headed up a small unit covering trade and commerce intelligence worldwide. Andrew Trivett had returned to civilian life working in security a few buildings away in Whitehall, also under Graham Stokes. They met regularly for a drink whenever Trivett stayed up overnight, and Matteson had enjoyed the occasional Sunday lunch with Andrew's family at his home near Oxford. As with Hong Kong, Trivett had gradually embroiled Matteson into his world, using his travel on trade and commerce work to undertake occasional simple tasks – deliver, collect, observe. Matteson never felt in any danger and even enjoyed the challenge of these undercover ventures.

It was late October and the weather had begun to turn, becoming more overcast and colder. Matteson was walking up Park Lane heading to Oxford Street. As he passed Claridges, he noticed the porter loading luggage into a waiting limousine. There was an emblem in the corner of each case and as he moved closer, he saw that it was a white serpent. He caught his breath and looked at the woman emerging from the hotel. It was her. It was Suen Ling, wearing a military style coat, with leather boots and gloves. As he approached, she looked at him, her face changing from apprehension to the shock of recognition, and then to the warmest of smiles.

"John. It is you, isn't it?"

"Yes, it's me," he said.

Suen Ling moved quickly to embrace him.

"It is so good to see you again John. You've really grown. So handsome."

He smiled at her. Although she had lost some of that freshness of youth, it had been replaced with a more mature beauty.

"Oh John, I am so sorry. I am just on my way to Heathrow. I have to fly back to the States this morning. I can't delay the trip."

"I can't let you just walk back into my life and then out again after just a few minutes. At least let me come with you to Heathrow. We can at talk on the way."

"Yes, that would be wonderful. The driver can bring you back."

The chauffer opened the limousine door kerbside and Suen Ling slid across the back seat. Matteson got in beside her and the car set off for Heathrow. Suen Ling linked her right arm into his and clasped his left hand.

"What are doing now, John? Do you live in London?"

"Yes, I do. I have flat just across the river. I'm still working in trade and commerce. A bit boring, but I get to travel a lot." He looked into her eyes as he talked. "And you? How are you? Are you well and happy?"

"Yes. I am OK. I live in San Francisco, and like you, I travel a lot although it is mainly Asia and Australia. But I will start coming to London more now." She squeezed his hand as she spoke.

Matteson was silent for a few moments before asking, "What happened in Repulse Bay, Suen Ling? I need to know."

"That was a long time ago, John. I really don't want to talk about it."

But Matteson kept looking at her, not taking no for an answer. Finally, she responded.

"They were bad people. They wanted me to do something to you, but I couldn't. I just couldn't do it. I had to defend myself. And then I had to hide. From the Police and those people. You must believe me, John I hadn't planned what happened. What I felt for you was….it was real."

"Yes, I believe you."

He leaned over and kissed her on the cheek.

"Your friend saved me, you know, Shao Xiao, the Major. He let me get away."

"Andrew Trivett? Let you get away.? How do you mean?"

"I knew his men were around, but he let me get to the airport and away, when he could have turned me in to the police. Things would have been very different then. Really bad, I mean. Please, can we now talk of other things. We have such little time."

Even though he still had so many questions, he could see that they were already on the Hammersmith flyover and would soon be speeding along the M4 towards Heathrow. The journey was going too quickly and perhaps this wasn't the right time.

"When you come back, can we spend some time together? I mean, go out to dinner and talk about everything?"

"Of course, I promise. Now, I want to know what has happened to you since you left Hong Kong."

They chatted through the rest of the journey, snuggled up Together in the back of the limousine, but it wasn't long before the car slid into the drop off at the Heathrow terminal.

She clipped open her bag one handed and gave him a small note book and pen.

"Can you write down your number please John. I caught my hand in the hotel bathroom," she said raising her left hand in gesture.

"Yes, sure."

He wrote down his name and his mobile number and dropped the notebook back into the open handbag.

The chauffer helped Suen Ling out of car and proceeded to unload the luggage onto a trolley whilst Matteson escorted her into the departure hall. She steered them to an empty British Airways First Class check in and pulled her ticket and passport from her coat pocket which she handed to the BA check in desk. At the same time, the chauffer was starting to load the cases onto the baggage conveyor. Procedure completed, the BA hostess handed Suen Ling her passport and boarding pass.

"You're in seat 3A, Mrs Lee. The First Class lounge is straight through. Have a pleasant flight."

"Mrs Lee?" Matteson queried, as they turned away from the desk.

"Yes. I married. But it was necessary. A marriage of convenience. But it is OK. I am free to come and go as I please. And my husband is kind and understanding. But very old," she laughed.

"I must go through now, John. I will phone you when I come back. Please do not tell anyone that we have met."

"Yes, of course......if you wish. But what about Andrew Trivett? He would like to know you're OK, I'm sure."

"No, no one please John. I will explain when I come back"

She leaned forward and kissed him on the lips. The embrace lasted for several moments. She went through to Departures, turned and waved, and then was gone, leaving Matteson to return to Park Lane in the limousine.

Chapter 38

"Of course!" he said out loud, "The Major! She said "Your friend saved me, Shaio Xiao – the Major!"

There it was, the final piece of the puzzle! The Major – Shaio Xiao – SX. Matteson still did not want to believe it and checked the spelling in the Chinese dictionary but there was no mistake. His best friend, the man he thought of as his mentor, had all this time been masterminding this group of killers! He had to confront Trivett, but now he could take no chances. This had to be a different kind of meeting.

On Monday morning, he was back in the office and phoned Andrew Trivett's secretary who confirmed that he would, as always on a Monday, be staying in London overnight. Although at first Matteson felt nervous and apprehensive about what he had planned, gradually during the day, he became calmer and more determined to see it through.

That evening, he waited until after nine when the sun had started to dip, and left Battersea, walking across Albert Bridge, up through to Sydney Street and then to Andrew

Trivett's flat in South Kensington. He had been to the flat a few times before. It was a small, one bedroom bolt hole on the second floor of one of those elegant double fronted terraced houses which had been converted into six flats and a basement.

Matteson was wearing a light raincoat and thin gloves, with the Walther and silencer in one pocket. He had cleaned the Walther of all traces of his handling before leaving and was now holding it firm with his left hand inside the coat pocket. He reached the house where Trivett lived and saw that thankfully no one had thought to put a camera at the front since his last visit. He could see only three lights on, one on the second floor which he knew to be Andrew's, one in the basement, and the third on the first floor on the other half of the building. He pressed the buzzer alongside Trivett's name.

"Yes, who is it?"

"It's me John. I wondered if I could come up and see you."

"This is a bit late, John. Can't it wait until the morning?"

"Not really. If you don't mind….it won't take long."

"OK. Come up. I'll leave the door open."

The entrance door buzzed, and Matteson pushed it open and went up the stairs. He took care at each landing not to be seen, and heard the TV coming from the first floor flat on the other side.

Trivett had a concerned look on his face, as he turned away from the door of his flat. He would normally have sat with Matteson in the two armchairs by the fireplace, but this time he went back to his desk, partly opening the top right-hand drawer.

As Matteson reached the second floor, he pulled out the Walther, fitted on the silencer and thumbed the safety catch off. He then walked in switching the gun in his right hand pointing ahead, and pushing the door shut behind him.

"What the hell is this, John!? What are you doing with that gun!?" yelled Trivett, remaining seated at his desk.

"I'm not sure yet, but I feel a lot safer with it at the moment."

"Well I bloody well don't! Put it down and tell me what this is all about!"

Trivett tried to command the situation, but Matteson felt calm and completely in control.

"Put your hands on your head, Andrew. For the moment. I want you to look at something."

Trivett hesitated, and with the anger showing on his face, he then put his hands on his head. Matteson pulled out a thin wad of folded papers from the left-hand pocket of his raincoat, walked forward a few paces and placed them on the desk, all the while keeping the gun pointed at Trivett's chest. He then stepped back.

"OK, Andrew, you can take your hands down. Read those. It's a statement from a man who asked you to arrange the shooting of the Russian, Lanskoy. The other paper is a print out of your numbered bank account showing movements in and out. You'll find the names Beck and Turan alongside the last entries. That's you paying them off for carrying out the killing."

Trivett left the papers where they lay. He leaned forward on the desk and then back in his chair.

"This is preposterous! You know me, John. You've known me for over ten years. I work for Gerald Stokes. I don't understand where all this is coming from."

"Just read the papers, Andrew."

Trivett just stared at Matteson willing him to back down, but he didn't.

"All right. As you wish, but you have landed yourself in a lot of trouble, I can tell you."

Trivett sat reading the documents, before again leaning back in his chair, catching the drawer with his elbow and easing it out a little further.

"This is obviously a set up. Anyone can see that. There's no name on this confession, and who can get a statement of a numbered account, I ask you. There is nothing to link this to me, nothing at all."

"The source is impeccable. And Stokes would, I believe, be able to exert government pressure to get the Swiss bank to reveal details of this account, once they are told where the proceeds came from. I am also sure that a search of this flat would uncover the voice synthesiser and the phone you keep for clients to contact you."

Trivett went quiet, and his tone changed.

"Have you told Stokes about this?"

"Not yet. I was planning to see him tomorrow, but I wanted to give you a chance to confess it all to him first."

"The result would be the same, John, would it not?"

Matteson said nothing. Although it was a light gun,

keeping the Walther trained on Trivett's chest was beginning to make his right arm and hand ache, so he switched to a double hand hold.

"You have to know, John, that I never did anything to harm my country. It was all commercial transactions, no secrets, nothing like that."

"But you killed people! Innocent people, like Dr Culver, although that was meant for me."

"I had nothing to do with that, John, you have to believe me. Beck acted entirely on his own, and you must have caused him to do so. So, don't blame me. There is no way I would have ordered you to be killed, no way."

"Possibly. But it's strange that after I told you about Beck, he mysteriously fell from his balcony. Was that you, Andrew?"

"I was really angry about that bomb. And he was becoming a liability, drinking too much. I couldn't have him around anymore."

"So that's Beck and Turan gone. Would you have recruited others?"

"What do you mean, John? Beck and Turan gone?"

"Turan's dead. I killed him."

Trivett was half smiling and shaking his head.

"I don't believe that. You killed Turan!? When? How?"

"A week ago. At his garage in Colombes. If you read the French newspapers, you will see that it is being reported as an accident. Just like Beck's."

Trivett was quiet for some moments, and Matteson was about to ask him if he would now phone Stokes, when he started talking again.

"Listen, I was in the process of closing this operation down. It had run its course, and if Turan's gone as well as Beck, it seems the right time to finish."

"What about the others? You must have had others in the loop?"

"No", Trivett lied, "just the two of them. If I give you my word that it is ended…….and also, that I will sort a time and a reason to leave the service in the next few months, can you find a way to forget this?"

"How can I, Andrew? It wasn't one petty crime. You've been at it for years. SX? Remember?"

"Yes, SX. A stupid touch of vanity. I dropped it before someone cottoned on to its meaning. But you worked it out?"

"Sort of. It was Suen Ling who called you Shao Xiao, the Major. And what with the description in the confession, it just had to be you."

"Suen Ling? That is ironic!"

"What do you mean?"

"Nothing. Forget it, John. Look, let us work something out. As you can see, I have plenty of money, enough to share. If not for me, then think of Dawn and the children. Look at them? Do they deserve all this?"

Trivett gestured with his left hand towards a large family portrait on the side wall. Matteson automatically turned to look at the picture and that was when Trivett went for the gun in his top right-hand drawer. But Peter Veldt had taught Matteson well, and he moved only his head, keeping his body and the Walther still facing front. He pulled the trigger. It was first time he had fired the Walther, not knowing for sure that it actually worked, but it did. The shot was wild, clipping the top of the desk and hitting Trivett in the right groin. Matteson kept pulling the trigger and two more bullets struck Trivett, the first in the chest and the second straight into the heart. He slumped down in the chair dead.

Matteson stopped squeezing the trigger. He felt in shock at what he had done. He walked forward and looked at Andrew Trivett's face which was a mixture of pain and surprise. Matteson had to fight back the tears. Although he now knew that Trivett was going to shoot him, he still felt a deep sadness inside at the loss of someone he had known as a friend for so long. Someone he had come to look upon as an older and wiser brother.

This was not how he had planned it to be, but it was done. And he knew he must now get out of there as quickly and as silently as he could. Remembering what the man called David had said, he left his gun on the desk with the confession and bank statement. Then, with one last glance towards his dead friend, Matteson left the flat, again pausing on the stairs at the first and ground floor to make sure they were clear, before going out the front entrance. He was relieved to be out in the street, thankful that no one in the other flats had heard the shots and raised the alarm. As soon as he was clear of the building, he pulled off the gloves which he discarded into a waste bin near Knightsbridge. He also then took off the light raincoat and folded it down enough to carry in his hand and walked to the West End avoiding as much of the CCTV en route by taking the side roads. Eventually he reached Leicester Square, and cut down to the Embankment near Charing Cross, and without even pausing, dropped the raincoat at the feet of a sleeping vagrant in one of the arches, and walked back up to Leicester Square, where he checked the cinema listings at the Odeon. Finally, he found a bar in Covent Garden and sat with a much needed drink, still not fully able to take in what he had just done.

Despite having several drinks, he found it difficult to sleep that night. In the two months since he first got involved in the shooting of Andrei Lanskoy, four people had died – Lilly's father, Beck, Turan, and now Andrew Trivett. And the last two, he had killed. He wondered how it would all end.

He arrived at his office the next morning, trying with great difficulty to act normal, wondering if he had been seen or if there had been a camera he had missed, and would the Police come marching into the office to arrest him. But nothing happened. Nothing except a call from Gerald Stokes late afternoon telling him "the awful news" that Andrew Trivett had been found dead in his flat, apparently shot by unknown intruders. Stokes said that nothing more was known at this stage, but he would keep him posted.

Chapter 39

"Ivan, I need to explain something to you."

The General had ushered his aide to a chair.

"The President is aware that Lanskoy's assassin died in Paris in an apparent accident. You know that the person behind all this is Feodor Krupin, but for reasons of my own, I do not want to take any action at this time. There must be no mention of Krupin or Zorich."

"Yes, Sir. I understand."

"And your men? They will keep quiet?"

"Absolutely. They will not be a problem."

"Good. I have a plan in mind for Krupin which I need to discuss later. But, do you still have the woman on board his yacht?"

"Yes, General. She is almost part of the family now."

"Good. See if you can get someone else on board to help her. We have until next May. Oh, before you go, Ivan, I have put you forward for promotion to Colonel."

"Thank you General, thank you!" said the Major smiling broadly.

"You deserve it. And when I finish here, you can go back into the field if you so wish."

"I would like that, Sir."

"Fine. Now I am expecting Garnovski. Show him in as soon as he arrives."

"Thank you for coming, Stepan," said the General.

He was seated in his armchair at the small table in his office, opposite Stepan Garnovski. Both men were sipping coffee, with a bottle of ice cold Vodka and two glasses on the table, should either wish something more.

"It is always good to see you, Leonid."

The two men went back a long way. In fact, General Shepilev, then a Colonel, had been Garnovski's commanding officer for part of his time in the Army. He went on to the KGB, whilst Garnovski left to go into industry. But they had stayed in touch, and met on occasions, whenever their commitments allowed.

"Have you found out who killed poor Andrei," Garnovski asked.

"We will talk about that a little later, Stepan. First, I need to know about these meetings with the others. I am led to believe that it was solely to agree on the hospitals for the poor. Do I have your assurance that there was no other, perhaps more sinister, purpose?"

Garnovski leaned back in his chair.

"There were other things discussed but I wouldn't call them sinister, Leonid. Everyone is interested in what will happen when the Presidency changes. Who will be in charge, what will they expect of us. I think it would be very unusual for those discussions not to happen."

"I agree. It affects us all. But curiosity about what will happen is different from conspiracy to make things happen, is it not?"

"No, Leonid. There was no conspiracy, I can assure you. Some were perhaps more vocal than others, but it was just noise. A noise that has been silenced by the trial of Mikhail Khodorkovsky and the killing of our dear friend. You have my word that there is nothing that I know of or am involved in that threatens the President in any way."

"Good. Some Vodka, yes."

The General poured two generous measures, and after the customary toast, both men drank it down in one satisfying shot.

"Now, I can tell you that yes, I have found the man who killed Andrei Lanskoy and he is now dead."

"At last!" Garnovski said with a clenched fist. "Who was he?"

"He was a professional assassin, part of group operating in Europe and beyond."

"And do you know who ordered the killing? That's who I really want to get."

"I have a good idea. But my job is to protect the President, or strictly speaking, the President's office since they do, of course, change. And with that in mind, there are matters afoot which I do not wish to become public. I have a document that I want to show you, but it must go no further than this room, yes?"

"You have my word, Leonid. I swear on my children's lives."

"Don't say those things, Stepan. Not on you children's lives. Yours will do!"

The General started to laugh, but it soon turned into a coughing fit. It lasted only a few moments, but enough for Garnovski to express his concern.

"It's not got any better then, Leonid."

"No. It comes and it goes," the General said with a shrug of his shoulders.

He then passed over a copy of the confession written in the name of Neylev, that his men had found in Zorich's flat in London. He watched Garnovski's face, which changed from eager curiosity to dark, explosive anger as he read the document.

"What the hell! What is this man saying? I arranged the murder of Andrei? This is all lies, Leonid, you have to believe me!"

"Yes, I do believe you, my friend. What this man says happened is true, except that it wasn't you who ordered the contract, but someone else."

"You said you had a good idea who it was. Can you tell me?"

"No. Not yet. It will become apparent later on, but I need more time to get things into place."

"And what about this…this little shit Neylev? What's happened to him?"

"He is no more. His absence will become noticeable and presumably get reported to you. Please do not look too deeply into his disappearance. Let the dog stay dead."

With that, the two men drank more vodka, and inevitably, the conversation slipped back to "the old days".

Fyodor Krupin was deep in thought as his personal jet crossed Uzbekistan on its way to the Indian capital of New Delhi. His men had reported that Neylev had disappeared and had not been seen for over a week. Neylev's fiancee said that she had received a phone call from him saying that he was going away, but since then nothing. She was getting worried and had contacted his office and they said they would look into it. Arrangements had been made for the two of them to move to Canada under assumed names at the end of June, so why would he disappear now? Worst still, his men had got into Neylev's flat in London and searched everywhere but could not find the written confession implicating Garnovksky, who appeared to be walking around still free as a bird.

Something had gone wrong. But what? Krupin had obviously checked out everything to do with Neylev and uncovered his previous identity and disappearance. He had planned to use this if necessary to blackmail Neylev, but the money and the new life in Canada proved enough.

There were reports of him being seen getting into a car in London with three other men and it could be that his past had caught up with him. But if that were the case, the confession would still be in his flat.

Krupin had already started tying up the loose ends, eliminating the employee who dealt with Neylev, and making sure the payments were suitably masked, but Neylev was the weakest link and he realised he should have got rid of him earlier.

He shook his head. He knew that he couldn't take any chances and had to abandon any idea of influencing the President. He also had to get out of Moscow. He called over one of his assistants.

"Cancel my meeting in Delhi and get the captain to change course for Malaga. Get onto to Moscow and arrange for my wife and daughters to move immediately to Spain. Make sure that they are well guarded. Say it is a kidnapping threat. Oh, and tell my business team to be in Malaga on Friday morning. No protests, no exceptions, understood?"

"Yes, Sir."

The assistant went back to the rear of the plane and set about carrying out his orders. Krupin picked up his phone and dialed a private number in Zurich.

"Doctor Loenhert, it is me Fyodor Krupin. I need you to come to Malaga early next week."

Krupin listened to the protests on the other end of the phone.

"I know you are busy but cancel what you have for next week. I need you there for one or two days," he said, closing off his phone.

Krupin spent the rest of the journey listing his different companies and working how and when to start disposing of them to the best advantage.

Chapter 40

It was now nearly two weeks since the shooting of Andrew Trivett. Everyone in the office was shocked when the news came out. They knew that Matteson would be affected the most since he had known Trivett since their days in Hong Kong, and to have this come on top of the car bomb incident only weeks before. But for Mattteson, it had become more of a case of had he got away with it? Was he in the clear?

In the middle of this period of speculation, he went, as promised, to the crematorium on the afternoon of Friday 24th June for the funeral of Derek Beck. There was just a small crowd, mainly friends and relatives of Janice Painter. Beck's mother was apparently considered too infirm to leave the nursing home. Matteson sat at the rear of the hall and stayed only long enough after the coffin had disappeared, to express his condolences to Janice, declining her offer to join them back at the shop for drinks and a buffet.

"Well, thank you for coming, Alan. Perhaps we could stay in touch? I would like that."

"Yes, of course. I'll give you a call. It would be nice to

meet up under different circumstances. Bye Janice."

Matteson was sitting in his office, wondering whether to call Lilly to see if she was free any time over the coming week-end, when Lindsay buzzed him, to say he was needed at the office of Graham Stokes. He looked at his watch – nearly five thirty. What did the old man want at this time? The doubts over his actions resurfaced as he left his building to walk down Whitehall. He was cleared through and escorted into Stokes' office.

"Ah, Matteson, come in. Pull up a chair."

Matteson was somewhat re-assured by the friendly tone and smile.

"It's not too early, do you think," said Stokes, opening a drawer and pulling out a bottle of single malt and two glasses. He poured a generous measure for both of them.

"Thank you, Sir."

Matteson sipped his whiskey, still wondering what this was all about.

"I wanted to talk to you about Trivett. The Police contacted us as soon as they knew he was one of ours. We went in and took away one or two things more relevant to us than the murder team, and we've uncovered something….well, rather sinister. There was a statement, well more of a confession actually. No names, no dates nothing, just what appeared to be a copy of a transcript of a question and answer session which stated that the Russian, Lanskoy, had been assassinated to order. And the man described in this confession as having arranged the shooting for three million dollars looks remarkably like Andrew Trivett."

"Andrew! Are you sure, Sir? There must be some explanation."

"Well, our search of the flat uncovered a voice synthesiser that was mentioned in the confession. Also, there was a statement of money movements in and out a numbered account. We have tried initially to have the account holder named, but so far, the Swiss bank have refused. They are insisting that we present a case of criminal activity. However, with a lot of leaning, the manager agreed to look at some photos of Trivett that we wired over to the Swiss authorities. Without any legal commitment, he has gone so far as to say that the man in the photo resembles someone who has visited the bank in the past."

"I still don't understand. Andrew Trivett! Do you know why he was killed?"

"As far as the public are concerned, it was someone who forced their way in thinking Trivett had cash and valuables, which he did not. So, they shot him. But, of course, the Americans just wouldn't buy that, so we've told them that he was getting close to uncovering who was responsible for the assassination of Andrei Lanskoy, and we believe he was silenced before he could make his findings known. You see, if we had to prove criminal activity to the satisfaction of the Swiss, we would automatically blow both of those stories."

Graham Stokes paused, and looked at Matteson for a few moments.

"I would normally throw all the resources I could muster to get at the person responsible for killing one of my men. And they would pay the price. But in this case, I am in a perverse way, grateful to whomsoever removed the rotten apple from the barrel. Who knows where Trivett's activities could have led. We already suspect that there were other people involved in this ring and other bank accounts. He would have eventually been exposed, but probably by others and in such a way that it would have brought me and my department down. As it is, the boat has been rocked, but we are still afloat."

Matteson didn't know what to say. There was something in Stokes' voice that made him wary.

"By the way, I am told that you asked on that Monday if Trivett was staying overnight. Why was that?"

"I was thinking of having a beer with him. We did meet up sometimes."

"Yes, I know. And what made you change your mind?"

"Nothing, really, Sir. I just decided to go to the pictures instead."

"What did you see?"

There was nothing casual about the question.

"It was called Mr and Mrs Smith. The usual thing - a lot of guns and bullets."

There was a pause in the conversation before Stokes resumed talking.

"Now that you mention guns, John, the Police have been unable to get any good trace on the pistol that was used. It was left on the desk. A clever move, don't you think? There was one other thing I needed to ask you about. There was a notation on the side of the bank statement. Two names, Turan and Beck. My French counterpart tells me that a man called Phillipe Turan was found dead in his garage on the outskirts of Paris, having apparently been under a car he was working on when it toppled and fell onto him, breaking his neck. They found a stash of guns and ammunition and now believe this man Turan could have been a professional killer. Obviously connected to Trivett."

"This gets more extraordinary as it goes along, Sir."

"Yes, it does, doesn't it. What I wanted to ask you about was the other man, Beck. The Police told us that Trivett had asked to look at Beck's flat after he had fallen from the balcony and been killed. This made me curious, so I ordered a deep forensic check of the flat which uncovered traces of RDX and PETN, which as you may know, are used to make plastic explosives. The sort that blew up your car and killed Dr Culver."

Matteson's mind raced. He was beginning to realise that Stokes knew an awful lot more than he was letting on. He had to open up on something.

"I know, Sir. I think it was Beck that planted that bomb. There was a sighting of two men in a car in Guildford just before Lanskoy was killed, described as one big and one, well, smaller. Frew Douglas on my team remembered a similar description of two men seen near the titanium plant last Spring where there was a suspicious explosion. I did some work and that led me to Beck – a big man, and a wine dealer and ex Army bomb disposal. I told Andrew Trivett about my suspicions."

"You told Trivett? Then Beck puts a bomb under your car, and a little later, he mysteriously falls from his balcony. Yes, I see."

Matteson was content to let Sir Graham assume that he told Andrew Trivett before the bomb explosion, and not after as was the truth.

Again, there was a silent pause.

"I want you to come and work with me, John."

"Pardon, Sir?"

Matteson could not hide his surprise.

"Until I can get a replacement for Trivett, I need someone for back up. Someone who can look at a problem and give me some answers. And I think that is you."

"What about my unit? I don't want to leave them."

"You won't have to. You can still run the operation and get your man Douglas to act as your deputy when you're away. Keep your office over there and have a desk here. I won't need you all the time. You'll have to get a higher clearance, of course, and you'll also go up a couple of salary grades. What do you think? Do you want the job?"

"Yes Sir, I do, thank you."

"Good. But just remember, I need to be told what's going on. Talk to me before you take any action, is that clear?"

"Yes, perfectly."

"Fine. Come by in the morning, and we'll sort you out a place and get things started."

Matteson went to leave, but Stokes called to him before he reached the door.

"Oh Matteson, one last thing. I'm pushing to get the formalities over Trivett's death speeded up, so his body can be released to his family. The sooner he is in the ground, the sooner this whole business will slip into the background. I want you to attend the funeral on our behalf. Plus of course, you are a friend of the family, so to speak."

Matteson didn't answer. This was the last thing he wanted to do.

"That won't be a problem for you Matteson, will it?"

"No, Sir. It won't be a problem."

Chapter 41

Matteson had only been in his dual role for five days, when on Thursday 7th July, 2005, three terrorist bombs exploded on the London Underground, followed an hour later, by another bomb which detonated on a bus in Tavistock Square. Many people died, and many more were injured in the four attacks. Life in the capital, and in the rest of country changed, not least for the security services whose job it was to protect the people of Britain.

Following the July bombings, Matteson had been seconded almost full time to work directly for Stokes, attending security meetings and providing in depth analysis and projections on terrorist activity. He had used his team at times, particularly Russ Sterne with his background experience of the Middle East and Pakistan.

The bombings also overtook any further reporting in the newspapers of Andrew Trivett's murder. In fact, the subject of Andrew Trivett was hardly mentioned again, although Matteson couldn't shake off the feeling that Graham Stokes knew what had really happened in that flat in South

Kensington. He never learned the outcome of the fourteen million dollars, nor if the money paid to Turan and Beck was ever recovered, or if any other members of the ring were exposed. He was relieved that the department's official view was that Andrew Trivett had died whilst in service, and his widow would receive all the benefits due.

He knew Andrew had legitimate funds, and presumably life policies, so Dawn and the children would not suffer financially.

Attending the funeral was one of the most difficult thing he ever had to do. He was trying to comfort Andrew's wife, knowing that he, a friend of long standing, was the one who had killed her husband. He hadn't visited Oxford since, but did receive a Christmas card from Dawn, with that family portrait from Trivett's office downloaded onto the front of the card.

The card was edged in black and underneath the portrait were the words "You will always be with us".

His life with Lilly was becoming difficult. They had several dates during late summer and even managed a holiday away together in September. But, whilst to the outside world he was still just a trade analyst working for the government, he knew that the closer he got to Lilly, the more inevitable it would be that she would learn what he really did. Then she would understandably believe he had been lying all along and that the bomb in the car park was intended for him, and not a case of mistaken identity. It was unlikely she would ever forgive him. That, coupled with the fact that her mother Heather still made it known that he was not welcome, meant that there really was no long term future for them. The last thing he wanted was for Lilly to end up hating him. With Lilly building more of a life in Guildford, he thought it best to start letting their relationship ease away. But Lilly was having none of it. Although she knew that they could not spend Christmas together at her family home, she wanted to be with him for New Year and had booked a hotel in Cornwall for the three nights. Thus, John Matteson welcomed in 2006 on the dance floor of the Carlyon Hotel, happy to be holding the woman who meant so much to him, but unsure of what the future would bring.

In Paris, Oscar was inside the Cafe Louis looking out across the Place de Clichy to the closed shop of Phillipe Turan. It was now early February, and eight months since Turan had died and still the shop stood empty. He had apparently left everything to his two sisters in Teheran, but relations between France and Iran were not so good now that Mahmoud Ahmadinejad was President. The sale and transfer of funds had stalled. There had been a constant stream of people coming into his cafe asking if he knew what had happened and when would the shop reopen. What with that and a shortage of staff after his young waiter left abruptly at the beginning of July, Oscar decided to stick a notice on the shop door telling everyone that Phillipe Turan had sadly died and the business has closed down. The notice was still there but faded and surrounded by a number fly-posters stuck on the shop front.

He saw a woman approach the shop. She wore a scarf over her head, and a winter coat buttoned up against the chill. She stopped and scanned the posters until she obviously caught sight of Oscar's notice. Her hand went suddenly up to her face. She must have reached the word "mort" which everyone recognised, no matter how little French they knew. Was it one of his sisters? Should I go and speak to her? Tell her he didn't believe any of the stories about Phillipe and those guns. That it wasn't the Phillipe he knew. But the woman turned away and walked towards the cafe. As she passed, her head was bowed, and her face etched with sadness, and he realised it wasn't one of the sisters, but the elegant woman from Teheran who used to visit his old friend Phillipe.

Chapter 42

Christmas and New Year had passed in Russia, and the winter had gripped hard. The snow that had first settled in November stayed until the end of March, and there were many weeks of severe freezing. It was now well into May and General Shepilev welcomed the warmth of Spring. He had whenever possible spent time with his daughter and granddaughter, hiding the worsening of his health as the shadow on his lungs spread.

The President had agreed that he could step down and enjoy his well-earned retirement but asked that he would be available for "consultation" if any emergency arose during the last two years before a new President was elected. The General had asked to stay on full time until June 2006, to allow him to properly hand over to whomsoever the President chose to replace him, presumably someone from the FSB. There was however another reason.

He had watched Fyador Krupin dismantle his business empire, selling the various components to other Russians, all needing the nod from the Kremlin. The reason given was that he had a serious illness, believed by many to be advanced prostate cancer, and would not be able to properly run his organisation, and needed to be with his family. He had also left Moscow and now based himself and his family in a fortress mansion estate he had bought in Berkshire, England, and his vast holiday complex in Spain.

The General had debated long and hard what to do about Krupin. He knew the illness was, of course, a sham. But if he exposed Krupin, there was no doubt that the President would have demanded justice for Andrei Lanskoy. But the publicity would have had disastrous consequences. The third oligarch to go down – the fingers pointing at Moscow would become fists, and confidence in the Russian economy would certainly falter or worse. As it is, the offloading of Krupin's companies had gone smoothly, helped by the sympathy many felt for his illness, and also by the guiding hand behind the scenes of the experienced and trusted Stepan Garnovski. So, the General had not told the President of Krupin's treachery, only that the actual assassin had been killed in Paris.

But Krupin would not escape justice. He was an ardent fan of Formula One and had invested a great deal in one of the racing teams. Despite his "illness", he was still able to attend every Grand Prix, and would be in Monaco in May. Ivan, now Colonel Guragin, had already put his people in place. The arrangement was for Krupin to be poisoned and have a cardiac arrest which would look as if he had naturally suffered a heart attack. There might be a few rumblings, but as a year would have passed since the trial of Khodorkovsky and the killing of Lanskoy, it should not trouble Moscow too much. And anyway, Fyodor Krupin was serious ill was he not? His death would come as no surprise to anyone except himself. After it was done, General Shepilov would explain to the President that Krupin was believed to be behind the death of Lanskoy, and the case would be closed.

However, if it proved too difficult to arrange the ingestion of the poison, an alternative plan would be put into operation. A marksman would be posted on the upper floor of a building some 400 metres from the landing jetty.

Krupin always came ashore for the Monaco race, but the window of exposure would only be five paces from jetty to car. Guragin's people on board would signal the departure from the yacht so the sniper would be ready the second Krupin stepped onto the jetty. It would be almost poetic justice, thought the General, for Krupin to die from an assassin's bullet the same as poor Lanskoy.

An assassination would undoubtedly create a backlash. He would have to step in and take full responsibility. Not the ending to his career that he had planned, but the doctors had not given him long before he succumbed to the disease destroying his lungs. His old friend, Stepan Garnovski knew something was afoot, but the General did not want him involved. He needed to stay clear of any possible repercussions but had agreed without hesitation to look after the General's family.

Whatever the outcome, General Leopold Shepilev would know that he had done his duty, and Krupin had paid for his treachery.

THE END

Made in the USA
Monee, IL
03 March 2022

92204896R00174